A Lost Touch of Bliss

Amy Tolnitch

Amy Tolnitch

**JEWEL IMPRINT
AMETHYST
MEDALLION PRESS, INC.
FLORIDA, USA**

Dedication,

For Styrling, always.

Published 2004 by Medallion Press, Inc.
225 Seabreeze Ave.
Palm Beach, FL 33480

Cover Illustration by Adam Mock

Printed in the United States of America

Library of Congress Cataloging-in-Publication Data

Tolnitch, Amy.
  A lost touch of bliss / Amy Tolnitch.
     p. cm.
  ISBN 1-932815-26-0
  1. British--Italy--Fiction. 2. Haunted houses--Fiction. 3. Spiritualists--Fiction. 4. Nobility--Fiction. 5. Italy--Fiction. I. Title.
  PS3620.O33L67 2005
  813'.6--dc22

                                    2004025442

Acknowledgments

Many thanks to my endlessly supportive husband and daughter for their belief in me. Thanks also to the fabulous writers in my critique group, Mary Lennox, Jacqueline Floyd and Sarah Hankins, all of whom have patiently kept after me until I finally got it right.

Chapter 1

Wareham Castle, Cumberland, 1196

"Please come to Falcon's Craig," the note read. "I am in need of your unique services. I own Villa Delphino on the Italian coast. It is yours if you will aid me." Amice de Monceaux read the Earl of Hawksdown's boldly scrawled letter for the second time and crushed the vellum in her fist.

Then she started shaking. How could Cain ask this of her? Tempt her with the one thing he knew she had always dreamt of ever since her brother told her stories of the sun-drenched land. And why did he own the villa? That was *her* dream.

Her stomach churned with memories, too many, too clear even now. After five years, she could still feel Cain's arms around her. And could still hear his calm voice saying, "I am betrothed," before he walked away.

The door to her chamber opened slowly. "Amice, dear? Are you in here?"

"Aye, Mother." Amice stuffed the vellum under her mattress and crossed the rush-covered floor to take her mother's arm.

Lady Eleanora pulled free and paced across the chamber, her pale fingers fluttering like butterflies in a meadow. "I cannot find Beornwynne's Kiss. Your father, the whoreson, must have hidden it again."

Amice took a deep breath, no longer startled by her mother's language. And, truth be told, she accurately described her late father. "Mother, the necklace is right here." She opened a trunk and lifted out a carved box, placing it in her mother's hands. " 'Tis safe, as always."

Her mother sat on the stone ledge in front of the window slit and opened the box. She gathered up the heavy gold and amethyst necklace in her gnarled fingers.

Amice laid a hand on her mother's shoulder and felt bones, as if she held a tiny bird beneath her palm. "Would you like to go sit in the garden, Mother?"

Her mother's brow furrowed, and she tilted her head to stare at Amice. "Where is Isolda? I told her to get my blue gown ready for the feast tonight."

"Mother, Isolda died last year." Amice kept her voice even, though she wanted to scream at the loss of the vibrant person who had been her mother and friend.

Blinking quickly, her mother looked around the chamber, as if she expected Isolda to pop out from behind the bed at any moment. "Aye, of course." She gave a small laugh. "I was confused for a moment. Poor Isolda. How I miss her."

Amice squeezed her mother's shoulder and took a deep breath. "Come with me outside. 'Tis a beautiful day."

"What were we talking about?"

"Beornwynne's Kiss."

"Of course. I . . . forgot." Her mother dropped the necklace, grabbed Amice's hands and squeezed tight. Too tight. Amice felt her mother's frail body tremble.

"Mother," she began.

Her mother's gaze clouded. "Beornwynne's Kiss will protect me, see me safe across the river when I die."

"And you have it."

When her mother looked up at her, her gaze was far away. "Is this it?" she asked, her lips trembling.

Amice stared down at the top of her mother's head, the strands of silver hair mixed with white, and her heart splintered. "Mother, all is well."

Her mother patted Amice on the hand and rose. She wobbled and caught herself for a moment with her hand on the seat, waving Amice away with the other. "I believe I shall go down to the kitchen and see if Cook has prepared any meat pies."

" 'Tis a good idea." Amice watched her mother's departure with a heavy heart, the knowledge that she was dying an aching lump in her belly.

The' only reason Amice remained at Wareham was to care for her mother. And by Michaelmas, her brother, the Earl of Wareham, would be wed to a woman who made it clear Wareham would have only one mistress.

Soon, she would have no place.

She closed her eyes and envisioned soft sand, a sparkling blue sea, and golden sunlight. Yes, there she could find peace. Take what Cain offers, her inner voice urged. Take it and flee to warmth and beauty.

How simple it sounded, but in her heart she knew it would take every scrap of strength and pride she possessed. Five years ago Cain Veuxfort had nearly destroyed her. Had taken her heart into the palm of his hand and then crushed it in his uncaring fist.

Her mouth curved in a wry smile. Now, it appeared he had a troublesome ghost who would not leave him alone. *He* needed *her*, the Spirit Goddess. She would be a fool not to take everything she could gain from Cain Veuxfort. Aye, he would give her what he offered and more.

And she would be free.

❧ ❧ ❧

Cain strode into his solar, wiping sweat from his forehead. He unbuckled his sword belt and poured a cup of ale, which he downed in one long swallow.

"Any survivors, my lord?" his seneschal, Nyle, asked.

"Geoffrey is improving, but he still swings like a maid." He sat and leaned his sword against the wall. "How are the figures, Nyle?"

Nyle rubbed his eyes and looked at the columns of numbers running down the parchment. "Good."

"Well done. What do you think of—"

The door to his solar suddenly crashed open. "There you are!" His Uncle Gifford blew in, closely followed by Cain's brother, Piers. Gifford carried a jug with him and spared not a glance for Nyle.

Gifford and Piers came to an abrupt halt in front of Cain. His uncle gazed at him with twinkling eyes. "Is the . . ." his voice dropped, "Spirit Goddess coming?"

Cain gave him a stern look. "I *am* attending to important matters here. And that . . . title is *supposed* to be secret."

Gifford snorted.

Piers waved a hand in dismissal. "You are *always* attending to *important* matters."

Gifford took a swig from the jug, plopped it down on an empty space on the table, and sat on the remaining stool. "Well, answer my question. Is she coming?"

"Aye. Lady Amice shall arrive soon."

"Ha! Wonderful news. Go on now, Nyle. We need to speak to the lord about something *truly* weighty."

"Some might judge keeping a roof over our heads and food on the table of concern," Cain suggested.

"Pah. Time enough for that later. Now, we want to know about our guest."

Giving up, he nodded to Nyle. "Go. When these two release me, I shall send for you."

Nyle's lips twitched. "Good luck, my lord."

He exited quickly, and Piers grabbed the vacated stool. His brother drummed his fingers on his thigh and gazed at Cain expectantly. "When will she be here?"

"I do not know exactly."

Gifford rubbed his hands together. "We shall put her in the rose chamber. It has a lovely view of the ocean and, of course, the garden. We want her to feel welcome."

"Gifford, the *only* reason she is coming is to get rid of that damned ghost," Cain reminded them. God knew, he reminded himself of that fact twenty times a day.

Piers elbowed Gifford, who reluctantly handed over the jug. "Wonder what the girl looks like."

"Visited Wareham once," Gifford commented. "Cannot say I remember the girl. Her father, though." He shook his head. "A brute of a man."

Cain's own memory surfaced and he nodded. "Aye, that he was."

His uncle peered around the solar and lowered his voice to a near whisper. "Got to be a sad case, what with not marrying and engaging in this ghost business." He blinked at Cain and snatched back the jug.

"Amice de Monceaux is the most comely woman I have ever seen." At the flash of suspicion in Piers's eyes, Cain realized his slip.

Piers leaned forward and there was a brief tussle between his uncle and him for the jug. "Give it to me, you old sot."

"I brought the jug. Get your own."

Cain watched them go back and forth and shook his head, wondering how his life had gotten so out of control. All the scene needed now to make it complete was an appearance from the ghost of Falcon's Craig. "Enough," he barked.

The two looked back at him like guilty boys caught stealing custard tarts from the kitchen. "Sorry, Cain," Piers said with a sheepish grin.

Gifford coughed. "So, how well do you know the wench?"

For a moment, Cain could not answer. It was a simple question, but impossible to answer. Did he know her? He had thought so once, but he was not sure he ever truly had. And knowing was far too mild a term to describe his tangled feelings for Amice. "She is a *lady*, not a wench. And when I fostered at Chasteney, Amice was there as well."

Piers took a pull from the jug and glanced sideways at Gifford. "Uncle, I sense a tale here. What do you think?"

Gifford settled back and crossed his thin legs. "My boy, I believe you may be correct." He stared at Cain. "Well?"

Cain was beginning to feel besieged. "As I said, Amice was at Chasteney the same time I was."

"And? Did you bed her?"

He fought a flush. His uncle was never one to hold his tongue. Had he bedded her? Oh, aye, though rarely in a bed. Five years had not dimmed his memory one bit. Or his guilt. Heat puddled in his stomach and raced down to his groin. He shifted on his chair and gave Gifford a stern look. "I am not answering that question."

"What does she look like?" Piers asked with a gleam in his eyes.

"You shall not try to add Amice to your collection of women." Piers was the kind of man women fought over. His boyish good looks and lighthearted view toward life drew women in like the tide to shore.

"Why not?"

Cain just looked at him.

"Ah, so that is the way of it. Brown, blonde, or red?"

Making a vain attempt to smooth down his white hair, Gifford noted, "I prefer red on a woman, myself."

"Brown, blonde, or red what?" Cain asked.

Gifford slapped a hand on the table. "Hair, of course."

Cain rolled his eyes. "Dark brown hair."

His brother leaned forward. "And? What else?"

For a moment, he let himself remember. "Big dark eyes. Tall, slender, with the longest legs I have ever seen on a woman."

Piers stared for a moment, then said, "Damn. Are you sure I—?"

"Aye."

Gifford started cackling and reached for the jug. "You just answered my question."

Well, hell. Cain shrugged.

Piers made a pass at the jug, but Gifford clutched it tight. Turning back to Cain, he asked, "What happened?"

He drew a mantle over his expression. "You know what happened. Mother saw fit to tell me I had been betrothed to Luce. Honor demanded I marry her." He silenced Piers's protest with a raised hand. "It was my duty as the earl. To keep both of *you* in home and," he paused, "ample drink."

Gifford gave another snort and passed the jug to Piers. "Luce. Naught but a twisted bit of fluff. Why Ismena liked her is beyond me. God rest both their souls, of course."

"Mother liked Cain's wife because she could deliver Styrling Castle," Piers reminded him. "And enough coin to pay the King's amercement."

"Not right," Gifford muttered.

Cain rubbed the back of his neck. He refused to think of his late wife, let alone discuss her. "None of it matters now. Luce is dead. As is whatever Amice and I might have shared." How he managed to utter the last with such certainty he could not fathom.

Piers's gaze narrowed. "Some things have a habit of lingering."

"Like that demented wraith who keeps mucking up my experiments," Gifford groused.

"Which is why Amice is coming here. She shall rid us of the ghost for good."

Gifford popped up and started toward the door. "I shall make sure Hawis gets the chamber ready."

"I have already spoken to her, Uncle."

Half turning, his uncle said, "I had better make sure." Opening the door, he muttered to himself between swigs from his jug.

Piers gazed at Cain and lifted a brow. "I have always wondered why you bought Villa Delphino."

Cain gritted his teeth. "I like Italy."

"Hmm. But you have only visited once."

"I am busy." He kept his gaze blank. It would only encourage Piers to learn the truth, that the villa reminded him of what could have been. He had seen Amice everywhere at Villa Delphino, imagined her in every room. It took only once to convince him he should never have bought the place, never tried to keep a memory alive.

"You have been alone too long, Brother."

"I like being alone."

"A man alone shall forfeit the sweetness of life."

Cain scowled. "More of your nonsense."

"You have an obligation."

Heirs, he meant. "Why don't you legitimize one of yours?"

Piers shook his head. "I am too careful to sire bastards. And you are the earl."

Cain stood and placed his hands atop the old, scarred table. "I married once. 'Twas a farce."

"Not all women are as corrupt as Luce. Perhaps, this Amice—"

"Nay!" He shook his head, mentally crushing an unruly surge of hope at the thought. "Nay, Piers. Put it from your mind."

"Very well." His brother's expression said the topic was far from forgotten. "I shall be in the stable. Pleasance is nearly ready to foal."

"Good." Cain watched his brother depart, and he dropped back into his chair, burying his face in his hands.

What had possessed him to send for Amice de Monceaux?

Just as he gave in to the thought, his inkpot went sailing into the air, landing with a wet plop on top of Nyle's carefully written accounts. As he watched the black ink drip across the parchment, he knew he had no choice.

Amice would rid him of the ghost. He would happily give up Villa Delphino and return to his life. Naught more. He was the Earl of Hawksdown now, not a young man swept away by beautiful eyes, a sweet mouth, and the body of a goddess. I am strong, he reminded himself.

"I am in control," he said aloud.

The inkpot rose from the parchment and did a little twirl in the air.

Cain grabbed up his sword and strode out of the solar.

❧ ❧ ❧

The next morning, Amice and her companion, Laila, were mounted in the bailey bidding farewell to Amice's brother, Rand, when a shout rang out.

"Who is it?" Rand called up to one of the guards.

A bellow rolled in from outside the castle, and Amice cringed. She knew that voice. Lugh MacKeir of Tunvegen, Highland laird and frequent visitor to Wareham.

Rand started laughing at the expression on her face.

"Rand, please. I must go."

Her brother looked up at the guard and ordered, "Raise the portcullis. 'Tis a friend."

With a heavy, grinding sound, the iron portcullis slowly lifted, and a huge, roan destrier pounded into the bailey, blowing air from its nostrils. The MacKeir easily balanced atop the beast, clad in his green and black plaid and an impressive collection of blades. Behind him rode a troop of his Highlanders, all nearly as massively built and armed as if they approached the greatest battle of their lives.

The MacKeir came to a halt and gave her a graceful bow. "Lady Amice, you are even lovelier than last I saw you."

"Thank you, my lord." She smiled in what she hoped conveyed a cool distance.

He gestured with an arm like a tree trunk. "Is she not the most beautiful woman you have ever seen, men?"

Caught between the temptation to blush or laugh, she watched as ten battle-hardened Highlanders all bobbed heads in unison, chorusing, "Aye." One of the men shouted out, "Make a fine bride for you," and she wanted to press her heels to her horse and flee.

"I have decided 'tis time, my treasure." The MacKeir glanced down at Rand and nodded an acknowledgment.

"Time for what?" And why in the world was he calling her his treasure? She frowned down at her brother, but Rand just stood there grinning.

"Why, to claim my bride, of course." The MacKeir's smile broadened, and he inched his mount closer to hers. He seized one of her hands in a meaty grip. "Your wait is over. The MacKeir has come for you at last."

She stared at him in astonishment. He clearly expected her gratitude. True, she was well past marriageable age, but still. "What . . . what are you talking about?"

Before he could answer, Rand loudly cleared his throat. "Chief MacKeir, I do not recall having an agreement for Amice."

"Details, my friend. I shall agree to whatever you require for the privilege of possessing this rare jewel."

She tried to pull her hand free but it was like trying to escape a lion's paw. "Rand?"

"Chief MacKeir, Lugh, please come into the hall and share a cup. You must be thirsty from your travel."

With a last squeeze, The MacKeir released her hand

and leapt from his horse. "Fine idea, my lord." He clapped Rand on the back. Luckily, her brother was a big man himself, or he would be sprawling on the ground from the force of the blow. Of course, during his long friendship with Lugh MacKeir, Rand had learned to brace himself. "Come, Amice," The MacKeir said as he held out his hand to her.

"Unfortunately, I cannot, Chief MacKeir. I am leaving."

Heavy black brows furrowed into a single line. "Leaving? But 'tis too soon, my precious. My men and I need to remain overnight and rest our horses."

She sighed. "Not with you. I must journey to Falcon's Craig."

"Nay. I forbid it." His forest green eyes flashed with possession. "My bride stays with me."

The whole conversation was so ridiculous, she was tempted to laugh. But she knew Lugh MacKeir well enough to clamp the urge. She had always thought of him as a gentle giant, but underneath dwelled a formidable Highland chief. She forced herself to smile politely. "I am not your bride, my lord."

He waved a hand. "Merely a matter of time. Do not worry, Amice. You shall be mine."

"I am not worried."

Obviously, he understood her response as assent and shot her an approving nod. "Let us discuss this in the hall. I have a powerful thirst on me, and I would look upon you."

"Chief MacKeir, did you not hear me? I must leave. Now."

He took a step toward her, his expression hardening.

Rand grabbed his arm and whispered something to him. As Amice watched, The MacKeir allowed Rand to pull him a small distance away and the two men held a soft, but clearly heated discussion, punctuated by several sharp looks in her direction from Chief MacKeir.

Finally, he stared at her brother and slowly tipped his head.

Amice looked at Rand, but his expression told her nothing. The warriors flanking The MacKeir stepped forward as he returned to her side.

Swallowing thickly, she waited for him to speak.

"You may journey to Falcon's Craig." He scowled. "Though I like it not, your brother convinces me 'tis important to you."

"Thank you, my lord."

"But when you return, I shall be here, ready to take you to Tunvegen where you belong."

Tunvegen, deep in the Highlands, far from anything or anyone familiar. Far from a villa perched over the warm sea. She gripped the reins tight. "Has my brother agreed to this?"

"Nay. But he will. As soon as we come to terms." He stepped closer and before she could get out an objection, swept her down to the ground.

She peered up at him, all at once aware of just how big he was. Normally, she was nearly as tall as a man, but next to The MacKeir she felt almost fragile.

"You are mine, Amice."

She opened her mouth to protest but found it plundered by another. And plundered it was, his firm lips capturing hers, tasting her, stroking her tongue, and sweeping through her mouth with gentle force.

He broke the kiss and cocked a brow. " 'Tis only the beginning, my flower." He puffed out his broad chest. "The MacKeir shall make you cry with joy."

Her jaw dropped. Dear God, how was she to escape this wild Scot? A journey to Falcon's Craig suddenly did not seem long enough. Before her bewildered eyes, Chief MacKeir and his men trooped into the great hall with Rand, talking and laughing like the greatest of friends. Surely, Rand would not give her to this big bear of a man. He knew her heart's desire, supported it in fact.

"Come, Amice," Laila said. "We should go before your Chief MacKeir changes his mind."

Amice was on her horse and outside the gatehouse faster than she had ever been in her life. Surrounded by her guards, she spurred her mount to a gallop and never looked back.

❦ ❦ ❦

Four days later Amice, Laila, and their guardsmen finally approached Falcon's Craig. Amice pulled her horse to a stop on a low rise to study the castle. High curtain walls loomed deep red in the setting sun, and the wide moat swirled with shining ribbons of gold. Beyond the walls, she could hear the pounding of waves upon the shore, and a fresh, salty smell scented the air.

Laila pulled up beside her. " 'Tis impressive."

"Aye." An image of Cain smiling at his wife cut through her body like an arrow, and Amice did not move forward. Apprehension shivered down her spine, and she wondered if she had the strength to continue. Dear Lord, how could she do this?

"Shall we go? 'Twill be dark soon." Laila laid a hand on her shoulder.

Villa Delphino, Amice reminded herself. She clucked to her horse and the group made its way across the grassy outcrop toward the castle gatehouse. They rode past a troop of watchful guards atop the gatehouse and into the bailey.

No Cain.

As she swung to the ground, a man ran toward them from a building she assumed from its size was the great hall. "Lady Amice?" he called.

"Aye." As the man got closer, she noted a resemblance to Cain. He was nearly as tall, with the same lean, hard build. Light brown hair framed a friendly face, but instead of Cain's vivid blue eyes, this man's gaze was a lively brown.

He smiled. "Welcome to Falcon's Craig. I am Piers, the Earl of Hawksdown's brother."

Amice forced a slight smile. "This is my companion, Laila."

"Welcome to you both. Please, join me in the hall. Your guards may stable the horses, then come inside as well."

Amice gave a nod to Thomas, her head guard, then followed Piers. They climbed smooth stairs to the second floor of an immense stone structure and stepped into the great hall. Her legs trembled, and she forced herself to look toward the dais, stiffening in preparation for seeing Cain and his wife. To her puzzlement, the dais was empty, save for one white-haired man.

A Lost Touch of Bliss ❧ 17

"My Uncle Gifford." Piers tapped the side of his head with a finger. "A bit mad, but most amusing."

"Oh." She was not sure how to respond. "Where . . . where is the Countess of Hawksdown?" *The sooner I meet Cain's wife the better*, she thought. The prospect of the encounter was making her belly ache.

"Who?"

She looked at Piers with increasing confusion. "The lady of the castle. The Earl of Hawksdown's wife." Why she was explaining such an obvious thing she could not imagine, but perhaps Cain's uncle was not the only one with problems of the mind.

"Oh, you mean Luce." Piers shook his head. "Dead."

"What?" Surely she had not heard him clearly. A frisson of heat crackled along her nerve endings as she stared at Cain's brother.

"Dead three years ago, my lady. My . . . cousin Morganna acts as lady of the castle."

Cain's wife was dead. The news shot through her head like a bolt of lightning, ringing her ears and heating her face. For a moment, she could not catch a breath. She gazed into Piers's curious eyes and lifted her chin. "Where is the Earl of Hawksdown?"

Piers shrugged. "Up on the battlements, most likely."

Suddenly, pure, cleansing anger cut through her discomfort. Damn Cain. Damn him for failing to mention his wife's death, and damn him for not even appearing to greet her. Why should she be surprised? Cain had made his indifference to her clear enough in the past. Painfully obvious.

"My lady? Would you like to dine here in the hall or

shall I have something brought to your chamber?"

"If you would take me to the battlements, I shall speak to the Earl of Hawksdown. In the meantime, Laila can unpack our things. We will take a light supper in our chamber."

"Of course, my lady." Piers looked around, then called out "Hawis!"

A small, round woman rushed over. Her sparking brown eyes took quick measure of Amice and Laila, lingering on Laila's dusky skin and black hair.

"Where is Morganna?" Piers asked her.

Hawis rolled her eyes.

Piers said something under his breath, then told Hawis, "This is Lady Amice Monceaux and her companion, Laila.

Hawis flashed them a bright smile. "Welcome to Falcon's Craig."

"Thank you," Amice said,

"How may I serve you, my lady?"

Amice's face softened at the woman's friendly manner. "Could you show my companion, Laila, to our chamber?"

"And bring food and drink, Hawis," Piers instructed. He turned to Amice and tilted his head. "Come with me, my lady."

They left the great hall and walked over to another square tower built into one corner of the inner curtain wall. " 'Tis the best view," Piers offered.

She forced her feet to move up narrow steps behind Piers, focusing on not tangling her feet in the folds of her mantle. At last, they emerged onto a flat platform, and Amice could see the stone walkway stretched atop the long wall.

"There he is," Piers said close to her ear. "I shall leave you and make sure your companion is settled."

"Thank you, my lord."

"Call me Piers," he said with a wink, before disappearing into the tower below.

For a moment, she just stood and studied Cain, a solitary figure outlined by the fading sun. He had changed. An air of remoteness cloaked him like a shadow now. She had always thought of him as her tall, fair-haired, elegant knight, but that man was gone.

As if he sensed her presence, Cain turned and stared at her.

Amice caught her breath. She stared into his blue eyes, so familiar even after five years, and heat surged through her veins to pool in a tingling at her fingertips. Ocean eyes, she had called them once. Knowing eyes.

He walked toward her, his broad shoulders briefly blocking the fading light. His face was full of harsh angles and a jagged scar crossed his left cheek. "Amice. Welcome to Falcon's Craig. Thank you for coming." His voice was cool, stiff.

The heat died. "I came for Villa Delphino as you knew I would."

His gaze was utterly blank. "How have you fared?"

A thousand thoughts tumbled through her mind, things she would like to say but never would. Pride forbade it. It was as if all of the defenses she had constructed over the years melted into the blue of his eyes. A longing settled into her joints like an unrelenting ache. Damn him. And damn her for her weakness. She lifted her chin. "Well. And you?"

He frowned slightly. "Also well."

She gritted her teeth. In one moment she wanted to scream at him and slap the bland expression from his face, and in the next it was all she could do not to reach for him. Anything but standing here pretending to be naught but old friends. She drew in a deep breath and hardened her expression. "I was surprised not to see you awaiting us in the bailey."

Cain looked out over the sea and the wind blew back his shoulder-length, blond hair. "I apologize. I did not realize you had arrived."

She bit her lip. If his manner were any cooler, she would freeze to ice in place. He had become even more closed to her. And she was still a fool. "What do you want of me?"

"I need the Spirit Goddess."

She was right in her guess. He would have never asked for her if he were not desperate. "I see."

"Amice." He took a step toward her, and she stiffened. "I understand. You wish me to get rid of a ghost."

"Aye." His jaw looked like sculpted marble.

"You will give me Villa Delphino."

"Aye."

"And arrange for travel and provisions."

"That was not part of my offer."

"It is part of my acceptance."

He hesitated, his face like the ocean itself, deep and unreadable. "Very well."

For a moment, she just stared at him, willing him to say something, a word to show he felt *anything* for her other than a need for her services. When time passed in silence, she drew her angry pride around her like an impenetrable mail hauberk. "It has been a long journey. We can speak more of this on the morrow."

"You agree?"

"Of course. That is the only reason I am here." Before his perceptive gaze could brand her a liar, Amice turned and made her way back down to the ground. She would not cry, she swore to herself. She cared nothing for Cain Veuxfort. Just as he cared nothing for her.

Chapter 2

Cain gave serious thought to flinging himself into the roiling sea. He knew he had not handled things well. Not well at all.

He should have been there to greet her. But when he heard she approached, he had fled to the battlements in a futile effort to prepare himself for meeting her again.

Even so, he had not expected seeing Amice to be this difficult. Over the years, he had convinced himself that she was not as beautiful as he pictured her, that the vulnerability he saw in the depths of her eyes was mere illusion.

He had even managed to persuade himself that his experience with Amice was simply youthful folly, physical desire, not a matter of the heart.

Amice, the girl, was beguiling, lovely, like a honeyed wine. But Amice, the woman, was a heady brew, dark and still, promising everything and yielding nothing.

It struck Cain then that he was every bit as cursed as he had been five years ago.

❦ ❦ ❦

Hawis was waiting for Amice at the foot of the curtain wall and guided her to a chamber in yet another tower within the walls, chattering all the while about how nice it was to have visitors. Thankfully, Amice did not have to say too much. Her emotions seethed like water in a boiling pot, and she desperately wanted to smash something to bits.

When they climbed the spiral steps and entered the chamber, Amice found it unoccupied. "Where is Laila?"

Hawis gestured to a door on one side of the room. "There is an adjoining room with space for her there." She bustled into the chamber and poked at a fire.

Amice looked around with growing surprise. She had not expected such luxury. With Hawis's ministrations, the fire burned merrily, warming the chamber. A bed nestled against one wall, encircled by velvety, rose-colored hangings. Two trunks sat against another wall. Though the shutters were closed, it appeared that the chamber possessed two large windows, with wide stone windowseats tucked below them.

Gesturing to a small table next to the bed, Hawis said, "There is cheese, beef, bread, and wine, my lady." She gestured toward another arched doorway. "The garderobe is through there."

"Thank you, Hawis."

The other woman turned and surveyed the chamber,

then nodded. "There is a bowl of clean water and cloths on that trunk. Do you need anything else?"

"Nay. The chamber is lovely."

Hawis pointed to one set of shutters. " 'Tis even nicer during the day. That window overlooks the sea, and the other, the garden."

Amice smiled. Apparently her arrival pleased someone in the castle. "Good night, Hawis."

"Good eve, my lady."

After Hawis left, she poked her head into the adjoining chamber. Laila was already asleep, her soft snores echoing through the darkness. She returned to her chamber, poured a cup of wine, and sat down on the rush mats in front of the fire.

Tomorrow, she and Laila would attempt to contact Cain's ghost. In her mind, she began making a list of what they would need. Sage. Her white bliaut. She tried to focus on their task, but images of Cain's face kept interfering with her thoughts. Curse him and his false heart.

Finally, she gave up and just stared into the flames as memories poured over her. The taste of him, the deep satisfaction of his touch. His smile, the expression in his eyes when he looked at her. People used to comment on it, how intensely he looked at her. Talk in wonder about how his gaze bespoke a deep love.

Until he decided she was not to his advantage. Not good enough for the future Earl of Hawksdown. Until he told her farewell as if they had barely known each other, and left to marry another.

She blinked back a tear.

"You are not wanted here."

The smallest breeze drifted over her hair and she turned.

So, there is a ghost.

A woman stood before her, or rather floated above the floor. Long tendrils of reddish hair twirled around her, brushing against a dark green gown. A gold circlet sat atop her hair, and jeweled rings glimmered in the firelight. A noblewoman, then.

Her voice was surprisingly strong. Amice did not move. "Why?"

"I shall not leave. This is my home."

The breeze quickened, causing the flames to sway. "Who are you?"

" 'Tis none of your affair. Pack your things and leave this place."

"Why are you still here?"

The ghost just glared at her.

Amice tried again. "I may be able to help you."

"I do not want your help. Go away."

"What is your name?"

The spirit glided closer, and a strikingly fair face stared down at Amice. A smile twisted her lips. "Cain Veuxfort never loved you. He never intended to ask for you. 'Twas all a lie. You were naught but a dalliance, foolishly willing to grant him the use of your body."

Heat stung Amice's face. For a moment, she was too shocked to say anything. How did this spirit know anything about her and Cain? And was she right? It was a question Amice had asked herself many times over the years. She shoved back the burn of shame and squared her shoulders. " 'Tis of no matter."

The ghost laughed then, a strangely bitter sound that danced across Amice's skin like pinpricks. "Leave now."

"I cannot."

With a swish of green, she simply disappeared.

Amice took a big gulp of wine and stared at the space the wraith had just occupied. The air still shimmered with a faint echo of her presence. So, there was to be a battle. Surely, between them, she and Laila could handle one determined ghost.

Even one who knew that she had given all of herself to a man who walked away without a thought. Pray God, the ghost did not know Amice's most deeply buried secret as well. It was the one that finally broke her. Neither time nor her strongest efforts had ever made her whole again.

Cain Veuxfort had taken too much of her with him.

🐎 🐎 🐎

The next morning, Amice sat in the great hall with Laila, a bite of golden cheese partway to her mouth, when the man Piers had identified as his Uncle Gifford burst into the hall, waving a sword, his eyes flashing with fervor.

"Hellbound bitch!" he shouted. "Damn you." He whirled and struck at something invisible, managing to send a platter of cold meat flying though the air. A brace of hounds sprang to fight over the morsels, snapping and tumbling across the floor.

Amice put down her cheese and looked around for signs of the ghost. "Do you see anything?" she whispered to Laila.

"Nay, but it appears he does."

She and Laila watched in fascination as the man rushed about the great hall, brandishing his sword. Chunks of bread flew into the air like stones from a trebuchet. People hid under the trestle tables and Piers sat next to them atop the dais laughing so hard his eyes teared. There was no sign of Cain.

"Ah hah!" Gifford hollered, just before he slashed down, bouncing cups into the air. Ale splashed over the table onto the floor. "I shall get you this time, cursed wench!"

As he wound up for another swing, Cain rushed into the hall. He shot Amice an aggrieved look before yelling at Gifford, "Stop! Stop this at once."

His uncle paused and glared at Cain. "Damn wench spoiled another experiment."

"Uncle Gifford, you cannot kill a ghost with a sword." Cain blew out a breath, then ducked as his uncle gave a shout and charged toward him.

"There she is! Hold on, boy."

Amice clapped a hand across her mouth.

Cain managed to catch the older man by the legs, and they fell on the soiled rushes in a heap. "Give me that damn sword," Cain ordered.

Somewhat sheepishly, his uncle handed it over.

Cain stood up, brushed a piece of bread from his hair, and set the sword on a table.

"Dear Lord, what is going on here?" another voice demanded.

Amice turned to find a young woman staring at the scene with disbelief. She heard Piers groan.

Cain's sigh was audible across the expanse of the hall. "Hello, Sister. How nice of you to visit."

This was Cain's sister? Amice's mouth dropped open. The woman's cheekbones stuck out from pale, taut skin like sharp mountain peaks. A white linen wimple and veil covered her hair, and a voluminous, grey bliaut encased her figure. The only spot of color was her lips, tightly pursed in what Amice suspected was a habitual look of disapproval.

The woman strode over to Cain, sparing a glance of displeasure at Piers. "I asked a question."

Cain reached down and helped his uncle up.

"Good morrow, Agatha," Gifford beamed. "How nice of you to journey from Styrling Castle to see us."

Agatha sniffed. "What were you chasing with that sword?"

"Accursed wraith." Gifford frowned. "Almost caught her too."

"What?" Agatha looked at Cain and, amazingly, pursed her lips even tighter together.

Piers snuck out of the hall.

"A ghost, Sister. We have a ghost who enjoys making trouble."

His sister's mouth gaped open like someone had just

prodded her stomach with a needle. "Are you mad? There is no such thing as a ghost."

Amice waited.

A pitcher of ale rose gracefully into the air and upturned directly over Agatha's head.

"Ahhh!" she sputtered, swiping ale from her dripping cheeks.

Cain looked as if he wanted to flee but held his ground. "As I said. But worry not, Sister. I have taken steps to rid us of this scourge." He gave Amice a pointed look.

"Perhaps we should get started," Laila murmured.

Nodding, Amice stood.

Noting the movement, Agatha whirled and spotted Amice. She pointed and asked, "Who is that woman?"

"I am Lady Amice de Monceaux, my lady. This is my companion, Laila."

Cain stepped forward. "Lady Amice is here to . . . help."

His sister looked so perplexed that for a moment Amice felt sorry for her. Agatha's mouth opened and closed but nothing emerged. Finally, she grabbed her attendant by the hand and reeled from the hall, shaking her head and muttering.

Gifford swaggered over to Amice and Laila, followed slowly by Cain. "Ignore Agatha's poor manners, my dear. Welcome to Falcon's Craig. I am Cain's uncle, Gifford Blanchard. Just Gifford to you lovely ladies." His bright green eyes sparkled with mischief.

Amice grinned. " 'Tis a pleasure, my lord."

"What happened?" Laila asked.

" 'Twas the ghost, of course. She is forever tampering

with my work, just out of spite. Never did a thing to her."

"What kind of work?"

Cain put an arm around his uncle's shoulder and squeezed. "Naught of interest."

Gifford rolled his eyes. "My nephew is such a dull boy, no imagination at all. He does not approve of alchemy."

"Ah." Amice heard the interest in Laila's voice. "What do you hope to discover?"

Leaning closer, Gifford whispered, "The greatest secret of all. Merlin."

Amice started to think Uncle Gifford was more than a "bit" mad.

Cain frowned. "Gifford, please."

Gifford shook off Cain's arm. "I must return to my workroom. Who knows what that infernal sprite is up to in my absence." He nodded to Amice and Laila and trotted off, pausing to retrieve the sword from where Cain had left it.

Slowly releasing a sigh, Cain said, "I would advise you to steer clear of Gifford's workroom. He is not always as careful as he should be."

"Does he . . . he really believe he can find Merlin?" Amice asked.

"Unfortunately, yes." Cain rubbed the back of his neck. "At least it gives him something to do."

Five years ago, she would have smoothed away the lines of strain bracketing his mouth, but she clenched the skirt of her bliaut instead, reminding herself she was charged with a task, nothing more. "I met your ghost last eve, my lord."

Cain lifted a brow. "And? When will she be gone?"

"She is insistent on remaining within the castle."

"I want this finished and my home back. Now." His sea blue eyes held her gaze fast.

A tendril of hurt coiled through her chest. Amice lifted her chin. "And I want Villa Delphino. But we have not yet been here a full day, my lord. I fear you shall have to endure our presence a while longer."

Laila touched her shoulder.

Amice gazed down into Laila's dark brown eyes gleaming with reassurance and felt the hurt ease.

"I shall gather our supplies while you question Lord Hawksdown, my lady."

Amice nodded. "Thank you, Laila."

Cain just stared at her. Finally, he said, "I do not know anything about her. Other than she has succeeded in turning my life into utter chaos."

"You do not have any idea who she is?"

He shook his head. "Nay, nor why she haunts us. She has never spoken to anyone."

Amice gulped. "She spoke to me."

Cain narrowed his eyes. "Who is she?"

"She refused to tell me."

"What did she say?"

"She ordered me to leave, told me she would not go." Amice dropped her gaze, remembering what else the ghost had said.

As if he read her mind, Cain asked, "What else? What are you not telling me?"

"Naught of import."

Cain grabbed her arms. "What are you hiding this time, Amice?"

She gritted her teeth against the insult, and lifted her gaze to glare at him. "She told me I never meant anything to you except a willing body to slake your lust upon."

His face flinched as if she had slapped him, and his grip on her arms tightened. " 'Tis not true."

Her face burned. "Oh? I think' 'tis exactly the truth. I was a fool not to have seen it at the time."

"Amice, I cared for you, you must know that. But—"

"Cease," she snapped. "I remember your actions very clearly. But worry not, I shall stay until your ghost is gone and I get my villa."

He dropped his hands and stepped back. "You are wrong," he said softly. "As is that damn ghost."

For a moment, she looked into his eyes, desperately wanting to believe him. But the facts denied his claim. The past could not be changed.

She whirled and rushed from the hall before he could give her more lies. It was bad enough to know the only man she would ever love had once *cared* for her.

Why had she come here? Every glance, every word from Cain was like another jagged splinter stabbing into her heart, reminding her what a fool she was.

Well, she might still be a fool, but she had become a strong fool. Strong enough to deal with Cain Veuxfort and get what she came here for.

🕯 🕯 🕯

Cain watched Amice and her companion enter the great hall for supper and reconsidered the wisdom of summoning her to Falcon's Craig. Amice wore a deep purple silk bliaut that outlined her lush body, and her rich hair tumbled down her back in glossy waves. Every time he looked at her, he felt as if his skin itched. Itched to feel hers.

He took a deep breath and reminded himself once again of the reasons why he could not have her. It was all that kept him from throwing himself on her like some kind of ravenous beast. That and the fact she rightfully despised him.

Next to him, Piers twirled a cup and shot out an arm to prevent Gifford from pulling the jug of wine closer. "Ah, the lovely Lady Amice."

Gifford chortled and made a successful lunge for the wine. "Like a bright flower in a barren desert, she is."

From the end of the table, Cain's cousin Morganna's blue eyes glared at them. As usual, she wore a bliaut carefully constructed to expose as much of her breasts as possible, her blonde hair arranged to look tousled. Her full mouth was set in a pout. Agatha had yet to make an appearance, hiding in her chamber most likely.

As Amice and her companion neared the dais, Cain rose. When she noticed the empty chair next to his, Amice halted.

The hum of conversation from the lower trestle tables stilled, then resumed in a buzz of speculative whispers.

Before Cain could move, Piers bounced up and leapt off the dais to offer Amice his arm. "Good eve, my fair lady. May I escort you to the table?"

Cain's stomach tightened when Amice looked up at his brother and giggled. Actually giggled. He scowled at Piers as they stepped up onto the dais, but naturally his brother's only response was a grin.

"Good eve, Amice," he said as she took her seat, and the woman called Laila settled at the other end from Morganna.

Amice stared straight ahead. "Good eve, my lord."

"Can you not call me by name?"

Slowly, she turned and stared at him. God, but she was beautiful. A man could get lost in her eyes for a lifetime and more. Her lips thinned. "I prefer not to."

He blinked. "Why?"

Before Amice responded, Gifford called over, "You look lovely this evening, my dear. Do you not think so, Piers?"

Piers smiled. "Enchanting."

"That reminds me of a song," Gifford began.

Oh, no, Cain thought. Not one of his uncle's songs. God only knew what the lyrics would be. "Uncle Gifford, we do not need a song."

"Dull. Dull as dirt. Piers?"

"Aye?"

Gifford jumped to his feet and linked arms with Piers. In a deep, carrying voice, he started singing. " 'Come ouer the wooods fair and green, the goodly maid, that lusty wench; To shadow you from the sun; Under the woode there is a bench.' "

Piers and Gifford swayed back and forth, accompanied now by the musicians on the side of the hall with their rebec and harp.

" 'Sir, I pray you do not offence, To me a maid, thus I make my mind; But as I came let me go hense; For I am here myself alone . . .' "

Cain buried his face in his hands as at that moment,

Agatha decided to come out of hiding. Following some idiotic verse about lying down in a bed of flowers with a not so vague reference to the man's "stamen," the two fell mercifully silent.

From the trestle tables below, clapping began, and grew in volume, his people stamping their feet and shouting encouragement to Gifford. Cain leaned back in his chair and filled his cup to the brim with wine.

He tensed as hands suddenly stroked his shoulders. Twisting back, he saw the hands belonged to Morganna, who gazed down at him with a sly smile on her lips. From the corner of his eye, he noted Amice's surprise, then an instant of something that actually looked like distress before she shielded her expression. Was it possible that another woman's attention bothered her? Nay, that was ridiculous. Amice had no particular affection for him. Men had always panted after her. But a persistent voice inside him asked, why had she not married?

"Pay no attention, my lord. You cannot control those two," Morganna purred.

"Aye. Well I know." He shot Gifford a chastising look, which his uncle blithely ignored. Cain abruptly became aware that Morganna's hardened nipples pressed into his back, and he inched forward. "Thank you, Morganna. 'Tis enough."

She sighed, her fingers lingering at his neck. "Very well. I shall see to your needs later."

He whipped around to correct her absurd implication, but Morganna was already gliding toward the end of the table.

"Lusty wench," Piers muttered.

The edge of a smile tickled Amice's lips before she suppressed it.

Cain fought the urge to smile back. "Piers, do not speak so of your cousin."

"Hardly a cousin, the connection is so far removed."

"Still, Morganna is family."

"Don't act like family," Gifford added. "Acts like a wench after a title."

Cain motioned the servants to begin serving, noting that Agatha had seated herself as far as possible from Morganna. He could not blame her. With Luce dead, he had taken pity on Morganna when she appeared at Falcon's Craig, figuring they needed a lady to look after things. He had since come to realize that her sad story of life at Marrick Abbey was most likely a falsehood to conceal the true reason she had been tossed out. Morganna might be of noble blood, but her morals were that of the lowliest whore.

He turned his attention to Amice. "Did you make any progress today?"

"Not very much." Amice turned down her mouth.

"Did you find out her name?"

"Nay, naught but the fact she is often seen at the east tower. We searched there, but found no record of her."

"The east tower overlooking the sea?"

"Aye."

"What shall you do next?" Despite his doubts, he found himself intrigued by Amice and her companion's unusual undertaking.

Amice glanced at him. "We shall attempt to summon

her and ask her who she is."

"She refused before."

"This time, Laila shall be with me. And we will be prepared."

Gifford peered around Cain. "How do you prepare to call a ghost?" He sounded like an excited child.

Amice gave him a mystical smile. "Now, that is my secret."

Cain hid his disappointment. He too was curious. More than curious. This was a part of Amice's life he knew nothing about. It made him feel even more distanced from her, and he found he did not like it. "How did you become involved in this sort of thing?"

"We had a bit of a problem at Wareham, a displaced lord who did not wish to leave. I asked for aid from an encampment of the Rom on our lands. 'Tis a long story, but in the end, I discovered I can reach out to a ghost and help him move on."

Gifford and Piers both gazed at Amice wide-eyed. "The Rom? You mean those thieving Egyptians? They *helped* you?"

Amice's back stiffened. "Aye. And refused payment."

Piers let out a whistle. "Odd, that. They must have taken to you."

Amice shrugged.

Cain gazed at her thoughtfully. There was more to this story than she was telling. Much more. But then Amice had always been one to guard her secrets. He peered over at her companion, Laila, and noted her small stature, brown skin, and bright black eyes with interest. "How many of these ghosts have you helped to . . . move on?"

"Enough." She looked at him clear-eyed. "Do not worry, I shall solve your problem. And then I shall be gone."

The idea of her leaving brought a pang of dull hollowness to Cain's chest, but he shoved it away. Whatever he and Amice once had was long gone. You could never go back.

Not that he wanted to. The image of Amice in the arms of the Earl of Stanham fluttered at the edge of his memory. Oh, she had claimed innocence, but the guilty expression on her face and the triumphant one on Stanham's told the truth. He swore on that day never to let his heart be that vulnerable again.

And then he had followed what he believed was the honorable path, only to discover it led to utter emptiness.

Still, he had other memories of Amice too, memories fresh and alive despite the passage of time. He remembered it all—feeling like the luckiest man in the world, the simple joy of just holding her hand, the way her eyes darkened with passion, the paradise of sinking into her body. And above all, the sense that his very soul merged with hers in pure completeness.

Perfection that turned out to be false illusion.

Cain set his jaw.

There was no going back.

"I look forward to the end of this as well, my lady."

❧ ❧ ❧

By the time Amice escaped to her chamber, her head ached and her stomach felt as if someone were twisting it in his fist. It was bad enough to be close to Cain, but to endure Morganna's obvious hostility and Agatha's scrutiny as well was too much.

She retrieved a ewer of wine and a cup, then walked over to the window seat. The shutters opened to show the black sea below. It swirled endlessly, a dark, deep abyss lit by splashes of moonlight. A breeze lifted her hair and brushed her face with warm, salty, moist air. Amice closed her eyes and took a deep breath.

She heard a sound behind her and turned. Laila gazed at her with compassion. "Are you all right, *te' sorthene*?"

Her heart-friend. It was the finest name anyone had ever called her. "Ah, Laila, 'tis so hard." Amice sat on the stone seat and poured some wine into the cup.

Laila sat next to her. "Amice, I believe the Earl of Hawksdown still has feelings for you."

Feelings. Amice took a sip of wine. A bleak sadness settled into her chest.

Laila took her hand. "The way he looks at you." She drew in a sharp breath. "Such hunger, such intensity. I can feel the force of it in the air."

"Lust."

"More than lust."

A part of her wanted to believe Laila, but there lay the path to new torment. She would not allow herself to be so poorly used again. "Nay."

Laila gazed intently at her, then rose and patted Amice on the shoulder. "I am to bed. Do you wish me to help you with your bliaut?"

She forced a smile to her face. "Nay. Goodnight, Laila. Dream well."

As Laila walked toward the next chamber, she turned and gave Amice an encouraging look. "Do not worry, my lady. All will be as it should."

Amice nodded. After Laila left, she stripped off her bliaut and undertunic and stood at the window in her chemise, gazing down at the rocky beach and watching the moonglow dance on the waves. How she wished she could just fly into the sky, free as a falcon, living just to live, unhindered by past pain and impossible longing.

She stared down at the beach, gradually realizing what she was looking at. With a gasp, she took half a step back. Cain strode out of the waves, beautifully naked, his sleek contours bathed in pale light. The sight hit her like a dagger to the chest. She suddenly remembered every inch of his body, remembered gliding her fingertips over his warm skin, remembered how perfectly he loved her as if it all had happened but a moment ago.

A woman emerged from the shadows and threw her arms around Cain. Amice sucked in a breath. Even from the distance, she recognized the woman. Morganna. Cain's "cousin," who sought to ease his tension. Morganna, who reminded Amice of a pretty doll, all creamy skin, golden hair and large, round blue eyes.

She slammed the shutters closed and took a big gulp of wine. She should be thankful, she told herself. It was a reminder to her not to weaken.

A tear leaked from her eye and the wall around her heart split open. She gulped in air, willing her emotions back behind her shields. But she felt as if Cain had sliced open her chest and no matter how hard she tried to keep them in, her long-buried feelings bled out of the fissure. *Fool. I am naught but a fool.*

"Please, dear Lord, help me to finish my task quickly. Let me send this ghost away at once so that I might depart. Please help me to be strong. Help me, Lord."

Amice dropped to the floor and clamped her hand against her mouth to stifle her sobs.

❧ ❧ ❧

"Morganna, let loose." Cain unwound his cousin's arms from his shoulders and stepped back, looking for his clothes.

Morganna pouted. "Oh, Cain, do not be so serious."

"There is nothing wrong with being serious. Someone needs to be."

She ran a fingertip down the side of his forehead. "But you seem so tense, so frustrated. I can relieve that, bring a smile to your face."

"I appreciate your concern, but I am fine." Cain drew on his braies and began walking back toward the castle. He heard a sputtering behind him but he did not pause. *Silly woman.*

"Cain, wait."

Without turning, he called back, "Come, Morganna."

Her response was a loud huff of irritation.

Cain gritted his teeth. He was in sore need of release, but bedding Morganna did not appeal. She was easy enough on the eye, but he saw calculation in her gaze. Despite his inability to swim, he would rather immerse himself in the cool sea than risk involvement with her.

Not that it would help anyway. The only true source of release for him lay abed in the rose chamber, no doubt praying she would be able to leave without delay.

He stalked in through the small sea gate and locked it tight after making sure a sullen Morganna came inside. "Go to bed."

She took a step toward him. "Are you sure you do not desire company?"

He frowned at her. "You should value yourself more highly, Morganna."

"Oh, but I do." She sent him a siren's smile.

"Goodnight."

Her mouth drew down in a scowl. " 'Tis *her* fault."

"Who?"

She scoffed. "Amice de Monceaux."

He straightened his shoulders. "Nay."

"Aye, it is. You still want that amazon. I can scarcely believe it."

"You do not know what you are talking about."

Morganna gave him a sly smile. "Oh, but I do. I have ears. And I can see it in your eyes."

"You are imagining things. Get to your bed."

With a final mocking look, Morganna turned and flounced away.

He stood and stared across the bailey toward the tower containing the rose chamber. The strength of his longing astounded him. It was as if the years vanished in the span of a heartbeat, the countless times he admonished himself to forget Amice de Monceaux meaningless.

He should not be surprised. Amice had always had the ability to slice through to his heart while safeguarding her own.

But he had accepted that he could not satisfy his goddess long ago.

It was bad enough to witness betrayal by a woman for whom he held no affection.

Amice's betrayal would destroy him completely.

Chapter 3

After verifying nothing appeared close to exploding, Piers slipped into Gifford's workroom. His uncle was busily pounding on something with a heavy metal mallet. When he spotted Piers, he set down the mallet and reached for a nearby jug to take a drink.

Piers looked down at Gifford's project. "What are you doing?"

"Had an idea to help that dull nephew of mine."

"Not sure how a pink rock is going to make Cain start to live again."

Gifford snorted. "Not just a rock. I am going to use it to create a special elixir." He winked and took another drink.

"You are sotted."

"Nay. I am never sotted."

Incredibly, Piers had to admit Gifford was right. His uncle soaked up drink like an endless trencher. "What is it?"

"Rose quartz. Once I distill it down, we can add it to Cain's wine."

"And?"

Gifford shrugged. "It will aid him to open his heart."

Piers started laughing. "You jest. A pink rock can achieve that kind of miracle?"

"Mayhap not alone." Gifford chuckled. "Have you another idea?"

"Nay." Piers scowled. "Damn Cain and his rigid sense of duty. He should have taken the way out Luce's father offered."

"And Ismena, the domineering bitch, should never have betrothed Cain to a woman like Luce. Ismena was never one to consider anything but her own aspirations." Gifford picked up the mallet and smacked it down upon the quartz, breaking the stone into smaller pieces. "But 'tis all in the past."

Piers grabbed the jug and took a swallow of ale. "What do you think of the Lady Amice?"

As Gifford placed the pieces of crystal into a pot hanging over the fire, he said, "She has promise. I must admit, I am most intrigued by this," he paused and quickly looked around the chamber, "vocation of hers. Remarkable talent, that."

"Aye. And I think there is much more to what happened between her and Cain than we know."

"Undoubtedly."

Piers grinned. "I believe I shall see if I can find out the story."

"You do that. With a bit of luck, perhaps we can stir something up there. She *is* a beauty."

Piers left the workroom whistling. They needed something to breach his brother's complete devotion to training and managing his estates. He had a strong feeling that Lady Amice de Monceaux was just the weapon they needed.

❧ ❧ ❧

Amice gaped at the old woman in surprise. She and Laila had been all over the castle asking questions about the elusive ghost of Falcon's Craig and had come up with nothing. Until now. "Malina, are you sure?"

Malina stopped kneading bread and nodded toward Amice. "Aye, I heard the story when I was but a wee one."

Amice glanced at Laila with excitement. "Tell us what you remember."

"Well, let me think." Malina began kneading again, the rhythmic motions of her gnarled hands seeming to aid her thoughts. " 'Twas said she threw herself from atop the east tower, straight over the cliff down to the beach."

"Why?"

"That I do not know." Malina frowned and paused her kneading. "I seem to remember something about her heart having been broken, but naught more."

"Who was she?"

Malina shook her head. " 'Tis all I remember, my lady. I am sorry."

Amice put her hand on the old woman's shoulder. "Nay, do not be sorry. You have been very helpful."

She gave Amice a gap-toothed smile. "Never seen her, meself, but I know she's caused the lord a bushel of trouble."

"Aye. Not for much longer."

Malina nodded and returned to her kneading.

Laila laid a hand on Amice's arm. "Come. We must prepare."

"Aye. Malina?"

"My lady?"

"Where can I obtain a bath?"

The old woman grinned. "The bathhouse, most likely."

"Bathhouse?"

"Aye, in the garden. Ask one of the grooms to build up the fire for you and fill the tub. The water is drawn from the pond. One of the young lord's ideas."

Amice was astonished. She had heard of such a structure, but never imagined finding one at Falcon's Craig. "Thank you, Malina."

As they left the kitchen and emerged into the bailey, Amice hailed a passing groom and made her request.

He bobbed his head and turned to go toward the garden.

Like a biting wind, a shaft of apprehension slid down her spine as she followed Laila up to her chamber. "Laila, something feels different this time."

"Aye." Laila frowned as she carefully sorted through cloth bags of herbs. Briefly, she closed her hand around their dreaming stones and shut her eyes.

"You feel it too?"

"There are powerful emotions in this place. Strong *tattipani*."

"Spirits? You sense more than one."

"Aye, but I know not who it is, or even if it is man or

woman. Just a shadowy sense of another."

Amice swallowed. "Evil?"

Laila shook her head. "Nay, but troubled certainly."

Forcing back her unease, Amice nodded. "They all are. But soon, at least Falcon's Craig shall be free of roaming spirits, and we can return home."

Laila opened her eyes and stared at Amice. "You are anxious to depart?"

Her heart lurched. "The sooner I leave here, the happier I shall be."

"But, the Earl of Hawksdown, I thought perhaps—"

"Nay! He dallies with Morganna."

Laila's eyes grew huge in her face. "Are you sure?"

"Aye." She twisted her lips in a bitter smile. "I saw them myself last eve on the beach."

"Oh." Laila walked over and gave her a hug. "I am sorry, *chav*."

Amice blinked back a tear. "As you said, all shall be as it should."

Laila gave her a mischievous grin. "Well, you do have The MacKeir."

"Oh, Lord. I had almost managed to put him from my mind." Shaking her head, Amice could not help but laugh. "I can only hope Rand has dissuaded him from claiming me."

"Perhaps." Laila giggled. "He does appear rather devoted though."

"Aye, like an overgrown puppy." Amice turned to go, still chuckling at the memory of Lugh MacKeir. She could not dislike the man. In fact, he was somewhat endearing, though outrageous. As she made her way down the steps and across the bailey to the bathhouse, she briefly considered Lugh as a prospective husband. He made no secret of his adoration and he was a handsome man. He made her laugh, even without trying.

She sighed. Maybe it was selfish, certainly the dream of a young girl, but she wanted to love her husband. Pray Rand had enough care for her not to agree to The MacKeir's request.

Across the bailey, she spotted Cain riding in under the gatehouse and increased her pace. After last night, she had carefully reconstructed her shields, painstakingly fortified herself. She was safe again.

But Cain was the last person she wished to see at the moment. With luck, she and Laila could finish tonight and leave on the morrow. Amice ignored a twinge of regret.

It was for the best. She would return to Wareham and never see Cain Veuxfort again.

✦ ✦ ✦

Cain tossed his mount's reins to one of the grooms and paced across the bailey, mentally listing the supplies needed in Hazelstone. Several of the villagers' huts required repairs, and Ranaulf needed a new team of oxen to pull his plough.

As he neared the great hall, he heard his sister's voice and stopped. Her tone told him some poor soul was the subject of one of Agatha's lectures. If only he could find a mate for her, a man to soften her, but her demeanor discouraged even the bravest hearts. Thank God she preferred to live at Styrling.

Turning, he made his way to his chamber, retrieved a change of clothes, and headed for the bathhouse. Perhaps an hour's soak would clear his mind and allow him to focus on things of importance. Making sure the planting proceeded on schedule. Seeing to his villeins' welfare. Training his men. Doing his duty. Carrying out his responsibilities.

Not dwelling on the blood-tingling fact that Amice was in his home.

He flung open the door of the bathhouse and froze. Amice had her back to him, her arms raised to soap her hair. Damn. Even her back was beautiful, all lush curves and smooth skin. His breath caught in his chest and his skin prickled with heat. She looked like a glistening statue of some mythical goddess. Cain shut the door with a soft thump.

Amice whirled around. Her eyes opened wide and her hands dropped to the water.

He knew he should turn and leave, but God help him, he could not look away. Her full breasts seemed to float on the water, the sight holding him fast. Somewhere Cain found his voice. "I . . . I did not know anyone was here."

Amice slid deeper under the water. He sniffed, realizing the small bathhouse smelled of lavender.

She gazed warily at him. "I shall be finished soon."

He stepped closer to the sunken pool and sat on a bench.

As she crossed her arms over her chest, her expressive eyes veiled.

His heart pounded an uneven rhythm and he felt warm. Nay, hot. The knowledge that Amice was naked, wet, and only a few feet away was making him daft. He had to be out of his mind not to run. "You like," he tried to swallow, "lavender?"

"Aye. 'Tis part of our ritual."

"Would you like help with your hair?" As soon as he asked the question, he could not believe his words. Why not just jump into the bath and do what he really desired? He was an addle-brain.

"Nay," Amice said quickly. "Cain, please."

"Please?"

"Go."

He studied her and let the moments pass in silence. It was all he could do not to join her. His body was as hard as iron, swollen with aching desire. He remembered with the sharp clarity of heartache what loving Amice had been like, and held on to his control by the thinnest thread of reason. "Are you sure?" he asked softly.

She turned away. "Aye," she whispered over her shoulder. "Leave now. Please."

Slowly, he stood and walked toward the door. He paused and looked back. Amice's shoulders were rigid, but just before he opened the door, Cain saw a tremor flit across her skin. He bolted from the bathhouse.

❧ ❧ ❧

Amice stared at the closed door for a long time after Cain left, trying to make some sense out of what had just happened. She splayed her hands and swished them through the warm water.

For a moment, she had thought she saw the same longing in his eyes she was sure shone from her own. But, no, it was impossible. They were back to the same thing. He desired her. She knew that. But desire was not enough. Not for her.

Quickly, she finished washing her hair and pulled on a fresh chemise and bliaut. Taking a deep breath, she opened the door to the bathhouse, half-dreading, half-hoping Cain would be waiting for her.

Instead she found his sister, Agatha.

Agatha sat on a bench facing the door to the bathhouse. She stared intently toward the doorway, her body tensed, her grey eyes open wide and blinking rapidly. She so closely resembled a hare, Amice would not have been surprised to see her nose twitching.

When Agatha spotted her, she leapt up. "Lady Amice, may I speak with you?"

Amice hesitated. Had Agatha seen Cain enter the bathhouse? Did she know what happened at Chasteney? She squared her shoulders. "How may I assist you, Lady Agatha?"

Edging closer, Agatha lowered her eyes, then raised her chin in a firm expression Amice recognized from Cain. "I want you to teach me."

"Teach you? Teach you what?"

Agatha fiddled with the folds of her drab, blue bliaut. "To be like you."

"I . . . I do not understand. Be like me in what way?"

Agatha bit her lip. "I know I shall never be a great beauty like you, but I wish to at least be passable." She gave Amice a forlorn expression. "If 'tis possible."

"Uh, yes, of course, 'tis possible." Amice's mind reeled to find the right words of reassurance.

"Good." Agatha beamed a smile, and Amice realized for the first time that it might indeed be possible. "When do we start?"

"Agatha, is there a particular reason you wish to change? A certain man?"

"Nay. Not yet, but someday I hope." Her eyes softened into a dove-like expression. "An elegant, learned, fair-haired man who will write me poetry. Perhaps one who can play an instrument and accompany me in song. A man who will walk with me to view my flowers." She looked at Amice. "I am a keen gardener, you know. The gardens at Styrling Castle are beyond compare."

"I did not know that," Amice said faintly.

"But of course the main thing I want is the mating." Agatha sniffed. "I am exceedingly tired of being a virgin."

For a moment, Amice just stared at her, vaguely aware her mouth was hanging wide open. "Mating?"

"Aye."

"Good God."

"I have shocked you."

"Uh, well, aye, a bit."

Agatha drew in her lips. "I prefer to be honest. And it is not as if I plan to sing silly songs about it, like my older brothers and crazy Uncle Gifford. Well, Piers anyway. Cain is not much for that sort of thing. Not anymore."

"What happened to change him?"

"Perhaps *you* can tell me."

"What?"

"And, of course, there was Luce." Agatha said the name with a sneer.

"He must have been very distraught at her death," Amice managed to say.

Agatha gave her a narrow look. "Aye, but not for the reason you might think."

"What do you mean?"

For a moment, Agatha stared back at her, but then shook her head. "Nay, that is a story to come from Cain, not me."

"But—"

"When do we start my lessons? You will help me?"

"Aye. Tomorrow?"

Wrinkling her nose, Agatha said, "I hoped today."

"My first duty is to . . . persuade your ghost to leave Falcon's Craig."

"Ghost." Agatha shivered. "Do not say anything more. Very well, tomorrow. When?"

"Sext?"

"Aye." Agatha's expression turned solemn. "Thank you, Amice. And thank you for not laughing at me."

"You are welcome."

Agatha nodded and walked away, leaving Amice staring after her in total befuddlement. Who could have imagined Cain's dour sister held such desires? And who could have imagined that she may have found an unlikely friend?

☞ ☞ ☞

The golden shimmer of a setting sun illuminated the chamber Amice and Laila had chosen to contact Falcon's

Craig's ghost. Situated on the upper floor of the castle's east tower, the chamber was largely empty, save for a bench, a few broken pieces of furniture, and a fireplace set into one wall, sooty black from inattention. Amice took in the bare timber floor, the large, open windows facing the sea, and felt a familiar sense of anticipation spread through her body.

She shot a sideways glance toward Cain and frowned. He had insisted on being here, claiming he had a right to see his bothersome spirit. He stood leaning against one wall, his brow curved, his arms folded across his chest. Watching. Wearing what Amice privately called his Knowing Expression.

He caught her scrutiny and gave her a bland look. As Laila set candles in iron holders upon the floor, Amice hung a small copper pot over the newly built fire and poured in a measure of water. She threw sage atop the burning wood, then reached into a pouch and began to add handfuls of herbs to the simmering water. Borage, fennel, fumitory, pennyroyal, rosemary, mugwort. And finally, a sprinkle of amber fragments.

For a moment, Amice just breathed in the herbal scent, blinking from the smoke as the sage caught fire.

She slipped off her enveloping mantle, and the fragrant air floated over her nearly bare skin. She wore only a plain, white silk bliaut. No chemise. No undertunic. Only the bliaut.

And, of course, the torc. An ancient Celtic gold collar, with two lion terminals, their eyes shiny red. Where Laila had obtained such a piece, Amice did not know, but on the eve of their first meeting, Laila had looked into her eyes, gone inside her tent, and emerged to place the torc around her neck.

"The Lion's Heart belongs to you," was all she had said.

Amice ran her fingers across the warm metal, then slipped off her shoes, and loosened her hair from its plaits.

She could feel Cain's eyes upon her like warm fingertips brushing across her skin. Studying her. Branding her.

Laila held a stick into the fire and began to light candles. Amice turned and caught sight of Cain out of the corner of her eye. He gazed at her as if he half-expected her to start flying around the room. "You shall remain quiet," she admonished.

Cain straightened his stance. "Why? I might be able to help."

She tilted her head. "You told me you knew nothing about her. Was that a lie?"

His skin flinched over his cheekbones. "Nay, 'tis true, but I do know something of my ancestors."

"Leave me to do what I have trained to do. 'Tis why you demanded I come here."

Cain's eyes flared, and the chamber narrowed to just the two of them. "Demanded?" he asked smoothly.

"As much. You knew I could not resist Villa Delphino. You *knew* because I shared my dream with you. And," she halted, the warmth of embarrassment creeping up her neck.

"And?"

She met his stare directly. "You knew I would not wish to come here."

Cain's lips twisted into a bitter smile. "Aye. I well

know you would not wish to see me ever again if 'twas your choice."

Laila moved beside Amice. "We are ready, Amice." Her calm words brought Amice out of the past and back to the present task. She inhaled the fragrant scents from the bowl and clutched the folds of her soft bliaut. She could not respond to Cain's last statement, uttered in such a harsh tone and so utterly untrue. "If I have a question, I shall ask. Otherwise, you shall stay where you are and be quiet. Agreed?"

Cain's stare was fire blue. "Agreed."

Amice and Laila stood in the center of the flickering candlelight, hands clasped. A collection of stones from the river by Wareham lay at their feet. Dreaming Stones.

The soft whisper of the night wind swirled across Amice's face, lifting strands of her loose hair and casting the chamber deeper into shadows. She focused on opening her mind, her senses, closing her eyes and drawing in deep breaths of the herbal scent filling the chamber.

"*Togaidh mise chlach, Mar a thog Moire da Mac, Air bhrìgh, air bhuaidh, "s air neart; Gun robh a chlachsa am dhòòrn, Gus an ruig mi mo cheann uidhe.*"

Gripping Laila's hands tightly, Amice slowly opened her eyes. "Come to me, troubled spirit. Tell me of your woe, so that I might aid you to the other side. Come to me."

Just as she heard a gasp, the air within the chamber thickened, as if there were too much mass in the same space. Her bliaut rippled around her body as if an unseen wind seized the fabric, and her hair blew behind her. The candles fluttered and nearly went out.

Laila's black eyes glittered and she gave a small nod.

"So, Amice de Monceaux, you did not heed my advice," a woman's voice said.

Amice dropped Laila's hands and turned to face the apparition. She heard a murmur of excitement beyond the room, and realized that Gifford and Piers were huddled outside, like two children spying upon their elders. There was naught to be done about it now. She shot a glance toward Cain.

His face was pale, taut, his stance rigid.

Amice put out her hands, palms turned upward. "Nay. I cannot."

The woman's gaze narrowed, her otherworldly lips pulled back in a sneer. "I see the Earl of Hawksdown has also joined us this eve."

Amice expected Cain to respond, but he heeded their agreement and remained silent.

"My lady," Amice murmured. "By what name may I call you?"

The hem of the woman's bliaut skimmed over the timber planks as she came closer to Amice. Close enough that Amice could see she had indeed been a wealthy woman in life, the gleam of jewels blinking from her fingers, around her neck, and through her hair. "Why do you not go?"

Amice studied her for a moment, considering whether to reveal her purpose. "The Earl of Hawksdown has something I want. I have agreed to . . . to talk to you in exchange."

The ghost snorted. "To get rid of me, you mean." She shifted her strangely probing gaze toward Cain, and Amice fought the impulse to step back. It was a gaze ripe with hatred. But why?

Amice stepped outside the ring of candles. "To help you journey to where you should be."

"Nay! I belong here." The ghost turned her piercing gaze back to Amice. "Why are you really here?" she whispered.

"I told you."

Translucent green eyes studied Amice, then the ghost gave her a sad smile. "I see." She shook her head. "It seems we share a weakness, Amice de Monceaux."

"What do you mean?" Somehow, she managed to sound puzzled though she feared she knew exactly what the ghost meant.

The ghost just peered back at her, her gaze holding a mix of pity, empathy, and condemnation.

"Who are you?"

"I am Muriel." The ghost lifted her chin and held her arms out to her sides. The fire became part of her, the snapping gold flames glimmering through her body.

"One of the kitchen maids told me you jumped from the tower. Is that true?"

Muriel's form stiffened, then faded into wispy streamers of gold. "Aye, to my death below."

Amice pitched her voice as soft as possible, wrapping her tone in gentle sympathy. "Why?"

The ghost's voice was as faint as her presence, and Amice crept nearer to hear. "He cast me aside." The spirit gradually faded completely from view, leaving the sound of bitter laughter lingering in the stir of air.

"God's wounds," Cain cursed, coming to stand next to Amice. He stared wide-eyed toward the fireplace as if he anticipated someone or something to leap out of it at any moment and set upon them.

There was a scuffle of movement beyond the door, punctuated by a low voiced, "Nay."

When Amice could find her voice, she called out, "Gifford. Piers. You might as well show yourselves. I know you are there."

Cain turned toward the door with a frown.

With bright eyes, Gifford scuttled into the chamber, rubbing his hands together. Piers followed more slowly, his gaze every bit as shining as Gifford's, but shaded with a touch of guilt.

"Good work, my lady," Gifford chortled.

Piers shook his head. "Never have I seen anything like that." He eyed Amice. "You were quite brave, my lady."

"Thank you, Piers."

Cain crossed his arms and stared down at her. "Why do you think she remains bound to Falcon's Craig?"

Laila gathered up the pile of stones and placed them in her pouch, the dreaming stones clinking against each other. She put her hand on Amice's shoulder. "Perhaps 'tis the other spirit who keeps her here."

Gifford let out a yelp. "Another one? Zounds!"

Piers chuckled and patted his uncle's arm. "Soon, the ghosts shall outnumber us."

"Laila, what are you talking about?" Cain asked.

Amice sensed Laila's hesitation, and knew her friend would not share all she knew with Cain. At least, not yet. Laila did not speak unless she was sure of something.

Laila shrugged. "Or mayhap 'tis her memories of what could have been."

Cain turned his focus to Amice. "What do you do now?"

Suddenly, Amice swayed on her feet and Cain caught her around the waist. It all happened so quickly she had no time to brace herself for the contact. She grabbed his arm to steady herself, trying without success to halt the racing of her heart at the mere touch of his hand against her bare skin.

"Are you all right?" he asked.

Amice gazed into his eyes and lost herself. She had the vague sensation of leaning forward before she stiffened and stepped out of his embrace. "Aye, just tired."

He lifted a brow, his knowing gaze exposing her lie.

She ignored him and stumbled toward the door. "I must rest. I shall think on this and talk to you on the morrow." *I must get away*, she told herself. *I must get away.*

Laila rushed up beside her and grasped her elbow. "Slowly, Amice."

Just as Amice neared the door, she tripped and landed flat on the floor. In bewilderment, she glanced around her, but saw nothing to have caused her to fall.

She heard Cain growl, "Damn wraith," before he lifted her up into his arms. "You shall end up at the bottom of the stairs in your condition," he admonished.

"I—"

"Put your arms around my neck, Amice." The shadow of a smile curved his lips. "I shall not bite."

Heat snaked through her veins as she stared at his mouth, then into his eyes, soft blue in the candlelight. Slowly, she slid her hands around his neck. His gaze darkened, and he shifted her a little closer against his body. She swallowed and bit her lip. "Thank you."

Cain turned and started down the stairs, the dim light swallowing his expression. Engulfed by fatigue, Amice gave up the fight and laid her head against Cain's warm chest, breathing deep of his scent.

His arms tightened.

And for just the slightest moment, he pressed his face against her hair.

Chapter 4

Naturally, Cain's attempt to seclude himself in his chamber to drink wine and figure out what in the hell to do about Muriel and his irrational desire for Amice was completely spoiled by the arrival of Gifford and Piers. He sighed in resignation and eyed the two, both brimming with excitement.

They plopped down on the bench facing Cain's chair and grinned in unison. Gifford set his ever-present jug next to the ewer of wine Cain had placed on a small table. "Damned fine show your lady put on tonight, Cain."

"Aye," Piers chimed in. "Never seen anything like it. And the way she just calmly faced that . . . that thing, and asked questions. Balls of iron, your lady's got."

Gifford cackled and punched Piers's shoulder. "No

lady that beautiful has ballocks, you simpkin."

Cain rubbed the back of his neck and drained his cup of wine, quickly refilling it before Gifford could get his hands on the ewer. "Amice is a brave woman, no doubt." He scowled and leaned forward. "But she is not *my* lady."

Piers rolled his eyes. "Should be."

"Piers," Cain snapped. "Cease." He tried not to think of how wondrous it had felt to hold her in his arms. Tried hard.

Gifford coughed and reached for his jug. "Well, what do you think of this ghost? And what is this about another one?"

Cain shrugged. "I do not know any more than you two, as you no doubt saw and heard everything from outside the door."

"Hmpf. Entitled to know," Gifford murmured, obviously lacking any embarrassment in the matter.

Piers pulled a cup from a shelf against the wall and helped himself to the wine. "I have never heard of a woman named Muriel. Have you, Gifford?"

Gifford furrowed his brows and sipped ale. "Seems like there was a story like that. Never thought of it until now."

"Do you know what happened?" Cain asked.

Taking another chug of ale, Gifford gave a nod. "Believe it happened as the, uh, lady said. Gerard Veuxfort, the third Earl of Hawksdown it was."

Cain carefully sipped his wine, deepening unease gradually spreading through him. "What did he do?"

"Don't know exactly. I remember hearing that he

would not marry her, and she killed herself. Ended up marrying another wench, who gave him nothing but trouble."

"Sounds familiar," Cain remarked.

Gifford eyed him carefully. "Aye. Seems as if Gerard should have gone with this Muriel instead."

Piers reached for the wine ewer. "Why did he not marry her?"

"I do not know." Gifford leaned forward and fixed Cain with a stern look out of character for his jovial uncle. "Mayhap his *mother* persuaded him he should wed another."

Cain stiffened. "You go too far, Uncle. You know why I had to marry Luce. Not all of us have the freedom to spend our time playing with exploding rocks and ignoring the pending loss of everything."

Gifford frowned at him. "Foolish boy," he mumbled.

"She appeared of noble birth," Piers offered. "Wonder why the match did not take?"

"Probably something to do with coin," Cain said. "It is always about coin." *No matter how we might dream it otherwise*, he added silently. "Amice will find out."

Gifford stood and arched his back. "I am off to bed. 'Tis a good bit of excitement we have had this eve." He grabbed his jug. "Believe I shall have a bit of ale and get my rest." Winking at Cain, he added, "Who knows what the morrow shall bring, eh?"

Piers rose also, emptied his cup and set it back onto the table. "I shall accompany you, Uncle. I have something I wish to discuss with you. Good eve, Cain."

"Good evening."

As Piers passed him, he leaned down and murmured, "If you will not claim Amice, then why forbid me the pleasure?"

Cain glared at him.

Piers gave him a roguish grin, then draped an arm around Gifford's shoulders and began talking in a soft tone as the two exited. The only word Cain could make out was "elixir" and he briefly closed his eyes. Hopefully no one would get injured from whatever they planned.

Cain stared into the flames. He tried to think of the myriad responsibilities he had, the villeins who needed his attention, the fields that needed planting. But in the end, he just let his thoughts drift.

He closed his eyes and smelled lavender.

His hand shook as he raised his glass to his lips.

On the morrow, he would meet with Amice to devise a way to draw out this ghost of his. He would spend all day on the matter, if necessary.

All day with Amice.

Cain took a deep drink of wine and realized a sad truth.

It was the first moment in as long as he could remember that he had looked forward to anything at all.

❧ ❧ ❧

The next morning Amice went grave hunting.

She and Laila had found the Veuxfort family crypt beneath the chapel. But, of course, Muriel would not be buried there. She would find no welcome within consecrated ground.

A guard let Amice out of a small door on the east curtain wall, and she found herself at the beginning of a winding path leading down to the water. The sun was just beginning to rise above the sea.

Amice picked her way down the rock-strewn path and made it down to the sand just as the sun turned the water red. She slipped off her shoes, held up her skirt, and waded into the cool, smooth water. It was a beautiful sight, the ball of fire glowing red, then orangish-pink, then finally bright yellow, painting the waves with gold.

Amice turned and walked along the wide expanse of sand, dodging a flock of white and black puffins. For a long time she walked aimlessly, needing nature's balm to soothe her spirit. She paused to look back at the castle and caught a glimpse of green from the corner of her eye up beyond the beach. As she headed toward it, the sand warmed her bare feet, and the sun bathed her face in bright fire, lifting her mood.

Amice breathed in the sea air and her thoughts began to clear. In the light of day, last eve seemed a strange dream. Not Muriel's appearance. Amice had expected that. But Amice was developing the sense that the heartbreak binding Muriel to Falcon's Craig was eerily like her own, save the conclusion. Perhaps Muriel's own story had not yet ended, if Laila was right about another spirit.

Her mind shied away from how she had felt when Cain picked her up. She understood now how a person could become addicted to opium, craving it with an intensity no amount of reason could control. The way she craved Cain Veuxfort. Amice came out of her troubled thoughts to find herself walking on a grassy knoll.

In the center was a grave.

Amice approached it slowly, already knowing she had found the object of her search. The headstone was worn with age, but clearly had once been a fine piece of polished granite. She bent down to study the words, the carving softened by years of ocean air.

> To My Beloved Muriel
> This Was Not Our Time
> One Day
> I Shall Be Waiting
> Always

Around the gravestone bright blue wildflowers grew in abundance, carpeting Muriel's grave. Amice dropped to her knees and studied the inscription. Who had written it? Someone who obviously cared deeply for Muriel. Had Cain's ancestor regretted his actions? Did the dead Muriel even know of the epitaph?

Suddenly, tears flooded Amice's eyes, and she gazed at the tombstone through a watery veil.

Would anyone ever love her that much?

She needed to find Laila. Disgusted with her weakness, Amice brushed away her tears, stood, and turned to go back to the castle.

And found Cain standing below on the sand watching her.

Heat stung her face. She knew from the look in his eyes that he saw the evidence of her tears. "Are you following me?" she snapped.

Cain climbed up onto the grass. "Trying to. I did not see you at chapel this morn."

"I do not attend."

"You did once, if only for appearances."

She shrugged. "I care little for appearances anymore."

He halted at the stone and an expression of astonishment washed over his face. "What is this?"

Amice turned back to the grave. "It appears to be your ghost's grave. Have you never seen it?"

"Nay. I have no time to idle on the beach. And you know I have never been fond of the water. I have not been down here for years." He looked around them. "And 'tis a hidden spot."

Amice had to agree with him. The place was isolated, seemingly set apart on purpose.

Cain bent down to read the inscription on the gravestone. Amice knew the moment he finished reading by the way his body stilled. "How did you find this?"

She stared down at him, wondering the same herself. "I happened to walk in this direction, and I saw a patch of green."

He gazed back at her, plainly believing there was more to it than that.

Amice shrugged. "Mayhap somehow Muriel guided me here."

Cain straightened and glanced back at the stone. "What do you think it means?

"Perhaps he loved her after all, if 'twas your ancestor who had the stone made. But why reject her? It makes no sense." As she finished, Amice realized she could be speaking of herself and Cain. In her mind, she drew in her shields a little further.

But her eyes locked with Cain's and suddenly it

seemed as if she had fallen over a waterfall. High over-head, a falcon screeched and briny air swirled across her skin, but it all occurred in the background while a warm, blue pool enfolded her.

"Amice." Cain started to take a step forward, then paused. His eyes held an indefinable light. "Sometimes duty, circumstances, require one to follow a path the heart does not choose. Mayhap he had no choice."

Amice looked away across the glistening waves. "I see."

"Or perhaps he was just a damn fool," Cain said softly.

Tears stung her eyes, but Amice managed to keep them in. She would not cry in front of him. It was bad enough he no doubt had seen her doing just that when he came upon her.

Cain moved beside her. "Do you think he is the other spirit Laila mentioned?"

Amice shrugged, unable to speak through her clogged throat.

"According to Uncle Gifford, the man was Gerard Veuxfort, the third Earl of Hawksdown."

Swallowing, Amice asked, "Does Gifford know any-thing more about what happened?"

Cain sighed. "Not really."

Amice frowned, happy to focus on the problem at Falcon's Craig rather than the murky past she shared with Cain. "She seems to bear a dislike for *you*. Can you think why?"

"Nay, but since she began making trouble, 'tis clear she bears me a particular animosity."

"How can you tell if you have not seen her before last eve?"

He gave her a wry grin. "Oh, many things. Finding the records I have just spent hours on covered with ink, the contents of my chamber moving around seemingly on their own, suddenly finding myself tripping over nothing and falling on my face, usually in front of important guests." Cain gestured with his hand. "The list is long."

"Laila and I shall try to summon Muriel again."

"Aye, I agree."

Amice bit her lip. "I think we should try this time without you." She held up a hand to halt his protest. " 'Tis apparent she bears you ill will. Perhaps she shall be more willing to talk to me if you are not listening."

Cain's reluctance was clear, but he finally nodded. "Aye. This time."

Amice walked back toward the castle, but Cain caught her arm.

"Amice."

He stood so close she could smell him. His scent drew her in such an elemental way it was all she could do not to press her body against his. Instead she pulled her arm free and folded both across her chest. "Aye?"

"I *am* sorry if I hurt you."

Amice froze and her skin burst into tingling all over. She had not expected this. *If* he had hurt her? Did he truly not understand? Destroyed, devastated her, aye, but not hurt. Hurt was when someone said something unkind. Not when someone took everything from you and decreed it wanting. "It . . . it is of no matter. 'Twas long ago." This time she turned away and began walking quickly.

Cain fell in beside her in silence.

Precisely at sext, Amice met Agatha in the latter's chamber. She was glad for the diversion. Between Cain and Muriel, she felt oddly exposed, as if a window into her heart had opened for all to see.

Agatha stood rod straight in the center of her chamber, appearing to all purposes as if she girded for battle. As usual, her hair was nearly invisible, her face was taut, and her bliaut an unflattering drab brown. "Well?" she asked.

"Do you have any bliauts in brighter colors?"

"Nay, just greys, blues, and browns."

"Do you have any that actually fit?"

Agatha glanced down, pursing her lips and furrowing her brow. "Does this not fit?"

"Look at me," Amice advised. "Does your gown look the same on you as mine does on me?"

Peering closely at her, Agatha walked this way and that, until she had completed a circle around Amice. "Nay. Yours is . . . tighter."

Amice grinned. "Fitted. How is a man to know you have curves if you swath them in ells of extra material?"

Understanding washed over Agatha's face. "Ah, I see."

"And you have lovely grey eyes, but these dull colored bliauts do nothing to make them stand out." Amice frowned and stepped forward to pull off Agatha's veil and wimple. Thick plaits of shiny, flaxen hair lay underneath, wound around Agatha's head. "Agatha, you have beautiful hair."

Agatha blinked. "Do you think so? Mother always told me it was too bright, too much like brass. ' 'Tis a brazen look you have about you,' she often told me."

Which explains why you hide yourself, Amice thought. "Ridiculous. You have lovely hair."

"Oh. But . . . what shall I do?"

"For one thing, let the plaits hang down your back under the veil. Do you have ribbons?"

Agatha hung her head. "Nay."

"Hmm. Wait here. I shall see what I brought with me that might be of use."

By the time Amice searched her own chamber and returned to Agatha's, Cain's sister had stripped down to her chemise, brushed out her hair, and littered her bed with numerous bliauts and undertunics of varying muddy colors. She glanced up as Amice entered. "I am hopeless."

Amice stopped in surprise. Before her stood another woman. Without the enveloping garments and concealing veil, Agatha Veuxfort was lovely. "Not at all."

Within the span of the afternoon, Amice clad Agatha in a bright blue bliaut of her own, shortened of course, an undertunic of robin's egg blue and a wispy veil covering only a portion of Agatha's hair, now loosely plaited with blue and white ribbons.

The effect was truly amazing.

Agatha dug out a piece of polished silver and stared at her reflection in wonderment. "I *am* attractive."

Amice grinned. "More than attractive."

"Thank you. Thank you so very much."

"My pleasure. 'Twas not hard." Amice bit her lip. "But Agatha . . ."

Agatha's face fell. "What is wrong?"

"Well, it is just that, well, I have noticed you are some-what, uh, well, disapproving. That kind of manner will not draw a man to your side."

"What are you talking about?"

Amice swallowed, suddenly sensing she was wading into precarious waters. "For instance, when Gifford was chasing the ghost. 'Twas ridiculous, rather amusing."

In an instant, Agatha turned back into the woman Amice had first glimpsed in the hall. Her lips were pursed into a moue of distaste and her stance rigid. " 'Twas folly. Uncle Gifford likes to behave outrageously. Piers is nearly as bad. A legacy from our foolish father, I fear."

Amice raised a brow. "They are not the ones trying to figure out how to experience mating."

Agatha snorted. "Piers does not need to, the women throw their bodies at him, and I doubt Gifford cares."

"Still—"

"Enough." Agatha crossed her arms. "I thank you for your aid, but I am not going to turn into a simpkin."

"I am not suggesting that."

Agatha paced across the room and turned back to face Amice. "I do not know how to be any other way," she admitted in a small voice.

Puzzling over her confession, Amice remembered Agatha's mother. From the things Cain had told her, and her own brief but strange experience with Ismena Veuxfort, Amice could imagine the effect the cold woman could have on her daughter. "All I suggest is that you try to hold your tongue when you are tempted to criticize. Try to be a bit more merry."

"Merry?" Agatha looked doubtful.

Amice nodded.

With a sigh, Agatha said, "I shall try, but I fear my new appearance may have to suffice."

" 'Tis a fine one."

"Aye, thanks to you." To Amice's surprise, Agatha walked close and took her hands. "Thank you, truly."

" 'Twas my pleasure." Amice giggled. "Now, all we need to do is find the right man."

Agatha squeezed her hand. "Perhaps we both will."

Amice sobered and gazed into Agatha's eyes. "I fear 'tis too late for me."

"Mayhap not." Agatha shot her a mischievous grin. "Mayhap not."

Shaking her head, Amice went in search of Laila.

❧ ❧ ❧

Amice frowned and glanced over at Laila. "It is not working."

"Nay." Laila bent and blew out a candle. "Muriel hides herself this eve."

"But we need to speak with her! How shall we find out why she lingers?"

"We shall try again, Amice," Laila said patiently. "You know this happens sometimes." She gathered up their dreaming stones and blew out another candle.

Amice paced over to the fire and back again over the bare timber floor. "We shall try tomorrow."

Laila stopped cleaning up and came over to stand next to Amice. "*Te'sorthene*, what is wrong?"

Amice stopped and gazed down at Laila, the dew of tears stinging her eyes. She was rapidly turning into a weakling. " 'Tis too hard. I thought I could just complete the task, get the villa, and make a new life." Her throat tightened and her voice dropped to a whisper. "This is killing me, Laila."

Laila's eyes glowed with sympathy, and she put her arm around Amice. "Do you wish to leave? You could stay at Wareham. Your brother would not allow his wife to toss you out."

For a moment, Amice considered the idea. "Nay, I cannot. I need to find my own path."

"How can I help?"

Amice shrugged, helplessness choking her. "There is naught to be done. I must be strong."

"You *are* strong."

"Aye, in some ways. But with Cain..." Her voice broke off and she stared into the flames. " 'Tis different. It is as if my will is gone, as if some buried but powerful part of me wants him desperately, despite everything."

Laila reached up and stroked her hair. " 'Tis love," she said softly.

Amice stared at her bleakly. "Then God save me, for 'tis a love that will destroy me."

❦ ❦ ❦

After they failed to summon Muriel, Amice climbed up to the battlements. She stood at the edge, tilted her head back and flung her arms open wide, wishing with every fiber of her being that the wind would simply pick her up and carry her away. Away to a place where her heart was whole again.

She sighed and walked along the stone allure, her mind whirling with possibilities. Why had Muriel not appeared? Beneath the scornful pretense, Amice sensed Muriel wanted to tell her story, no, needed to tell it. For some reason, she held back. Pride? Embarrassment? Or maybe she just enjoyed trifling with them.

The battlements looked down toward the sea, a sharp cliff below the castle walls angling down to the beach. Amice stopped and leaned against a merlon. This must be close to where Muriel had jumped, she mused.

As her mind registered a shifting of stone, the merlon broke and she plunged into the air. Twisting, she caught the edge of the remaining piece with one hand. The stone cut into her fingers, but she held on even as her body smacked into the stone wall.

"Ahh," she cried.

"Amice!"

"Cain!" she shouted. "Help me!" Amice heard the sound of pounding footsteps, but her grip began to slip. He was not going to make it in time. For a crystalline moment, Amice realized the supreme irony. She would die in the same place as Muriel, both of them cast aside by the Earl of Hawksdown.

She looked up and saw Cain's face, tight with horror. Her fingers slipped, one, then another, then another.

"No!" he roared and flung himself down just in time to grab her wrist. "Take my other hand," he yelled.

With every bit of strength Amice still had, she swung her body up and seized his other hand. Cain yanked her up onto the allure.

He pulled her against his chest, his arms wrapped tightly around her. Amice burrowed in closer, clutching his tunic in her hands. Dear God, she had almost fallen. Another instant and she would have been gone. She lifted her head and gazed into Cain's eyes.

Intense, ocean blue eyes that held an expression her heart recognized. Hunger.

She knew it because she was sure the same desire shone in her own.

Cain's lips thinned and his nostrils flared. "Damn you, Amice," he said in a hoarse voice.

And then he kissed her.

Amice sank into his embrace like a bird returning to the nest, weeping inside with the sweetness of his taste, his smooth lips stroking, sucking, possessing her mouth until it felt as if she were inside of him.

Not close enough. Never close enough.

She arched into his body and put her arms around his neck, pulling his head even closer to hers, surrendering to her cravings, glutting her senses on him. Something alive rippled between them, and Cain pulled her up atop his thighs, rocking against her woman's mound, his arousal branding her.

It was the same way they had made love many times.

Amice gasped and broke the kiss. What was she doing? She stared at Cain in astonishment.

He stilled, his gaze slowly shifting from glittering hunger to disbelief.

Neither of them let go of the other, still clasped belly to belly atop the battlements.

Amice was not sure she could. Nearly dying had set free what she had spent years burying deep. With a shaking hand, she put her palm against his cheek.

Cain took a deep breath, closed his eyes, and turned his face into her palm.

The gesture tore into her heart like a fine sword, cutting through walls painstakingly erected as if they were no more than air. Then, almost imperceptibly, she felt him begin to withdraw, his body stiffening slightly beneath hers, moving her away so that they were no longer pressed against each other.

He opened his eyes. "Are you all right?"

Her impersonal Cain had returned, quite a feat since she still straddled his lap. Amice climbed off and stood on wobbly legs. "Aye, thanks to you."

Cain stood and half-lifted his hands. For a moment, Amice thought he would take hers, but he hesitated and returned them to his sides. "What happened?"

Amice turned to look at the broken merlon. She could not overcome fear to go any closer. "The stone gave."

"That makes no sense," Cain muttered, walking over to inspect the stone merlon. "I am careful to keep the battlements in good repair." He peered down, then ran his fingers along the broken edge. When he turned back to her, his eyes burned with fury. "The merlon was broken deliberately."

Ice spread through Amice's veins and she gripped her mantle in her fists, her eyes wide. "Then . . ."

Cain's lips drew into a tight, flat line. "Someone wanted

either you or me to fall. The guards would not linger to lean against the stone. And no one else ever comes up here."

" 'Twas her," Amice whispered. "Muriel."

He looked doubtful. "Can a ghost break stone?"

"I do not know."

"She has never attempted to seriously harm me before." He walked back toward her with a frown.

"Nay, not you. Me."

He gazed at her thoughtfully. "Why?"

Amice took a deep, shuddering breath. "She wants me to go. I believe she knows if I stay, at some point Laila and I shall figure out a way to get *her* to go, and she very much does not want that."

In the stillness of the night, they heard soft laughter.

Instinctively, Amice moved into Cain's arms, looking around her with a terror she could not subdue, wishing she were enclosed in the safety of her chamber.

A few feet away, Muriel slowly took shape, a pale glimmer of color that danced atop the stones. "How touching," she sneered.

Amice felt Cain brace himself behind her. He tightened his hold around her waist. "It *was* you."

A swirl of green and gold lifted in what still managed to look like an indolent shrug. Muriel glided closer and fixed her glowing eyes on Amice. "You are right. You must go." She burst into mocking laughter. "But not quite for the reason you think."

Amice swallowed a few times before she could speak. "Why, then? And why do you remain here?"

"So many questions. My reason for staying shall be my own."

Pulling her courage back together, Amice asked, "Is it because of Gerard Veuxfort? Is he still here?"

The ghost appeared stunned, and began to fade.

"Wait!" Amice called. "There is something I must tell you!"

But Muriel continued to fade, her whisper shattering the night like a thunderclap. "The reason is quite simple. I shall never allow the Earl of Hawksdown to be happy."

In the wake of her words, Amice stood motionless, unable to look at Cain. Inch by inch, he dropped his arms from around her. Amice gulped and fought for control, desperately attempting to wrap herself in reserve.

"Amice."

His breath brushed her ear. Amice took a step away, then turned. She just stared at him, wondering what she could possibly say to the ghost's absurd implication. *Please, do not tell me Muriel is mistaken, she prayed. I know 'tis true, that I have naught to do with your happiness. Please do not make me hear it from your mouth.*

"Amice. We need to talk."

"About Muriel, yes, I know. I do not believe she knows of the grave." Amice nodded. "Aye, that could be the key. Perhaps if she realizes——"

"Not about Muriel." His voice was soft but his jaw was set with determination. "About us. About what happened. Before."

Amice stepped back. "Nay, 'tis not necessary."

"I think it is. Particularly with my mad ghost's insinuations."

He said mad. Amice backed up another step. "Nay.

'Tis no point to it. What difference does it make now after so many years?"

Cain stared at her mouth, then lifted his gaze to hers. "Have you forgotten everything, then?"

"I have forgotten *nothing*, Cain." Her voice turned harsh, bitter anger rolling over her. "Nothing. You used me and threw me away to follow your mother's bidding. That is all. There is nothing to talk about."

"Amice, nay, 'tis not that simple."

Amice lifted her chin. "Aye, it *is* that simple! And I do not want to hear your lies. Go find your 'cousin.' I am sure *she* can accommodate you."

"Amice, nay, wait."

She whipped around and ran.

Cain stood watching her, feeling as if his bones were melting in an inferno of pain and guilt. The truth of it was that Amice was partially right. He *had* thrown her away, yielding to his mother's manipulation. In the process, he had gained the coin to pay the King's amercement and to save Falcon's Craig. He had obtained Styrling Castle for his mother.

And he had convinced himself Amice could never be a good wife for him. Amice drew men like Piers drew women, and she liked it. And she was forever dabbling in some kind of pagan rite.

But still. They had shared of themselves in the way of a husband and wife. His body tensed at the memory. They had made promises. Amice rightfully assumed they would marry.

Then, he had walked away, turning his attention to the

care of Falcon's Craig and telling himself his mother was
right to insist he marry Luce, that duty to family was more
important than anything.

God, what an idiot he was.

Amice was right to hate him. Even if he could bring
himself to trust her, he knew Amice well enough to be
certain she could never forgive him. Why should she?

Chapter 5

    After watching Amice flee him as if he were some kind of demon, Cain stopped in the hall to inform Nyle about the broken merlon. Needing solitude, he climbed to his chamber, stripped off his tunic and undershirt and built up the fire. The scent of lavender stirred in the air, and Cain breathed deeply.

When he thought of how close he had come to losing Amice, his gut turned over. Damned ghost. If she had substance, he would delight in permanently separating her head from her body himself.

He picked up his discarded tunic and held it to his nose. Amice's scent still clung faintly to the cloth. Cain closed his eyes and let his heart bask for a moment in remembrance.

Then jumped as soft hands crept around his neck and smoothed over his chest. For a heartbeat, his heart leapt with possibility, but knew before he turned that Amice would never do such a thing. Cain looked over his shoulder. "Morganna."

"Mmm," she purred as she stroked her fingers down to his stomach. She rubbed her body against his back like a cat looking to scratch an itch. A naked cat.

"Morganna, cease."

Instead, her small hands slipped beneath his braies so quickly that Cain had no time to act before she closed one hand around his still throbbing rod. He tore her hands away and jumped up. "What in the hell do you think you are doing?"

She stared back at him and put her hands beneath her breasts, as if she were offering him a sweet. "Come now, Cain. You can have these. And," she paused, gliding her hands down to the pale triangle cresting her legs. "Anything else you desire."

"I do not—"

Morganna laughed and gave him a sly look. "Oh, yes, you do." She gazed pointedly at his groin and licked her lips. "Aye, you do indeed."

Damn the wench. Cain knew he was hard, but what man would not be, faced with a beautiful, naked, albeit cunning, woman who dared to hold him in her hand? He crossed his arms. "I *am* a man. Not a eunuch."

She stepped closer. "Aye, you are. With a man's needs."

Cain gulped. She was right about his needs, but he was rather particular about the woman who could satisfy them. "Where are your clothes?"

Morganna sighed and closed the distance between them. She put her hands on his shoulders. "Cain, stop this foolishness. We shall be good together." She smiled and pressed against his crossed arms. "Very, very good."

Cain frowned. "How do you know, Morganna?"

She shrugged. "A woman can just tell when a man is right."

"Oh? An *innocent* woman? A virgin?"

A knowing smile slid across her lips. "No woman is truly innocent of men."

Cain stepped back. "Somehow, I have the feeling you are a little less innocent than most. Go away, Morganna. Get clothed and leave me."

Her mouth turned down. "Surely, you do not mean that, Cain." She turned in a slow circle, arching her back, her golden hair swirling around her. "Look well upon what I offer you."

Gritting his teeth, Cain looked around his chamber until he spotted her bliaut. He snatched it up and thrust it into her hands. "Go."

Morganna sniffed and dropped the garments to the floor. "What are you afraid of, Cain? Afraid you might come to care for me? Afraid once you have me, you shall never want anyone else again?"

"Hardly." Cain bent and picked up her clothes once more. This time, he put a hand on her shoulder and steered her toward the door. If she refused to dress within his chamber, she could do so without. It was obvious Morganna did not suffer from reluctance to display her body.

She shook off his hand as they reached the door and turned to gaze at him. "She will never have you, you know."

"Who?"

Morganna smiled. "I know what happened. I know what you did to her. Ismena told me. She shall never forgive you."

Cain froze and narrowed his gaze. "What did my mother tell you?"

"How you fancied yourself in love with Amice. How she let you claim her body without a betrothal. How you came to your senses and abandoned her." Morganna laughed lightly. "Such a sad story. And then you ended up with a wife who loved another."

"Enough."

"Poor Cain. And yet you refuse me, when I could make your pain go away."

"You can do nothing for me. Get out."

Morganna flounced out and Cain slammed the door, this time throwing the iron bar across it.

He turned back to hear soft, jeering laughter that oozed from all four corners of the room. A cold slice of air skittered across his shoulders and a voice whispered, "She is right, you know. Amice is too wise, too proud to ever give *you* another chance."

Cain whirled around but saw nothing. "Coward," he hissed.

The laughter slowly faded, mocking him even in its silence.

❧ ❧ ❧

The next morning, Cain found himself alone on the dais to break his fast. He looked up as Gifford sailed into the hall.

"Here, my boy." Gifford handed Cain a cup of some kind of liquid. " 'Tis a special brew I created just for you."

Cain did not take the cup. "What is in it?"

"Wine and a bit of my elixir." He plopped down and reached for a jug of ale. "Try it."

"Is it safe?"

His uncle gave him an irritated look. "Why would I wish to harm you? Of course 'tis safe."

Cain watched as Gifford drained the jug in one very long swallow and gestured to the butler for more. "What kind of 'elixir' did you concoct?"

Gifford sighed. "Good for you." He took another swig of ale. "Need to start living, Cain."

"I am alive."

Shaking his head, Gifford popped a chunk of cheese into his mouth. "Not really. You are so damned determined to be serious, you have turned yourself into a martyr."

Cain peered into the cup. It did not look harmful, but with Gifford, who knew what the ingredients might be? "I am no martyr."

"Oh? Then why are you sitting here alone? Where is Lady Amice?" Gifford stared at him with perceptive eyes.

"Probably hiding from me." Cain took a small sip of the drink.

"Hmpf. Girl has sense."

"Leave it, Uncle. She hates me, and justifiably so."

"Hmm. Don't look that way to me." Gifford grabbed up another piece of cheese and slid his elixir closer to Cain. "Drink."

The second sip felt a bit gritty on his tongue but Cain swallowed anyway. *What the hell*? he thought. He felt oddly off-center, as if nothing in his life made the same sense it had before Amice came back into it.

"What happened between the two of you? 'Tis obvious you are still in love with her."

Cain stilled and stared at nothing. Was Gifford right? He shook his head and forced down another gulp of Gifford's drink. It was definitely gritty. "What did you put in this stuff?"

"Not enough apparently. Well?"

"Well what?"

"Good God, you *are* thick-witted. Why are you sitting here instead of pursuing Amice?"

"Good question, Uncle," Piers pitched in as he took a seat on Cain's other side.

He was trapped. "Amice wants nothing to do with me. We shared something once but 'tis gone."

Gifford grunted. "Liar."

Cain's patience shredded. How could they not see the truth? "I appreciate that both of you care for my well-being, but you are wrong. I am perfectly happy with things as they are. I do not want another wife. I am the *last* man in the world Amice de Monceaux wishes to marry. And she is every bit as unfit for that role today as she was five years ago. For God's sake, she's a pagan."

Gifford just stared at him in horror.

The import of his expression slowly sank in, and Cain wanted to groan. "She is right behind me?"

Gifford nodded.

"Hell."

After a moment, Piers whispered, "She is gone."

"Dammit, Cain. You are a stubborn simpkin, boy."

Gifford drank deep and shook his head. "Damn near hopeless."

Piers coughed and pulled over a ewer of wine.

Cain felt as if he could bury his face in an entire barrel.

Gifford slammed down the jug and glared at Cain. "Stop being a fool!"

"Gifford—"

"Nay, you will listen. I am tired of watching you act like some kind of drudge. When is the last time you laughed? Really laughed? Got drunk? Did something just because it felt good? You have shut down, boy, and I cannot watch it anymore."

"I have responsibilities."

"We all do, but that does not mean we stop living," Piers murmured.

Cain rolled his eyes, stamping down the wave of yearning winding through him. The Earl of Hawksdown was not a man enslaved by weak emotion, he reminded himself. Again. "Enough! I know Amice is the first noblewoman we have seen in years but that does not make her an ideal candidate to be the Countess of Hawksdown. Stop trying to put Amice and me together, both of you. It is not going to happen. She is a faithless woman. *And* she despises me!"

"If she likes men so much, why is she not married, hmm?" Piers asked.

" 'Tis obvious. She does not want to confine herself to one man."

Gifford jumped up and put his hands on the table. "You damned idiot!" he roared. "Can you not see the pain in that woman's eyes when she looks at you? No, you cannot. And do you know why? Because you are too blinded by the pain in your own!"

Cain's mouth fell open. With a final angry look, Gifford swept up a jug and stalked away.

"Not sure I have ever heard him use that tone of voice," Piers commented. "Except that one time with Mother."

Draining his cup of wine, Cain turned to gaze at Piers. "It is this cursed ghost. She is turning Falcon's Craig into a place of madness."

"Do you truly think our ghost is the problem?"

Cain stood and picked up a ewer. He did not need a cup. "I shall be in my solar. Working." He left the table, feeling the censure of Piers's gaze every step of the way.

🐾 🐾 🐾

That evening, Amice made a fist and banged on the door to Cain's chamber. It had taken her the entire day, but she had managed to replace agonizing hurt with wonderful rage.

And she was *not* going to allow the coward to hide from her in his chamber.

"Who is there?"

"Amice." She smashed her fist against the door again. "I want to talk to you."

There was silence, then the door slowly swung open.

Amice blinked. Cain stood in the shadows, the fire lighting his hair to gold. He gazed at her with an oddly soft expression.

"Come in."

Steeling her resolve, Amice gathered her pride around her like a protective mantle and followed him into the room.

Cain picked up a cup and drank, then refilled it. "I apologize for my careless statement this morn. I had no idea you were there." He gestured to a blanket spread before the fire.

Amice remained standing. "I demand that as long as I must remain at Falcon's Craig, you not discuss me with your brother or your uncle."

Cain sat on the floor and stretched out his long legs. He drained his cup before gazing up at her. "Would you like some wine?"

"Aye."

Filling another cup, Cain held it out to her. Amice took it and settled herself onto a stone windowseat. She drew in a deep breath. "I must insist on this."

"Very well. But they bring up the matter continuously."

"Why do they care about a mistake that happened long ago?"

"Mistake?" His gaze turned indigo in the firelight.

Amice shrugged and gulped some wine. "Or, whatever you wish to name it."

"Why have you not married?"

Amice's breath froze in her throat. She could never tell him the truth. "I . . . I suppose I just never found the right, uh, situation. 'Tis an odd question coming from someone who deems me 'unfit' for matrimony."

"Your brother, he could not make a match for you?"

"Nay."

"Why not? You come from a good family and, God

knows, you are a beautiful woman."

Only Cain could make flattery sound like an accusation. Amice tossed down half her cup of wine. "Why are you asking me this? What difference does it make to you? And of all people, I would guess you could think of your own reasons why I have not married, false though they might be."

He turned and sent her a wry smile. "Mayhap not all men are as insistent on constancy as I."

Slowly, Amice rose and walked over to Cain, her face set into tense lines. She poured the rest of her wine over his head. "You ignorant bastard," she hissed.

Cain jumped up, swiping red droplets from his cheek. "Oh? Do you forget I *saw* you! Tightly tucked in the arms of the Earl of Stanham. I am sure he was one of many."

Gathering her breath, Amice slapped him across the face.

He caught her hand, his gaze glittering fire.

"I *never* betrayed you with another. You made your own conclusions without trusting me."

"Trusting you? When most of the men at Chasteney lusted after you and made no secret of it? You jest."

"You should have had faith in me."

Cain started laughing. "You truly must deem me a fool."

Hot tears stung Amice's eyes, but she blinked them back and yanked her hand from Cain's. "This is pointless. You persist in casting yourself as the victim, when indeed the opposite is true."

Cain dropped her hand.

Amice stepped closer and raised a brow. "Does that make it easier for you, Cain? Easier to justify using me then abandoning me? Easier to treat me in one moment like a precious jewel then in the next like mud on the bottom of your boot? Do you assuage whatever conscience you have by deeming me unsuitable?"

"Damn you."

This time, it was Amice who laughed.

Cain swallowed her laughter into his mouth.

Amice instinctively stiffened, but the touch, the taste of him was like healing balm to her bruised soul. She could no more pull away than a flower could resist rainfall.

Fiercely, she tore at Cain's clothes, vaguely aware he did the same to hers. The sounds of fabric tearing blended with harsh breaths, gasps of desire.

When they finally came together skin to skin, Amice felt as if she would die from the intense sense of rightness she felt, the sheer wonder of his warmth enveloping her body. He pulled her down to the blanket and onto his muscled thighs.

Amice's body stilled in anticipation. Cain broke their kiss and stared at her. His eyes were gleaming bits of sapphire, drawing her into a whirlpool of raw hunger. Amice smoothed her fingertips up the side of his face, the moment hushed, suspended.

Their gazes locked as Cain slowly, achingly, sank his thick, hot length into her body. The feeling was so incredible Amice could only gasp for breath, unable to look away from his gaze. She heard herself making soft panting sounds as her body quivered and stretched to take all of him in.

"Dear God, Amice," Cain growled, then Amice found herself on her back on the blanket.

She wrapped her legs around Cain's waist and hung on as he stroked into her, at first smooth and slow, then faster, deeper, both of them rocking, bucking as they joined. More and more yet, until Amice felt as if she drifted among the stars.

Floating free, Amice surrendered to feeling, savoring the brush of his tongue around hers, the taste of wine and dark desire, the scent of cedar and sage taking her back five years in a heartbeat.

Helplessly, Amice gazed into Cain's ocean eyes, sucked into a sea of wanting as if there were no longer any boundaries between them, only one perfectly combined being.

Deep inside, an elemental part of her broke apart and reformed, responding to a shift in the very fabric of her existence. Of their existence. She could see Cain felt it too, by the stark intensity in his gaze.

Then he stroked the swollen nub of her sex, and Amice spun into a glittering abyss. She cried out with the joy of it, clenching around Cain with an uncontrollable rhythm as he drove into her, desperately, frantically, in a moment adding his own cry of release to hers.

The world had surely stopped.

Cain gathered her close and smoothed the tangle of hair from her face.

Amice snuggled into his embrace as his fingers gently stroked her hand. "I always loved your hands. So graceful yet strong." She felt him draw in a sharp breath.

"Amice."

"Aye?"

"I am sorry."

Amice stiffened and lifted her head. Somewhere, she found a scrap of dignity and clung to it. "For what?"

He gestured to their bodies, slick with sweat, intertwined still. "You always were my strongest weakness." His expression was both apologetic and self-mocking. In one look, he demeaned all they had just shared.

Shakily, Amice edged her body from his and got to her feet. She wanted to shout at him, to rip out his heart with her own hands, but pride kept her moving. How could he act as if this meant naught but a weakness of the flesh? Was she the only one who felt the deep perfection of their joining?

It seemed to take forever, but finally Amice managed to put herself into some degree of order. She walked toward the door without once glancing at Cain.

But at the end, she hesitated and looked back. Cain sat on the blanket cradling a cup of wine, watching her.

"Do not be sorry, Cain. I am not."

He just stared at her.

Amice left without another word.

Chapter 6

Cain cracked open one eye at the loud explosion. As his chamber gradually righted itself, he realized the sound was a banging on the door. His head felt like someone had taken the flat side of a sword to it, and when he tried to sit up his stomach did not want to come with the rest of his body. He groaned and raked his hair back, just before Gifford opened the door and peered in.

" 'Bout time you woke up." Gifford wrinkled his nose and glanced around the chamber, his gaze sharpening with interest. "What went on in here?"

"I took your advice and got drunk." Cain swung out of bed and staggered to a bowl of water, dumping the cool contents over his head.

"You picked a hell of a time to do that."

Cain turned to stare at his uncle as he dried off. "Why?"

"We appear to have a bit of a problem developing."

"What have you done now? Did anyone get hurt?"

Gifford sniffed and drew himself up straight. "Nothing to do with me at all."

"What is it?" It took a couple of tries, but Cain finally managed to pull on braies, chausses, and a tunic.

"A band of Highlanders led by the largest savage I have ever seen is outside the walls. The savage demands you release Amice to him."

Piers bounded into the room. "He says he is the Chief of the MacKeirs and Amice is his betrothed."

Cain sat down on the bed. "Good God." Why was he surprised Amice had failed to mention her betrothal?

"The MacKeir appears to be under the belief you are holding Amice against her will."

"Where is she?"

Piers chuckled. "Hiding inside her chamber with her companion."

"You best see to the matter," Gifford said. "This MacKeir brought enough men and equipment to mount a siege."

" 'Tis easy enough. I am not restraining Amice. She is free to leave whenever she likes." And doubtless eager to do so after last night, he thought.

Gifford shuffled back and forth on his feet, peering into the corners of Cain's chamber. "What of Muriel?" he whispered.

Damn. He had to keep Amice here until Muriel was expelled. "Has Amice spoken to her betrothed?"

"Not yet. Got the feeling she's not sure what to say."

Cain frowned. "What a mess." He rose and started to leave his chamber.

Piers coughed.

"What?"

"Do you not think you should put on shoes? My lord."

Cain glowered at him and pulled on his boots. He tromped down the stairs, his irritation mounting with each step. What had Amice done to this MacKeir? And why did she not tell him she was free to go?

He strode across the bailey, dodging through a swarm of people rushing back and forth, already preparing for the possibility of attack. Stable grooms hurriedly led horses to the smith's forge for new shoes while members of the garrison ran for the armory. Cain nearly stumbled over a flock of chickens.

By the time he reached the rose chamber, Cain felt so angry that his head did not even hurt anymore. He banged open the door and anger turned to rage. "What the hell is going on here?"

Amice did not look up. She and Laila knelt on the floor within a circle of flickering candles. He caught the whispered words, "Beloved Eostre, hear my plea."

Damn it. His castle was under attack, and she was holding some kind of pagan ritual. "Amice!" he roared.

She looked up, her expression a mix of fear and defiance.

Cain took a deep breath. "What is going on?"

"I—"

"Just tell the man you are not a prisoner."

"I tried, but he does not believe me."

Cain gritted his teeth. "Come with me."

He half dragged her back across the bailey to the walkway on top of the stone gatehouse, Piers and Gifford following them. A line of archers had already spread out along the allure. His garrison captain stood to one side, looking apprehensive.

"Why was the drawbridge down?" Cain demanded.

His captain's gaze flitted back and forth. "We was receiving supplies, my lord."

"And failed to notice a troop of armed men approaching?"

"Aye." For a moment, it appeared the man would say more, but in the end he just bit his lip.

As Cain looked down at the Highlanders armed for battle, he resolved to replace his captain immediately. Some of the Scots were working on assembling a trebuchet while others were in the process of dragging an immense log toward the castle walls. "Which one is The MacKeir?" he hissed.

"The biggest one, right there." Amice pointed.

Amice's betrothed looked like a massive wolf. He had black hair with a braid on one side, wild green eyes, and sported a truly astonishing array of swords and daggers.

Just then, The MacKeir looked up. "Amice!" he bellowed. "Be strong. I shall rescue you from this knave. Hawksdown, you whoreson, release my woman."

Well, that was it. Cain turned to Amice. "Go to your betrothed."

Amice's face whitened. "Nay."

Cain shook his head to clear it. "Why not? You belong to him." He ignored the slice of pain the words produced.

"I do not."

"Explain." As Cain glanced down, The MacKeir drew one of his swords.

"I shall gladly fight you for my woman," he roared. "Come down here, coward, and settle this like a man."

"I am not holding her prisoner, you idiot," Cain called down in reply. He turned back to Amice and lifted a brow.

"He is not my betrothed. He . . . would like it to be so, but there is no understanding between us."

"Mayhap your brother made the agreement after you left Wareham."

Amice's face turned a shade paler. "Nay, he would not do that without my approval. And he knows my position on Lugh."

"Lugh? It sounds as if you and the man are on intimate terms."

"Aye, of course he has bedded me, but that does not mean marriage. You know that."

"Sarcasm is not helpful at the moment."

Amice glared at him. "Nor are more baseless insults."

Cain sighed and rubbed the back of his neck. "Perhaps if you went out there to talk to him, you could persuade him to leave."

"If I leave the castle, he will take me to Tunvegen, I am sure of it."

"Hell." Cain paced back and forth on the allure, nearly bumping into Piers and Gifford, who were naturally peering down at the Highlanders with excitement. If The MacKeir truly was not betrothed to Amice, how could he put her out, knowing the man would force her to make it so? He crossed his arms and studied Amice. "You swear to me that you are not betrothed to The MacKeir?"

"I told you I am not."

"Very well. I shall send a messenger to Wareham to make sure. Until I receive a response, The MacKeir will be barred entry."

Amice visibly swallowed. "Thank you, my lord."

Cain walked to the edge of the battlement. "Lady Amice does not wish to leave. She is under my protection, not my restraint."

A great bellow of anger rose up over the castle walls. "Liar! Cowardly whoreson!"

"And the lady informs me you are *not* her betrothed."

For a moment, there was silence, then The MacKeir spoke again. "You give me no choice, Hawksdown. I shall besiege your castle until I gain what is mine."

"You are making a great mistake," Cain responded.

"Nay, 'tis you who is making the mistake of going against The MacKeir. Amice, my precious, be brave. Soon, we shall be together."

Cain heard Amice give a heavy sigh, just before the walls shook as a battering ram crashed into the portcullis. The archers shot off a rain of arrows as Cain thrust Amice behind him. "Get down," he shouted at Piers and Gifford.

But just as they made for the steps, a strange cracking noise sounded. Cain half-turned, seeking his garrison captain. The man was standing with an expression of utter shock on his face. "Thomas, what was that?"

Thomas looked at Cain and shook his head. "The ram broke."

"What?"

"Aye, cracked apart with the first blow."

"The tree must have been diseased."

Thomas looked doubtful, then cast a wary glance around him. "I do not think so, my lord."

Cain could not help it, he glanced around also, half-expecting Muriel to be floating on the walkway. "Amice, you and Gifford get to the hall and stay there. Piers?"

"Aye, I shall fetch Peter to aid us with our mail."

❧ ❧ ❧

When Amice heard the knock on the door of her chamber, her stomach gave a lurch. Before she opened the door, Amice knew who it was. She was surprised he had not sought her out earlier when she failed to appear at supper.

Desperately trying to collect her pride and courage, Amice straightened her shoulders and opened the door.

Cain's gaze glowed like burning embers. He strode into the chamber without asking for entrance.

Amice steeled herself for his anger and made herself calmly pour a cup of wine. She did not offer any to Cain.

"What have you done?" he asked softly.

"Naught but try to aid *you*."

His face drew into taut lines, the planes of his cheekbones plainly visible in the dying light. "I asked you to get rid of that damned ghost. Not only have you failed to do that, now I have some Scottish madman battering at my doors to get at you. Why is that, Amice?"

"We are making progress with Muriel. 'Tis too much for you to expect me to accomplish the task in the span of five days."

Cain took a step closer and crossed his arms. "Why is The MacKeir here? What did you do to him to create such fervor?"

Amice gave him a bitter smile. "I know 'tis difficult for you to conceive, but some men actually find me appealing, valuable."

"I know well just how appealing you can be."

Something inside Amice crumbled, and she clenched her hands into fists. "I have never been with any man but *you*."

Cain glanced at her askance.

"Never."

"Amice, there is no need to lie."

"How nice it must be for you to be so certain in your judgment. Why, I cannot say, but to my shame, 'tis the truth. I have never wanted to be with another man."

"What are you saying? That you did not dally with the Earl of Stanham?"

"I did not bed the Earl of Stanham!" Amice yelled. God, it felt good to finally say it. "He made it appear that way to hurt you. Aye, he wanted me but I refused him. He was jealous of *you*."

Cain's eyes grew wide and his gaze turned incredulous. "Come now, Amice, are you claiming you were committed to me? In love with me?"

"You know I was."

"I was just another suitor to you," he said, shaking his head. Dismissing her feelings. Dismissing the power of what lay between them.

Amice gulped in a breath and fought back tears. "I

loved you more in an instant than anyone else could in a lifetime. How *dare* you discount that!"

Cain's jaw clenched and he took a step toward her. For one breathless moment, Amice thought he would take her in his arms, but he fisted his hands and turned away.

Chapter 7

As the siege wore into the second day, Amice sat in the hall and shared a suspicious look with Laila. From reports brought to them by a young page, Lugh and his men had unsuccessfully tried to ram through the portcullis, suffering four more inexplicably broken logs. When they tried to climb a ladder to the north tower, the ladder, seemingly on its own, fell away from the wall, dumping the men into the moat.

"It has to be Muriel." Amice almost felt sorry for Lugh.

"Meddlesome wraith," Gifford muttered as he paced back and forth. Suddenly, he whirled and clapped his hands together. "I *do* remember you."

Amice looked up. "What do you mean?"

Gifford plopped onto the bench next to her and

crossed his legs. "I visited Wareham years ago. You were a child."

"I am sorry, Gifford. I do not recall you."

"Your father hosted a great hunt. People came from all over the countryside. I myself saw your father take down a boar." He peered at her closely.

And Amice remembered. She had been six years of age. Hot shame flooded her at the memory. She had been so excited at the prospect of so many fine guests.

Gifford gave her a sympathetic look, and Amice stiffened. "I lost my way and came upon you in the garden."

"Aye." She had been hiding, barred from the festivities because of yet another "wrong" she supposedly committed to earn a beating by her father.

"You were crying," Gifford said softly.

"My sire was not an easy man."

"Nay. I recall that well." He wrinkled his nose. "But even then, it was as if you wore an invisible shield around yourself. I had never met a child with so much reserve."

"A lesson I learned very young."

Gifford patted her hand. "Perhaps it is time to learn a new one, my dear."

Before Amice could respond, Piers rushed into the hall, clad from head to foot in shiny mail, a gleaming sword in one hand and a cup of wine in the other. "You have to come see this!"

Gifford jumped up. "What is it?"

"You have to see for yourself. 'Tis the damnedest thing I have ever seen."

Amice, Gifford, and Laila followed Piers out of the hall and into the bailey.

"We can watch from atop that wall," Piers pointed. "Hurry."

Amice ran up the narrow steps to a partially concealed walkway and stared down at a scene of disorder. Lugh stood, legs spread apart, arms crossed over his chest, with a deep frown on his face.

Though the garrison lined the walls, many holding crossbows, no one was doing anything but watching.

Lugh lifted one hand and his men launched rocks from the trebuchet.

The stones rose high in the air, then higher and higher still as if an unseen force carried them in the wind. Amice watched open-mouthed as the stones continued their flight all the way over the far wall of the castle, to fall down to the sea.

Below them, Lugh threw down his sword in disgust and peered up toward the battlements. "Hawksdown?"

"Aye."

Amice could hear the amusement in Cain's voice.

"I wish to speak with my betrothed."

"You shall leave your weapons with my captain."

Though she could not hear him, Amice could see the sigh of frustration on Lugh's face.

He unbuckled his sword belt. "All of them?"

"All of them. And just you. Your men remain outside."

"I agree."

Amice scooted back against the stone merlon. What was she to do? Rand would not have betrothed her to Lugh. Would he? Laila laid a hand on her shoulder. "We should return to the hall."

"Aye." Amice gave Laila a worried look. "Rand would not have done this."

Laila shrugged. "Either way, you must talk to The MacKeir."

Taking a deep breath, Amice nodded. "Aye." She led the group back down to the bailey, stepping out onto the grass as the guards raised the portcullis and Lugh rode in. He stopped at the sight of her and gave her such a boyish grin she could not help but return it.

He leapt from his horse just as Cain emerged from the gatehouse. The two men eyed each other, reminding Amice of two roosters marking out territory.

Slowly, she approached them, noting the tremendous difference between the two. A sleek, golden lion and a brawny, black bear.

"Lady Amice," Lugh called out. "Come."

Amice stamped down irritation at his arrogant tone. "Chief MacKeir, why are you here? I thought you agreed to remain at Wareham."

He scowled. "I tired of waiting while you spent time in another man's holding."

"I have a task to complete."

Lugh crossed himself. "Aye, I see. Particularly after today."

"And I am not your betrothed." Amice could feel Cain's gaze upon her, suspicious and watchful. Piers and Gifford hung back just far enough to be polite while still listening intently to the conversation. Laila stood next to Amice quietly.

"Aye, *m'eudail*, you are."

In numbed shock, she watched as he took a piece of vellum from his plaid and passed it to Cain. All at once, her legs felt like butter and her vision blurred.

Cain bent to read the document and his mouth drew into a grim line. When he looked up, his expression was condemning. "He speaks the truth."

Amice fainted.

🌤 🌤 🌤

Cain caught Amice around the waist just as she crumpled. He swung her up in his arms, giving The MacKeir a stern look.

"I shall carry her," The MacKeir announced, as he reached for Amice.

"You have done enough. I have her." Cain ignored the titter from Piers and turned to go to the hall. Partway there Amice's eyes began to flutter, and by the time they reached the hall, she was blinking.

"What happened?" she whispered. "Was it Muriel?"

The MacKeir moved up beside them. "Are you all right? I did not expect the news of your good fortune to affect you so greatly."

Amice stared at him blankly.

Cain restrained the urge to run The MacKeir through with his sword and gently put Amice back on her feet. She gripped his arm, her eyes wide, and for a moment Cain feared she would faint again.

"Get you something to drink, my dear," Gifford muttered, and toddled off toward the buttery. As he left, Agatha walked into the hall.

She let out a squeak of fright, halted, and put her hand to her mouth.

Cain gaped at her. What had his sister done to her appearance?

The MacKeir stared at Agatha as if he had discovered paradise. "A goddess," he whispered. He glanced at Amice, then at Agatha, then back and forth again as if he could not decide what to do.

Agatha lowered her hand but did not move.

Cain looked over at Piers, who was barely constraining his laughter. "Chief MacKeir, may I present my sister, Lady Agatha."

The MacKeir drew in a breath, strode over to Agatha, took her hand and kissed it fervently. "Enchanting."

Agatha drew back her hand in horror. She shot Amice a pleading look, but Amice was apparently still in too much shock to respond. Cain guided her into a seat on the dais and looked pointedly at Piers, who just grinned back at him. "Do something," Cain hissed.

Piers wandered over to The MacKeir and Agatha. By now, Agatha had backed up against the wall, The MacKeir hovering over her. "Chief MacKeir, please take your ease. We shall have food and drink served."

The MacKeir took Agatha's arm. "Thank you. I have a mighty thirst upon me." He pulled Agatha toward the table. In response to her obvious agitation, Piers merely nodded approvingly.

Cain sat down and resisted the impulse to bury his face in his hands.

Along with Gifford, a cluster of servants bearing trays of drink and food arrived, followed by Morganna barely clad in a deep scarlet bliaut. Cain briefly closed his eyes, wondering how the situation could possibly become more complicated.

Of course, it was at that moment that Muriel decided to appear.

At the sight of her, The MacKeir jumped to his feet with a roar, reached for his missing sword and snatched up an eating knife from the table, brandishing it like it was a great war sword. "*Bana-bhuidseach*!"

Agatha tried to run, but The MacKeir caught her and thrust her behind him, holding her close with his free hand.

Muriel floated closer. "I am not a witch, you overgrown boor. I am a spirit."

The MacKeir looked wildly around the hall, clearly searching for additional weapons.

"Might as well have a seat, MacKeir," Gifford advised as he took another gulp of ale. He pushed a jug toward The MacKeir. "As my nephew reminded me, you cannot get rid of a ghost with a sword."

The MacKeir slowly released Agatha and lowered himself onto a stool. He reached for the jug and poured the contents down his throat.

Amice stirred beside him, thankfully finally coming out of her stupor. "What do you want, Muriel?"

"Pray accept my congratulations on your betrothal, Lady Amice."

Cain took a big gulp of wine.

"Why, thank you, Muriel."

"I was betrothed once."

"To whom?"

Muriel drifted closer. "To the Earl of Hawksdown, of course."

Cain narrowed his eyes. What was she talking about? Gerard Veuxfort's wife was named Elena.

"What happened?"

"He broke the betrothal."

"Why?"

With a bitter laugh, Muriel said, "He found me in an awkward position with another man. Instead of trusting me, he believed I betrayed him."

"Was he wrong?"

"Aye. It was all Elena's doing, the jealous bitch. She was determined to have Gerard."

"Did she get him?"

"Aye." Muriel laughed again. "She made his life hell, of course." She gazed into the distance. "I enjoyed those years very much."

"But why kill yourself? Surely, you could have found another to marry. Or entered a convent."

Muriel wrinkled her nose. "Convent life was not for me. And I did not want to marry anyone but Gerard."

"Death seems a harsh solution."

"The Earls of Hawksdown have never chosen their brides well, have they, Cain?"

Cain stiffened and set down his cup. "Nay."

"Muriel, why do you linger here?" Amice asked.

She stared at Amice for a long time. "Because I cannot leave."

"Why not," Cain asked. "There is nothing for you here."

"You are quite wrong in that. For one, I have gained

much enjoyment from watching you make a wretched marriage and punish yourself for it. Your unhappiness brings me great cheer."

"Demented wench," Gifford growled.

Muriel did not even look at him.

Cain glared at the apparition.

Muriel glared back, then said softly, "But you did seize a bit of happiness recently. Or rather, pleasure."

At a loss for words, Cain just looked at her. Damn her for knowing things.

Slowly, Muriel turned toward The MacKeir and raised a brow. "Pleasure with the Lady Amice."

The MacKeir jumped to his feet, his face instantly scarlet and set in angry lines. "What do you say?" He gave Cain a sharp look. "What does she mean?"

Cain glanced at Amice. Her face was white and she sat completely still. What in the hell was he supposed to say? That he did not know of the betrothal? He very much doubted The MacKeir would accept that explanation. That he was drunk? Hardly an excuse.

The MacKeir did not wait for an answer. He drew himself up and fisted his hands. "I challenge you to combat, Hawksdown. You have abused my betrothed. For that you shall die."

Cain stood. "I did not abuse Amice."

The MacKeir laid a meaty hand on Amice's shoulder. "I am sorry, beloved. I should have protected you from the attentions of this cur."

Amice opened her mouth but no words came out. She blinked and shook her head. "Lugh, please reconsider. Muriel lies."

"Does she?" The MacKeir looked at Muriel, who wore a sly smile on her lips.

"The Earl of Hawksdown did not abuse me."

"He forced you."

"Nay. Muriel lies."

"I think you seek to protect him. Do not worry. After I kill him, I shall take you to Tunvegan as my bride."

"This is absurd," Cain finally said.

The MacKeir lifted his chin. "Honor is not absurd. Do you accept my challenge or are you a coward as well as an abuser of innocent women?"

Well, hell. There was no way he could let that pass. Cain rubbed the back of his neck. "I accept. Tomorrow at prime."

"Weapons?"

"Swords."

The MacKeir nodded. "Done." He looked down at Amice. "Come. Walk with me in the bailey."

Cain could do nothing but watch as Amice left. She was betrothed. Pledged to this beefy Highlander with whom she was obviously well acquainted. He could scarcely credit it.

How could she love him as if her very soul blended with his while betrothed to another?

God, he was a witless fool.

❦ ❦ ❦

As soon as they were outside, Amice pulled her arm from Lugh's grasp. "Show me the agreement."

Silently, Lugh held out the piece of vellum.

It only took a moment to verify the truth. Rand had indeed given her to his boon companion, Lugh MacKeir. "How could he?" she whispered, then put her hand over her mouth.

"Let us walk," Lugh ordered, once more taking her arm, smoothly taking back the betrothal agreement.

Amice let herself be led across the grass, her mind still unable to accept her brother's betrayal. How could Rand do this? And why?

"Lady Amice, your brother looks to your welfare. He and I discussed this matter at length. You need a husband. I want you."

"Why?"

"What?"

Amice stopped and peered up at Lugh. "Why do you want me?"

He looked surprised at the question. "You are a beautiful woman. And you are strong enough to live at Tunvegen."

"Is that it?"

"I understand." Lugh smiled and took her hand. "You wish to hear love words." He stepped close. "I shall show you with my body, *m'eudail*. I shall wipe any memory of that knave from your mind."

Good God. He was serious. "Lugh, you must release Cain from this challenge."

He scowled and shook his head. "I cannot. 'Tis a serious offence."

Amice bit her lip. "Cain did not violate me, Lugh."

"I told you, you need not protect him. If you wish to journey to Italy, I shall take you in celebration of our wedding."

"It is not about the villa." She squeezed his hand. "I am sorry, Lugh, but I am telling the truth."

His expression turned so fierce, Amice tried to pull her hand free, but he held it fast. "You were willing?"

"Aye." Willing, eager, desperate. She had been all those things, to her shame.

"You did not know of the betrothal."

"Nay."

Lugh drew his lips together and his features relaxed. "I shall still take you." He puffed up his chest. "Once you have a taste of my skills in the bedchamber, you will never want any other man."

Amice fought it but in the end she had to grin. Lugh was so sure of himself and free about expressing it. Based on the way he kissed, his boast might actually be based in fact. "Lugh, I do not wish to marry you. I am sure you are every bit as skilled as you claim and I truly like you, but . . ." She held out her hands.

"You will come to love me, lass. When I fill your belly with our babes, you will realize how lucky you are."

Babes. Amice blanched. What was she to do? She could not reveal her past to Lugh. She could not bear to tell him. But he deserved to know she might be barren. Rand, how could you? "Do not fight tomorrow. Please."

"You fear for him." Lugh narrowed his eyes and studied her, reminding Amice that despite his bulk and manner, he was also a very astute man.

"He *is* good with a sword, but—"

"I am better," Lugh stated with his usual confidence.

"Mayhap." Nay, much better. And bigger. And stronger. And more ruthless.

"You care for him."

Amice looked away. "I did. Once. I would not wish to be the cause of his death."

"Forget the Earl of Hawksdown. You are mine."

"I have forgotten him," Amice lied. "But I have not agreed to wed you either."

Lugh just lifted one bushy brow. " 'Tis done."

"Not without my consent."

Lugh's brow furrowed and his eyes turned emerald green. "If I spare Hawksdown's life, you shall consent to the marriage."

A bleak hollowness settled deep into her body. To save Cain, she must give up any chance to be with him. Lose him forever. She wanted to wail in anguish, curse the fates and leap on her horse to gallop away without stopping.

Amice nodded. "I agree."

❧ ❧ ❧

The next morn, Cain paced back and forth across the bailey, staring suspiciously at Gifford. There was no sign of The MacKeir. Most of the people of the castle stood in the bailey waiting. "Where the hell are they?"

Gifford just shrugged. "Perhaps Piers cannot find him."

Cain turned toward Amice, who gazed at him with an innocent expression. "What do you know of this?"

She bit her lip, then said softly, "He will not fight you."

"What have you done?" He strode over to stand in front of her. Agatha and Laila flanked her, wearing identical expressions of dismay. "Where is he?"

"I do not know, but he agreed not to fight."

Something was wrong here. "Why? He seemed most anxious to avenge your honor last eve."

Amice flushed and looked down. "I told him the truth."

Cain noticed Gifford creeping closer and gave him a warning look, which Gifford of course pretended not to see. "The truth?"

"Aye."

As he stood staring at Amice, it sunk in what she had done. "Damn it, Amice, I am capable of fighting my own battles."

"Lugh is *very* good with a sword," she said in a small voice.

"So am I."

Finally, she lifted her gaze and stared at him. Her eyes were flat, as if something had been extinguished inside her. "He is better."

Cain knew his skill with a sword was impressive. He would have had at least a fighting chance. "I do not believe this. How did you persuade him to abandon the fight?"

Amice looked away. "I agreed to marry him."

Gifford made a sound of distress.

Cain closed his eyes against the jolt of agony that shot through him. "You agreed to marry The MacKeir to spare me from having to fight him?"

"Aye."

"Damn you, Amice," he growled. "You had no right."

"I do as I wish, Cain. I make my own decisions."

"And witless ones they are, if this is an example." Cain

looked around the bailey. "Thomas," he called to his captain.

"Aye, my lord."

"Find The MacKeir and bring him here. I do not care if you have to drag him." When Thomas just stood staring at him wide-eyed, Cain yelled, "Now, dammit!" Thomas and a group of guards fled.

Cain rubbed the back of his neck. "I cannot believe this."

" 'Tis for the best, Cain."

"Amice."

Slowly, she turned and gazed into his eyes. The expression he saw there made him want to howl to the heavens. It was as if a veil had parted to show her true feelings, but then her eyes went blank. "Do you . . . do you *want* to marry him?"

"Of course. Lugh is a fine man." Her voice held no emotion whatsoever.

"Amice—"

"What now, Hawksdown?" The MacKeir bellowed as he crossed the bailey, trailed by Piers, Thomas, and the other men from the garrison. He wore a sword strapped to his waist and carried a shield. The MacKeir stopped several feet from Cain and cocked a brow.

"We had an appointment, MacKeir."

The MacKeir looked at Amice. "Did my woman not tell you? I agreed to spare you at her request."

"You forgot to mention you compelled her to agree to the marriage in exchange."

"I compelled her to do nothing." The MacKeir gave Cain a mocking look. "We are betrothed."

No. He would not let her do it. Cain drew his sword and stepped close to The MacKeir. "Amice is a passionate wench. I shall always remember the feel of her warm curves beneath my body, her soft cries of pleasure."

For a moment, The MacKeir looked shocked, then his eyes darkened, he pulled his sword free and raised his shield. "For that, you *will* die."

"Give it your best try," Cain hissed.

With a roar, Lugh swung his sword.

Cain dodged the blow by inches and slashed back toward Lugh's neck. The sound of sword thunking against shield rang through the bailey.

"No!" Amice shouted. "Stop this madness."

"Piers, get her out of the way," Cain shouted, focusing on ducking another lunge by The MacKeir.

Shouts of encouragement filled the air, but the world narrowed to just The MacKeir and him. Though The MacKeir was bigger and stronger, Cain soon realized he was quicker and more agile. He used that advantage to leap and duck free from most of The MacKeir's blows, using his shield to absorb as few as possible.

"Whoreson!" The MacKeir grunted, as he swept his sword toward Cain's knees.

Cain jumped over the blade, and whirled back toward The MacKeir. He slashed with all his strength. His blade crashed into The MacKeir's shield, then slid off, slicing into the Scot's arm.

The wound inflamed The MacKeir, and he bore down on Cain in fury. In a move so sudden Cain had no time to prepare, he brought his sword up in a killing arc, the strength behind the blow so powerful, it wrenched Cain's sword from his hand.

The MacKeir paused and smiled at Cain.

Cain could not believe it. No one had ever been able to do such a thing. Failure was an acrid taste on his tongue. He raised his shield. He would be damned if he would ask this boor for mercy.

"Do you concede?" The MacKeir growled.

"Go to hell." Cain glared at him.

From the corner of his eye, Cain saw a flash of color, just before Amice burst between them. She gave Cain a look of sheer anguish, then turned to The MacKeir, palms up. "Lugh, please."

For a long moment, The MacKeir stared back at her, his lips flat and his eyes hard.

"Please, Lugh. I have already agreed to marry you. Let us not begin with death."

The MacKeir shifted his gaze to Cain and studied him. "He has earned it."

"Lugh." Amice laid a hand on his arm. "Please."

Slowly, he slid his sword into the ring attached to his belt and nodded. "For you." Then he grinned and shouted out, "Let us drink!"

Cain remained in place, watching with a growing sense of unreality as The MacKeir and everybody else in the castle trooped off to the hall to celebrate. Everyone save Gifford and Piers.

Gifford shot Cain a knowing look.

"Shut up," Cain snapped.

Piers handed him back his sword. "Fine bit of sword-play, there."

"I lost," Cain said half to himself. "I failed her."

"Lucky The MacKeir showed some sense," Gifford muttered.

Cain rubbed his neck.

Gifford handed him a jug. "Take a drink."

Cain tipped ale into his mouth.

"Go on, then," Piers said, shoving Cain from behind.

"Go?"

"Into the hall."

"I shall join you anon." Cain stomped off toward the training field before the two could argue.

Chapter 8

"Lugh, you are bleeding," Amice said.

He glanced at his arm and laughed. " 'Tis but a scratch. Now, will you toast to my victory and great showing of mercy?"

Amice sighed and looked past him to where Agatha hovered just out of reach. Her eyes were wide, and she gazed with clear fascination at Lugh as if he were some sort of dangerous creature, which of course he was. Hardly Agatha's vision of an elegant, learned, fair-haired man who would write her poetry. "You should let me tend to your wound."

"Drink first." He waved to Hawis, who came rushing over.

"Aye, my lord?"

"Bring your best barrel of ale, my fair lass! Sparing a man's life is thirsty work."

Hawis looked to Agatha, who nodded up and down in jerky movements. "At once, my lord."

As she scuttled off, Amice noted Gifford and Piers approaching. Where was Cain?

The two came to a halt before Lugh.

Abruptly, the buzz of conversation in the hall quieted.

Gifford lifted a brow. "Fine display of swordsmanship, MacKeir."

Lugh puffed out his chest. "Thank you. My skill with a sword is known throughout the Highlands."

"Perhaps while you are here, you can teach me that last trick you used on Cain," Piers said.

" 'Twould be my pleasure." Lugh winked. "Your brother clearly needs aid."

The people in the hall began talking again.

"Where is Cain?" Amice finally asked.

Gifford sniffed. "On the training field. Not used to being bested."

"Is he injured?"

"Nay, only his pride."

Hawis returned and put a ewer of ale into Lugh's hands, while other servants passed drinks around the hall. Gifford, naturally, had his ever-present jug with him, and Piers strode off to find his own.

Lugh took a long drink. "Ah, 'tis good." He grabbed a cup from a passing servant, filled it and handed it to Amice. "Join me, *m'eudail*."

"What does that mean," Gifford asked.

"My darling." Lugh filled another cup and motioned to Agatha. "Come, Lady Agatha."

Agatha glanced at the cup, then at Lugh, then back again. Finally, she inched closer and accepted the ale. Lugh shot her a lusty grin, and Agatha's mouth fell open.

Amice laid a hand on his arm. "Thank you, Lugh."

His grin faded and he gazed down at her, his deep green eyes probing. "I would talk with you. Alone."

"You shall allow me to clean your wound."

"Aye."

"Come to my chamber." Laila started to follow them, but Lugh raised a hand.

"Your lady shall be safe."

Laila looked to Amice. She nodded agreement and led Lugh from the hall. After stopping in the well-house for a bucket of fresh water, they walked across the wide bailey.

Lugh squinted up into the sunlight. "A fine day."

With each step, Amice grew increasingly uncomfortable. In the distance, she spotted Cain riding full-out toward the quintain. She felt the heavy weight of Lugh's stare upon her and wondered what he wished to talk about. He would no doubt be anxious to leave Falcon's Craig. But surely he would understand she must stay to complete her task. Amice bit her lip.

When they reached her chamber, Lugh shut the door with a solid thump, and drew off his tunic and undershirt.

Amice swallowed, suddenly realizing just how large and imposing her betrothed really was. She pointed to the windowseat. "Sit."

Without a word, Lugh sat and poured himself a cup of

wine from the ewer Hawis kept filled.

As she drew herbs from her bag and tore a strip of linen from a chemise, Amice felt him watching her. She put the water next to him, and gently dabbed at the gash.

"Well, shall I live?"

Amice twitched her lips. "Aye, but I should stitch the wound."

"Do with me what you will, Amice."

Her gaze shot to his. Lugh lifted a brow, then shook his head. "I know your secret," he stated.

Shock pooled in Amice's belly. Which one? "What do you mean?" She shifted her gaze toward Lugh's shoulder.

"You love him," he said softly.

Amice closed her eyes. "Nay. I did not want him to die, 'tis true, but—"

"Look at me."

Slowly, Amice let the linen drop into the bucket and looked at Lugh.

He gave her a small smile. "I know the look of a woman in love. 'Tis in her eyes," he said as he traced the side of her forehead with his calloused thumb. "In the way she holds her body when her lover is near."

"I do not love Cain," Amice choked out.

"Aye, you do."

"Lugh, you do not know about the past we share. He—"

Lugh waved a hand. " 'Tis of no significance."

Amice straightened. "It is to me. And I have given you my consent."

Lugh tilted his head toward his shoulder. "Finish your healing, lass, and I shall think on this."

🐎 🐎 🐎

"You have to help me," Morganna hissed.

Muriel glided closer. "Why? You failed to get Amice to leave."

"I tried." Morganna pouted. "It was not my fault Cain happened to catch her in time."

"I do not want her *dead*, just persuaded to leave Falcon's Craig. Do something else."

"What?"

"Have you no imagination, stupid girl?" Muriel narrowed her eyes into emerald slits, and Morganna's mouth went dry. "What was I thinking to enlist help from you?"

Morganna stuck out her jaw. "Because I am the only one willing to aid you."

For a moment, Muriel glared at her, then nodded. "True enough. I need her gone."

"I will think of something. But first, you must help me persuade Cain to bed me. He is so damned honorable he will force himself to marry me then. I want to be the Countess of Hawksdown, not some unpaid servant!"

"You should never have been so blatant. Cain is not the type of man to pounce just because a woman is naked."

Morganna sighed. "Aye, I know that now. But I thought surely the sight of my body would sway him. And he *was* ready."

"Not for you."

"Then help me."

A swirl of gold whipped through the chamber, filling it with strange light. Morganna stood frozen by fear.

Slowly, the gold solidified into a bag on the floor. Muriel gestured to the pouch with a gossamer hand. "Take it."

"What is this?"

"Something very special. Very rare and *very* potent. Put only a small amount into the wine Cain keeps in his chamber."

"What will it do?"

Muriel smiled. "Make him unable to resist you."

"Perfect. Then all this will be mine."

"Do not forget your part of the bargain."

"I shall be happy to take care of Lady Amice." Morganna looked down at the bag and slowly smiled.

❧ ❧ ❧

After smashing the hell out of the quintain for the better part of an hour, Cain finally admitted he was avoiding facing Amice. He had been bested. Accept it and move forward.

Cain went in search of The MacKeir. What to do with the man now?

He entered the hall to find The MacKeir regaling Gifford, Piers, Amice, Laila, and even Agatha with some undoubtedly exaggerated tale of when he and his men fought off a hundred McDougals.

"And then, I jumped over the blade, twisted in the air, and brought my sword down right across the bastard's neck," Lugh said.

"Did you manage to perform a backflip at the same time?" Cain asked dryly.

Lugh grinned. "Did not think of it. Mayhap next time."

Cain poured himself a cup of ale.

Rising to his feet, Lugh nodded to his audience then looked at Cain. "Hawksdown, I would have private discourse with you."

Amice jumped up. "Lugh, I—"

"Do not worry. I shall not kill him." He put his hands out. "I have no weapons."

"Come," Cain interrupted. "We can talk in my solar." He gestured to The MacKeir. They left the hall and walked up the steps.

Once in the solar, The MacKeir closed the door and crossed his arms. "Did you bed my woman?"

For a moment, Cain stared at him, considering how best to respond. "Aye."

"Why?" The MacKeir's jaw looked like it could break apart at any instant.

"I should think it obvious."

MacKeir took a step toward Cain. "Is it your habit to bed innocent women who happen to be within your holding?"

"Nay."

"Then why Amice?"

There was no way Cain would tell him the truth. He could no more resist Amice than a fly could resist honey. "I had too much to drink, Amice was there, and . . ." he shrugged his shoulders.

"That is your excuse?"

Cain rubbed the back of his neck. "I knew naught of any betrothal."

"Aye, but you do not answer my question. Amice is

not a wench to be trifled with."

"Nay, but she *is* a very beautiful woman."

The MacKeir studied him through narrowed eyes. "I have long wanted Amice to be my wife, but circumstances delayed me being able to claim her."

"And now?" Cain found himself half-hoping MacKeir had changed his mind.

"What happened between you and Amice in the past?"

Cain met the The MacKeir's stare. " 'Tis none of your affair."

"Anything affecting my betrothed is my affair."

"If Amice wishes to share the story with you, 'tis her choice, but you shall not hear it from me."

"Mayhap I *should* have killed you," The MacKeir said, rubbing his chin.

"You would have been next."

MacKeir shrugged. "Would not be the first time someone tried to slay me."

"Even you could not fight off my entire garrison alone."

"You shall give her your villa as recompense?"

"I shall grant it to her when that damned wraith is gone from Falcon's Craig."

"What kind of man forces a woman to his will and besmirches her honor?"

"A desperate one."

The MacKeir scowled. "Than I shall stay as well to ensure Amice's safety."

"Fine."

"And my men will be permitted entry. You have my word no treachery shall come of it."

Cain nodded.

The MacKeir cocked a brow. "Are you in love with her?"

Love? Cain's heart slowly twisted in his chest. He could not be. He was not sure he even knew anymore what that mysterious emotion was. "Nay."

The MacKeir gave him a knowing look and strode out of the chamber.

⚜ ⚜ ⚜

Agatha knelt on the ground in the castle garden, pulling weeds from among the plantings of rosemary and lavender. She loved gardening, usually found the rhythmic motions soothing.

But not today.

Today all she saw was Lugh MacKeir, wielding his sword like some kind of conquering hero from the legend of Camelot. Her hand trembled as she yanked a weed.

"Lady Agatha?" a voice rumbled.

Her stomach flipped over. Slowly, she peered up and swallowed. The MacKeir stood over her, his massive body blocking the sun. "Aye?"

He squatted down next to her.

Agatha caught her breath. His eyes gleamed just like the lush green of the grass beneath her knees.

"I would know more about you."

"Me?" Agatha's voice came out a squeak and she coughed.

"Aye." He planted each hand on the ground.

"I . . . I fear I am not very interesting, my lord."

"Chief." He drew his heavy brows together. "Why has

no man claimed you?"

Agatha lifted her chin and stood, clutching her bag of weeds. " 'Tis none of your affair."

The MacKeir rose and towered over her. "Has your brother not seen to your welfare?"

"My brother allows me the freedom to live at Styrling Castle."

"Without a man? 'Tis unnatural."

"I assure you, it is quite natural for me." Agatha's face heated as she recalled her conversation with Amice. This man's betrothed, she reminded herself.

He studied her and lifted a brow. "English men are blind indeed."

The heat in Agatha's face spread down her body. "I . . . I appreciate your concern, my, uh, chief, but I am content."

"Are you?" He seemed to come closer though Agatha would swear he had not moved a single sculpted muscle.

"Aye."

The MacKeir shook his head. "A woman needs a man's touch."

Agatha opened her mouth to dispute him.

"Just as a man needs a woman's. 'Tis as certain as the sun's rise each day."

Her mouth snapped shut.

"Mayhap you have not met the right man, Lady Agatha."

"Mayhap," she said weakly.

He winked. "Or perhaps you have."

Agatha stood in the garden watching him leave, and felt as if the air had just been sucked out of her in one great whoosh. *He is betrothed. He is a wild Highlander.*

He is absolutely the most provoking man I have ever encountered.

Dear God, what was she to do?

❧ ❧ ❧

Cain sat in the hall the next morning, nursing another cup of ale and trying very hard to remind himself of his goals. Keep the estate profitable. See to his villeins' welfare. Find a man to exert some control over Morganna's behavior. Figure out how to entice one to take Agatha.

None of it was working. He had never felt so helpless and frustrated in his entire life.

He cut a glance over at Amice, who sat calmly munching on a bite of bread. Damn it. Just watching her eat aroused him, the movement of her lips, the touch of her tongue catching a crumb from her mouth, making him ache for her taste.

Suddenly, his captain, Thomas, burst into the hall, his face taut and his eyes burning. "My lord!" he called.

Cain vaulted to his feet. "What is it, Thomas?"

"Woodford. He attacked Hazelstone. We just received word from Ranaulf's boy."

The MacKeir thunked down his cup and rose quickly.

"Sneaky bastard," Gifford cursed.

"How many of his men this time?"

Thomas shrugged. "At least a score."

"Gather a group of ten men. We ride at once."

The captain nodded and rushed out of the hall.

The MacKeir moved beside him, his face set. "My

men and I will go with you."

" 'Tis not your battle."

"When some filthy whoreson attacks an innocent village, I am pleased to make it my battle."

"Very well." Cain found himself looking forward to hunting down Harry Woodford. It was time to put an end to this. "Nyle," he shouted.

"Aye, my lord."

"See that warm clothes and food are taken to Hazelstone."

Amice laid a hand on his arm. She was shaking. Cain paused. Her face was ashen but resolute. "Cain, Laila and I are talented healers. Let us go to the village."

" 'Tis too dangerous."

"I will send a score of my men to guard them," The MacKeir injected.

Cain's gaze flicked to The MacKeir then back to Amice. It was obvious she wished to help. He nodded. "Be careful. Woodford has been a thorn in my side for years, though he has not attacked so close to Falcon's Craig before."

"Who is he?"

Before Cain could answer, Gifford spat, "The knave Luce wanted to marry."

"Aye," Piers added. "He blames Cain for her death."

Amice's gaze turned confused and she tilted her head. "Why? How did she die?"

Cain made his expression go blank. "There is no time to explain."

Within the hour, the group thundered out the gatehouse toward Hazelstone.

❧ ❧ ❧

They made it to Hazelstone in less than a day. Amice drew in a sharp breath at the sight, reminded of the massacre she had seen years ago. An entire village butchered for no reason but that she refused to marry the Earl of Atteby, an old man with claw-like hands and powerful allies. Her father had been almost glad of it, justifying his killing rampage as retaliation.

She shoved back the memory into the buried place she kept all memories of her sire.

Hazelstone was small, with no more than a tiny church and twenty or so wattle and daub houses clustered together. Wide expanses of open fields surrounded the village, spotted here and there with thatched huts, and criss-crossed with low, loose-laid stone walls.

In the center of the village the people had gathered to tend the injured, next to what appeared to be the only intact house standing. As they rode in, Amice smelled the acrid scent of burnt wood and saw tendrils of smoke still rising from burned dwellings. Outside the village, butchered sheep littered a blood-soaked field next to bodies of men, women, and children.

Cain vaulted from his horse. "Father Osbert, what happened here?"

Before the priest could answer, a man lying on the ground next to him shot Cain an angry stare. "Like demons they were. Clad in black. They rode out of nowhere and started killing."

Amice swallowed back the urge to retch.

"It was Woodford?" Cain asked.

"Aye. Heard one of the men say his name."

Cain pointed to Amice. "Lady Amice and her companion are healers. And my seneschal shall be here soon with food and clothing."

"Thank you, my lord. We are hard pressed to do much for the wounded."

"Is there adequate shelter?"

The priest shrugged helplessly. "Most of the houses are damaged, my lord. We have not been able to go in to discover whether they remain habitable."

"Everyone is welcome to take shelter at Falcon's Craig."

The priest nodded. "Thank you, my lord."

"Which way did they ride?" The MacKeir interrupted.

Another man standing on the edge of the group lifted an arm and pointed. "North, toward the hills, my lord."

Cain turned to look at Amice, his gaze hard. "See to the villagers then get back to Falcon's Craig."

Amice nodded and watched as he, Lugh, and a band of ten men galloped away.

❦ ❦ ❦

Amice was in the process of bandaging a young woman's burned arm when she heard the ominous sound of metal meeting metal. She jumped up and took a step back, her hand to her mouth.

Laila pulled at her sleeve. "Run, Amice!"

She glanced back to the battle, stunned at the sight of so many men clad in black surcoats cutting down her

Highland guard one by one. Shouts rent the air and the thwack of metal against shield was deafening.

"Now, Amice," Laila hissed. She dragged Amice behind a hut and pointed across a field toward a copse of trees.

"Come with me."

"Nay. I will slow you down. Go!"

Amice picked up her skirts and ran, her heart hitching in her chest with terror.

She was nearly to the trees, her breath rasping, her chest burning, when her feet left the ground. In one moment, she was running for her life and in the next she was face down over the back of a horse, the ground rushing by with sickening speed. Amice tried to lever herself up but a meaty hand shoved her down.

"Be still," a low voice growled.

Amice began to pray as the heavy sound of many horses rang in her ears. First she prayed to Brigit, then to Danu. During a prayer to Eostre her stomach rolled and she threw up, heaving violently onto the grass below.

Her captor never acknowledged any of it.

Finally, mercifully, the mount slowed and Amice realized they had entered a forest. An eerie quiet settled over the troop as they wound their way through the trees, the leafy groundcover muffling the hoofbeats.

When Amice could catch her breath, she demanded, "Who are you?"

"The last man you shall ever see."

Biting back her fear, Amice said, "As I have not seen you, I must doubt your words."

To her surprise, her captor laughed in response, and

hauled her up to a sitting position facing him

Dread snaked down her spine as she stared into obsidian eyes. A crude, dull helmet shielded the man's face and hair. The rest of him was cloaked in black and mail.

"What do you see, Lady Amice?"

Amice drew in a harsh breath. "A coward."

His eyes flashed like burning embers in a dead fire. "I advise you to watch your tongue. The method of your death is still undecided."

"Who are you?"

"Henry Woodford."

"The man Cain's wife favored."

"Aye. Favored." His lips parted in a grim smile. "Until that whoreson, Hawksdown, destroyed her."

"What do you mean?"

"He killed her. He was insane with jealousy. And he killed my beloved Luce."

Amice's skin turned cold. No, he must be lying. Cain would not do such a thing. "I do not believe you."

Woodford shrugged. "I do not expect you to. I know you *favor* Hawksdown. But the tale is true."

"Why have you taken me? I have naught to do with your quarrel."

As he guided the horse under a grey stone gatehouse, Woodford's eyes turned cold. "In that you are wrong." He cantered into a bailey and shoved Amice off the horse onto the dirt. "Rafe?"

"Aye, my lord," a male voice answered.

Amice slowly moved to a sitting position and wiped dust from her face. The voice belonged to a huge, black-haired man. Above a heavy beard dissected by a ridged scar, thin lips twisted in a grim smile.

"Take Lady Amice to the chamber I have had prepared for her." Woodford gazed down at her, and Amice lifted her chin. "Do not worry, Spirit Goddess. Your stay here shall be brief." He turned away, laughing.

The man called Rafe plucked Amice up as if she weighed no more than a leaf, slung her over his shoulders and entered the castle.

Chapter 9

"There is something wrong here," Cain said to his captain. "The tracks head north but Woodford's castle lies to the west." He drew his mount to a halt and dropped to the ground.

The MacKeir shouted, "Why do you stop, Hawksdown?"

"I am not sure. This does not feel right."

With a grunt, The MacKeir leapt off his horse and approached him. "Why?"

" 'Tis the wrong direction."

"Mayhap the man goes to another manor. Or to an ally's."

"Perhaps, but—"

"My lord!" A rider pounded into the center of the group.

As Cain turned, his feeling that something was awry solidified into conviction. The small figure jumped down and ran up to him.

Cain recognized one of the villagers from Hazelstone, and he braced himself for the news.

"My lord, they took the Lady Amice!"

The MacKeir let out a roar.

"When?" Cain bit out.

"Yesterday," the man said on a breath. " 'Twasn't nothin' we could do."

"My men?" The MacKeir asked.

The villager closed his eyes and crossed himself. "All killed, my lord. We been doin' nothin' but preparing bodies for burial."

"It was the same men?"

"Aye, not as many, but the same." The man spit in the grass. "Like demons."

"He must have taken her to Hexham," Cain said to The MacKeir. " 'Tis the only place he would feel safe."

"Then to Hexham we go."

Within a few moments, they thundered west. Fear choked Cain's heart, and he silently prayed to God over and over. He had seen too many examples of Woodford's brutal treatment. *Dear God, let Woodford be using Amice only to lure me to Hexham.*

❧ ❧ ❧

Amice woke in a cold, dark room and listened to a faint scurrying sound in the far corner. She stretched, kneaded her sore arms, and listened for any other noise. The silence was tomblike.

Her teeth chattered despite her strongest effort to calm herself. No, Woodford had ordered the man called Rafe to put her in a chamber, not a tomb. Amice gathered a thin coverlet around her and stepped onto the floor. She inched toward a sliver of light and willed whatever was making the sounds in the corner to stay there.

Just as she neared the light, the door opened, flooding the room with torchlight.

"Ah, you are awake. Good."

Woodford. Amice glared at him and rubbed her head, wincing as her fingers grazed a lump.

"Rafe knows not to hit any harder than necessary." He walked into the room and lit the fire.

As the fire took hold, Amice looked around at her surroundings. It was a poor chamber, small and dusty with neglect. Her bed was no more than a thin pallet, the single cover the one she had wrapped around her. A scarred table stood against one wall with a jug of water. The other wall had only two iron rings embedded into the stone. A length of white silk hung from one of the rings.

"Not the comforts you are accustomed to," Woodford said as he turned to face her.

"Nay. Not at all." As Amice studied him, she thought what a strange combination of beauty and wickedness he presented. He had the kind of looks that immediately made a woman think of long firelit nights of passion, his lush mouth alone evoking the image. But his eyes revealed the darkness inside the man. Flat, reptilian eyes. Amice suppressed a shiver.

He tilted his head and gazed at her with open curiosity. "You are very different from my Luce."

"How?"

"In every way, I imagine," he said softly. "She was a small woman, yet still lush-figured. Luce was all that was bright and beautiful."

"Why did you not marry her?"

His face tightened. "Her father disliked me."

"Why?"

"He was a fool." He paced the floor.

Amice sensed he was lying. "Did you love her?"

"Aye!" he roared. "And she loved *me*." He stepped close to Amice. "Luce was the other half of my soul. She shared the same desires as I."

"Desires?"

Woodford's face drew on a faraway expression, and he gave Amice a soft smile. "Aye. Luce was willing to do anything for the sake of pleasure." His gaze shot to the rings. "Anything. *She* was a goddess."

Amice made herself look away from the rings and what they suggested. "This has naught to do with me."

He just looked at her speculatively. "What do you desire, Amice?"

She fought against a surge of horror. "To leave this place."

"Nay. You shall never leave."

Panic twisted in her stomach, but Amice made her face remain expressionless. "Cain will come for me."

"Oh, I hope so, my dear. I truly do. 'Twill be all the more satisfying."

An aura of evil seeped from him like a stream of venom. Amice pulled the coverlet tight around her.

Woodford chuckled. "Rafe will bring you food and drink. Be nice to him and mayhap he shall procure a thicker blanket and some extra logs for the fire."

"I am not cold," Amice lied.

"Sweet dreams, my lady," Woodford said, then thankfully left her alone.

Amice stood in the dim chamber staring at the door. She fought it but in the end her body started to shiver, and it seemed nothing she did could stop it. She huddled before the meager fire and stretched out her hands.

How was she to escape this place?

When the door opened, Amice stiffened. The man called Rafe slid in, a rawboned, young woman behind him. He held a brace of candles aloft. "Put the platter and ewer over there."

The servant hastened to do his bidding, then turned back and waited, eyes downcast.

"Leave us," Rafe said.

Amice clutched at the edges of the coverlet and met Rafe's gaze. He stared back at her unblinkingly, then walked outside, returning in a moment with a heavy wool blanket which he tossed toward her.

"I . . . thank you."

He grunted. "Eat. You will need your strength."

"What does Woodford intend?"

"Naught good, you can be sure of that."

Amice stood. "He means to kill me."

"Aye."

"I have done naught to warrant such a fate."

"Life is not fair, my lady." He nodded toward the rings. "Mayhap you could persuade Woodford to change his mind."

Revulsion swirled in Amice's stomach, and she was glad she had not yet eaten. "Nay."

Rafe shrugged. " 'Tis your fate."

"How can you give loyalty to a man like that?"

He cocked a brow. "Not all of us are born into wealth, my *lady*."

"You know nothing of me."

"I know you are noble born. It is easy for you to talk of things like loyalty."

"Woodford is a sick man."

Rafe laughed. "Aye. You do not know the half of it. Best hope you do not have the chance." He turned to go.

"Help me. My brother will pay you whatever Woodford offers and more."

"Nay." He narrowed his gaze. "The last man to defy Woodford ended up watching his innards ooze out of his body into the dirt. I've no taste for that."

Amice swallowed. Dear Lord, how was she to get out of this mess?

Rafe set the candleholder down. He crossed his arms. "This old tower is an odd one, my lady. Many hidden passages, secret rooms. You be careful where you step."

"What?"

He left.

What did he mean? Amice dropped the blanket and

picked up the candleholder. She walked to the opposite wall and studied it. It was painted wood, the colors long faded into dirty grey.

Slowly, Amice ran her hand over the wall, knocking against the wood and listening for a different sound. Nothing. Had Rafe been wrong? Or had she misread his meaning? With a heavy sigh, Amice continued until she reached the corner.

And felt something move. She pushed hard and blinked in shock when a section of the wall swung open. The candlelight revealed narrow, stone steps winding down into darkness.

Amice ran back, wrapped the food in the blanket, took a gulp of ale, and started down the steps.

❧ ❧ ❧

Piers watched Laila pace back and forth across the floor in Gifford's workroom, whispering half to herself.

"Sit down, dear lady," Gifford said. "All that movement is making my head ache."

Laila sat on a stool and stared woodenly ahead. "Amice is in terrible danger. I can feel it."

Gifford reached over and patted her hand. He poured some wine into a cup and pushed it into her hands. "Drink."

"Who is this Henry Woodford?"

Before he smashed a chunk of pink crystal, Gifford shared a look with Piers.

Piers rubbed his chin. "Bad bit of blood."

"What do you mean?"

"Only met the man a few times, but I have heard, well, Cain will get Amice away from him."

"How?"

"He will do whatever he must. That is the kind of man he is."

"Why does Woodford blame the earl for the countess's death?" Laila took a sip of wine.

Before he answered, Piers tipped a long gulp of ale down his throat. He could still hear Luce's screams of fury and pain before she died. " 'Tis a bit of a story, my lady."

Laila gave him a grim smile. "I have naught else to do but worry."

Piers nodded. "Woodford and Luce both fostered at Wolfton Castle. Apparently, they fell in love, or at least as much as that evil bastard can possess such an emotion. Woodford had a sister, who befriended Luce and Luce spent a time at Hexham."

"Hexham?"

"Woodford's holding."

Gifford hit the crystal. "The old earl, Luce's father, did not like what he heard of Woodford."

"What do you mean?"

After taking a pull from his jug, Gifford's mouth turned down. "Stories of his cruelty, depravity. That when he was in the mood, he was uncontrollable. 'Twas rumoured he killed a servant in one of his . . . bouts."

"Oh, dear Lord," Laila said, her hand going to her throat. "My poor Amice."

"Cain will save her," Piers insisted. " 'Twill be all right."

"I hope so. Dear God, I pray so." Laila looked down,

then back up. "How did the Earl of Hawksdown happen to marry Luce?"

Gifford grumbled. "Ismena, my sister, persuaded Luce's father to give Luce to Cain. The two of them had some kind of past, not exactly sure what. I think Ismena knew something Luce's father wanted kept quiet. Anyway, he fetched Luce from Hexham and delivered her here along with a lot of coin and a grant of Styrling Castle. They were married within the fortnight."

"Oh."

"Nobody guessed how far Luce would go to be with Woodford. Turned out they often met at an old cottage deep in the woods."

"And then Luce turned up carrying a babe," Piers added.

Laila rose and paced. "Why would the Earl of Hawksdown not simply assume the babe was his?"

Piers scowled. "Because after consummating the mar-riage, Luce would not allow Cain near her. Truth be told, he did not want her either."

"She killed herself," Laila guessed.

"Aye, but not on purpose. Fool tried to rid her body of the babe. She bled to death."

"And Woodford blames the Earl of Hawksdown for it."

"Aye."

"There is no hope for Amice," Laila choked out.

This time, Piers could not say anything.

❧ ❧ ❧

By mid-morning, Cain caught sight of Hexham. He

nodded to The MacKeir. "That is it."

The MacKeir held up a hand and the group slowed to a stop.

Graceful, pale grey towers rose from the center of a clear, blue lake. High, crenellated walls encircled the towers and led to a huge gatehouse that sprawled over the narrow thread of land crossing the water. " 'Twill be difficult to breach," Cain said.

Under his breath, The MacKeir muttered in Gaelic. "I shall offer a ransom."

Cain lifted a brow. "I doubt Woodford will accept, but 'tis worth a try. Better from you. Anything I offer shall be rejected."

"Let us proceed, then." The MacKeir dug in his heels, and his mount shot toward the castle walls.

As they neared the gatehouse, archers took position along the battlements. They stopped just out of reach. The MacKeir urged his horse a few steps forward. "I am The MacKeir. I demand you release my betrothed, Lady Amice de Monceaux, at once."

Cain spotted Woodford above the gatehouse. There was no sign of Amice. Cain held his breath.

"Oh, how wonderful," Woodford called down. "Two men to fight for the lady," he mocked them.

The MacKeir's horse snorted and stepped sideways. "I am willing to pay a ransom for the lady's safe return."

"I do not need your coin. And I have plans for the fair Amice."

Cain nudged his horse forward next to The MacKeir. "Your quarrel is with me, not Lady Amice. Release her."

"Why?"

"She is innocent."

Woodford's laughter spilled over the wall. "No woman is innocent. You know that, Hawksdown."

"I shall happily fight you for the lady."

"If *I* win?"

Cain glared up at him. "You can take my life."

"Ah, a true pleasure. But what if *you* win?"

"I shall spare your life in exchange for the lady's safe release to me."

"To you? Or to her betrothed?"

"Either."

"Hmm." Woodford tilted his head back and forth. "No, 'tis too simple. I have a better game in mind."

"What do you want?" The MacKeir yelled.

"I want it all. And even now, Lady Amice is doing exactly what I hoped she would."

"What are you talking about? Where is Amice."

"Why, making her escape of course. Or at least she thinks she is."

"What have you done?"

"The lady has decided to take a bit of a swim. And you, Hawksdown, are the only one who can save her. If any other man makes the attempt, my archers shall shoot him down."

The MacKeir shot a glance toward Cain. "He is mad," he hissed.

"Aye." Cain's heart thudded in his chest. "She must be in the lake." Dread encircled his heart as he turned his horse and raced back across the causeway. He did not gallop far around the edge of the lake before he found her.

"Filthy whoreson!" The MacKeir roared.

Cain gazed across the water in horror. Trapped in an iron cage and slowly sinking into the water was Amice, her eyes wide in terror, her face white as bone.

It was obvious she had heard everything.

She knew she would drown.

For Cain could not swim.

Chapter 10

How could I have been so stupid?

Amice looked out across the deep blue water and saw the agony in Cain's eyes. Lugh stood next to him, his thick arms crossed, his face drawn into angry lines.

She had thought she was so clever, so brave. All the way until she reached the bottom of the winding stairs to find Woodford waiting to throw her into this damn cage. Her teeth chattered with cold as water splashed up over her foot. All night long, she'd huddled in the cage, kept awake by Woodford's threats and Rafe's mockery.

She had never hated another person as much as she hated Henry Woodford. What kind of woman had Cain's wife been to love such a brutal beast of a man?

The cage dropped another inch and water seeped into the blanket she sat upon. She gazed across the water into

Cain's eyes and bit her lip. He could not save her, she
knew that. He had never learned to swim, and the distance
between them was too great.

Pray God Lugh did not try. Woodford would cut him
down in an instant.

The cage rocked lower into the water, soaking into
Amice's skirt. She reached out, gripped the bars of the
cage, and closed her eyes.

She forced the cold water out of her mind, and she was
back in Cain's chamber, feeling the warmth of the fire and
his touch against her skin. She took a deep breath and
smelled cedar, not the damp mildew on the stone. She
heard her own moan of delight, not the venomous taunts
from Woodford.

But a loud splash shattered her dream.

In horror, Amice watched Cain stride into the lake, his
face taut with rage and purpose. His mail lay in a pile on
the bank. "No!" she yelled and rose to her knees. "Go
back!"

Woodford's cackling laughter surrounded her, and
Amice's grip on the bars tightened.

Cain did not say anything, but struck out in an awkward
kind of paddling motion.

For a moment, Amice held her breath. Could he do it?
Had he learned to swim?

And then his head went under.

"No!" Amice screamed. "Cain!" She tore at the ropes
binding the door of her cage, but they were wet and tied
securely.

A glimpse of fair hair sent her heart beating again as
Cain surged out of the water, his arms propelling him by

will alone. She could hear him gasp for breath.

"Kick your feet, dammit," Lugh shouted.

"I am trying," Cain called back.

"Move your arms, man. Like you are pushing the water away from you. And for God's sake, keep your fingers together!"

Cain's expression grew fierce as he slowly made his way through the water.

Amice thought she would never see such a sight again. Even Woodford's men grew silent as they watched Cain struggle to reach her. Every few feet, he sank under the surface, and Amice held her breath and prayed until his head popped back up.

Woodford had proudly informed her sometime during the interminable night that the lake reached a depth of thirty feet.

Tears half blinded her as she watched Cain's head slip under again. "Come on, Cain," she prayed.

And continued to pray when the water remained smooth.

Lugh roared a protest and put one foot in the water, but the ominous sound of arrows being drawn into place halted him. He paused, clearly weighing his chances.

"Oh, God," Amice sobbed. "Nay." The cage was halfway in the water now, the cold water swirling around Amice's waist. Tears ran down her face and she bowed her head.

Then, like some magical serpent from the deep, Cain shot out of the water in front of the cage. He caught at the bars, his breath coming in harsh rasps. "Are you all right?"

Amice could not manage a word. She just blinked at him.

In a moment, Cain drew out a dagger and cut through the ropes. He pulled Amice out and wrapped one arm around her.

"I cannot believe you made it," Amice choked out. "You cannot swim."

"Nay." He shot her a cocky grin. "But I was determined."

Amice smiled, knowing she had never loved him more than in this moment. She shivered. "Let us get out of this water."

Cain gazed back across the lake. "You are a good swimmer. You go on."

"I am not leaving without you."

"You must." He gave her a wry look. "My legs are going numb. I think a snake bit me. I will not make it."

"No." Amice gazed at him in horror. "I can help you."

"I am too heavy."

Amice set her jaw. "I am not leaving you here." She yanked his arm from the cage and struck out across the lake.

They managed to get about halfway to the shore when Cain whispered, "Be well, my love," as his head slid beneath the water.

❦ ❦ ❦

Amice kicked and paddled desperately as she slung one arm around Cain's neck. She had to keep his face out of the water. She looked toward shore. God, it was so far.

Lugh started to pull off his mail, and Woodford shouted to his men. "If the big man interferes, kill all of them."

"Bastard," Lugh roared, shaking a fist.

Between breaths, Amice called, "Stay, Lugh. I can make it." She wished she believed her words, but she would not be the cause of Lugh's death too.

When had Cain gotten so heavy?

Doggedly, she kicked and kicked, moving forward at an ant's pace, the cold water and her lack of sleep weighing her down. Keep going, Amice. Keep going. Do not think about the cold. Do not think about how tired you are. Just keep going.

She repeated the words to herself over and over until it was as if her mind were someplace else, reaching the shore the only thing that mattered.

After an eternity, she felt ground beneath her feet and stumbled toward the bank.

Ignoring Woodford's yell of fury, Lugh jumped into the water and hauled both Cain and her out. "What ails him?"

"Snake," Amice gasped as she fell to her knees.

Lugh threw Cain across his saddle and jumped up behind him. "Bran, take up Lady Amice."

Bran plucked her up and set her before him, wrapping a warm, weighty arm around her, before kicking his horse into a gallop. They fled Hexham under a shower of arrows.

Amice tried to stay awake but exhaustion drew her down and down until she fell asleep, a prayer for Cain unspoken on her lips.

❧ ❧ ❧

Cain peered up at the old monk in confusion. The last he remembered, he was going under the water in that blasted lake again. "Where . . . where am I?"

"Riveux Abbey, my lord."

He sat up and looked around the barren room in which he lay on a thin pallet. "How did I come here?"

The monk crossed himself. "A band of men led by some huge Highland savage brought you."

"Was a woman with them?"

"Aye. She rests in the chamber next to this one."

"Where is MacKeir? The Highlander?" Cain amended.

"In our refectory, ploughing through most of our stores."

Cain smiled. "I shall see you well recompensed, Father." He stood and tested his weight on his bandaged leg. It ached with a dull throb, but it was manageable. "Can you lead me to the refectory?"

"Of course." The monk turned and led Cain down a narrow passageway. They went through an arched doorway and across a grassy cloister surrounded by worn, stone walkways. The monk headed toward a large stone building which stood in one corner.

When Cain entered, a group of brown-robed monks stood in a circle around The MacKeir and the rest of the men. It was clear they had never seen men eat with the kind of gusto The MacKeir and his Highlanders brought to the table. Huge platters of fresh and smoked fish, loaves of brown bread and creamy hunks of cheese disappeared into mouths as fast as some of the other monks could replenish the table.

One of Cain's men spotted him and jumped up. "My lord. Are you well?"

"Well enough." Cain leaned down and grabbed a chunk of cheese from The MacKeir's hand.

"Hey!"

Cain grinned and popped it in his mouth, taking a seat on the bench next to The MacKeir. "I need to rebuild my strength."

The MacKeir gave him a somber look before filling a cup with wine and placing it before Cain. " 'Twas a brave thing you did."

"I had no choice. That whore—, uh," he looked at the monks. "Woodford would have let her drown. I have no doubt of it."

"But still, to brave the lake when you knew you had not the skill to swim was a courageous thing indeed." The MacKeir grinned. "Worthy of a Highlander."

Cain took a gulp of wine and chewed on a piece of smoked trout.

Around them, the other men told the monks of Cain's feat, the story growing with the telling until Cain sounded as if he walked across the water to get to Amice. Would that it were so, Cain thought, recalling the stale taste of the lake water all too well.

"Is Amice all right? The monk said she was resting."

The MacKeir nodded. "Aye, the poor lass was exhausted between no sleep in that infernal cage and coming close to drowning."

Cain frowned. "Woodford shall pay for that. I should have taken care of him before this."

"Why did you not?"

"I did not want to take the time away from Falcon's Craig." He twirled his cup. "Woodford was annoying, but I did not see him as a real danger."

"If you need aid in thrashing the bastard, send for me at Tunvegen." MacKeir chuckled. "I imagine Amice will wish to accompany me to make sure Woodford gets what he deserves."

The wine turned sour in Cain's stomach. He looked down, then up to find The MacKeir staring at him with a knowing expression.

" 'Tis obvious you love her," The MacKeir commented.

Cain froze.

"Aye," The MacKeir said with a nod. "I saw your face when poor Amice hung in that cage."

"I was enraged, as were you."

"More than that. As if you looked upon your own life ebbing away and would do anything to stop it." The MacKeir sighed and chewed on another bite of cheese. "You love her."

Cain just drank his wine and wondered if The MacKeir was the only one of them with any sense whatsoever.

❧ ❧ ❧

They returned to Falcon's Craig the next day.

When Amice rode into the bailey, Laila came hurtling from the garden, arms outstretched. "Oh, thank God," she shouted.

Amice slipped from the horse and rushed into Laila's embrace.

"You poor thing, I was so worried for you." Laila put

her hands on either side of Amice's face and studied her. "You are all right?"

Amice managed a shaky smile. "Aye." She bit her lip. " 'Twas horrible, Laila. What an evil, twisted man Woodford is."

"You should rest," a voice said next to her.

Cain's voice. Amice peered up at him. His expression was closed. "Aye," she said. "I am still a bit tired."

"I shall have Hawis bring food and drink." Cain started to walk away, then paused and turned back. "Would you like a bath first?"

For a moment, Amice just stared at him, the longing to bathe with *him* nearly uncontrollable. What sweet peace it would be to float in warm water with his arms wrapped around her, his skin hot against hers. Amice shivered. "I am too tired."

His eyes flashed for an instant then turned blank. "Very well. Take care of your friend, Laila. She has been through much at Woodford's hand."

Laila pulled her toward the rose chamber, clucking like a mother hen. Amice did not hear her words. She was so very tired. Tired of worrying about what she should do with her life, tired of fighting her yearning for Cain, tired of trying to get rid of Muriel. So tired of it all.

She recalled the story one of her brothers had told her before he died. Of the coast of Italy, a beautiful, sunny place he had discovered on crusade. It sounded so perfect, like a place outside time, outside normal worries. How she longed to run away and lose herself there.

Amice walked into her chamber and sat on a bench by the window overlooking the sea. She closed her eyes and breathed in the salty air, in a short time accepting a cup of wine Hawis pressed into her hands.

As she sipped the wine, her spirits lifted a bit and she gave Laila a reassuring smile.

"Are you hungry?"

"Aye. Famished." She broke off a piece of bread and cut a big slice of cheese. "There is something about nearly dying that makes everything taste better."

Laila patted her hand. "What happened, *chav*?"

As Amice told her of how she had been tricked by Woodford and his man Rafe to spend the night in a cold cage, she could not think of anything except the sight of Cain swimming to her.

Laila muttered a gypsy curse under her breath.

"You should have seen it, Laila. Even Woodford's men stopped to watch. 'Twas the bravest act I have ever seen."

Laila beamed a smile at her.

"How impressive," another voice interrupted.

Muriel. Damn, if the wraith did not have an uncanny ability to appear at the wrong time. "Aye, Muriel, he was."

Muriel came more into view, her features cast in a sly look. "Who would have imagined the Earl of Hawksdown could be so selfless, so heroic?"

"You misjudge him because of your own past."

She shimmered.

"Have you ever seen your gravestone?" Amice asked softly.

"Nay," was the whisper.

Amice sipped wine. "You do not leave the castle?"

"I cannot." Slowly, Muriel came back into view. "Where is my grave?"

"Above the beach, in a lovely, grassy spot. Blue wild-flowers grow there."

Muriel drifted closer.

"Do you wish to know what the stone says?"

Gold shimmered, then Muriel's voice, stronger now. "Aye."

A warm breeze slid through the chamber across Amice's face. She glanced at Laila, who gave a slight nod. Amice swallowed and told her, " 'To my beloved Muriel. This was not our time. One day. I shall be waiting. Always.' " By the time Amice finished, tears ran down her cheeks.

And just like that, it was raining. Warm sheets of soft rain poured down and blew into the chamber. Amice turned her face and let the rain wash the tears from her cheeks.

She looked back to see if Muriel remained. A swirl of gold and green lingered, but at the edge of Amice's vision, she saw something else. "Laila," she whispered.

"Aye, I see it too."

"Is it—?"

"The other spirit."

"Gerard Veuxfort."

"Aye."

Before their astonished eyes, it appeared as if Muriel turned toward the flash of blue and white, but it was gone. She gazed back at Amice. "Thank you."

Amice nodded and Muriel disappeared.

❧ ❧ ❧

Cain woke with Morganna's mouth around his rod and a fierce need for release. He heard himself panting, felt himself grinding into her warm mouth before he shoved her from the bed. "Leave me alone!"

Her mouth was wet with him and she smiled unashamedly. "You want me. You need me."

Dear God, he felt as if he were on fire. The urge to take her was overwhelming. He fisted his hands. "Get out."

Instead, she moved closer, so close that he could smell her own musky desire. She took her fingers and spread herself open, displaying the glistening folds of her sex. "Look at this," she whispered. "Take me."

Cain could not seem to draw a breath. He pressed his fingernails into his palms and tried to swallow.

Morganna caressed herself and let out a moan.

"Nay," Cain managed to rasp.

She knelt on the bed and slid her tongue down the length of him. His staff jumped and swelled at the touch. Morganna laughed. "You need a woman, Cain."

Damn right he did. He had never felt lust like this in all his days. It was like a drug.

A drug.

He drew in a sharp breath and glared at Morganna. "What have you done?"

She shrugged, then lay back, opened her thighs and arched her back off the bed.

God help me, Cain thought as he stared at the proximity of her body, open and inviting. He leaned toward her, helplessly. Yes, he needed this. If he did not plunge his staff into her body he would explode. Lust ripped through his consciousness, decimated his reason and he moved over her.

Morganna gave him a smug smile and reached for him.

With the small bit of sanity he still possessed, Cain asked, "What did you put in my wine?"

"Something for both of us," she purred. "You shall be like a stallion, and finally appease your needs and mine."

Cain felt sweat break out on his forehead. "What was it?"

"I do not know exactly." She stroked him. "Come. Take me now. Fill me."

Gasping for air, Cain positioned himself at the entrance to her body. Her dampness touched him like hot oil, at the same time painful yet so intense to be irresistible.

Morganna rubbed against him and moaned. "Take me."

You are drugged, his mind screamed. *You are being trapped by this conniving creature. This is not the woman you want.* But the creature was less than an inch away, begging to be taken. He could almost feel the heat of her body clench around his rod.

Cain reared back and leapt off the bed.

Morganna shrieked in outrage.

He yanked her to her feet, threw her out the door, and barred it.

She screamed and beat at the door but Cain made himself remain strong. He could relieve himself of his frustration, if need be. With short, jerky movements, he did just that and sat before the fireplace. Though the fire had burnt down, Cain felt as if it blazed heat.

It was going to be a very long night.

Finally, he heard shocked voices outside his chamber. Morganna mercifully shut up, or was silenced, he did not care which.

Tomorrow, he would choose a husband for her. Cain rose and paced back and forth across the chamber, considering the possibilities.

Then he thought of the perfect solution. Sir Edrik. A great bull of a man, reputed to have the largest rod in the garrison. He was not much to look at, but he would serve Morganna well and likely count himself fortunate to have a beautiful, young wife. That with a bit of coin should seal Morganna's fate nicely.

They could go live at Casswell Manor, and he would never have to deal with the scheming wench again.

Cain went over to the wine jug and sniffed at the remnants. It smelled no different than any other brew. What *had* Morganna put in his wine? He knew little of herbs, and she claimed not to know either.

Amice would know.

But just as he gathered up the jug, he stopped himself. There was no way in hell he could go to Amice's chamber in his condition and not bed her. It was hard enough to resist Morganna, and he had no interest in her under normal conditions. He would be on Amice like a beast in rut.

He made himself put the jug down. On the morn was soon enough to consult her.

All he had to do was get through tonight.

Chapter 11

🌿 "I have an idea, Laila," Amice said as they descended the steps.

"A potion from Gifford?"

Amice laughed as they walked across the bailey. "Nothing that dangerous. I want to search the castle. There must be something here from Muriel's time."

"Why do you think that?"

"I just feel it. And I think we need something more to draw her out."

"What of the other?"

"If it is Gerard Veuxfort, then he has a reason for remaining as well."

"Muriel?"

"Mayhap." Amice entered the great hall and halted in

surprise. At the high table sat Cain, Lugh, Piers, Gifford, Agatha, and her own brother, Rand.

"Amice!" Rand called out, then rushed over to envelop her in a tight hug. "How do you fare?" he whispered.

Amice pulled away. "How could you betroth me to Lugh?" she hissed. "How *could* you, Rand?"

He grabbed her hand and pulled her toward the table. "We shall talk on it later. But I *do* have your best interests at heart, Sister."

At her snort of disbelief, Rand stopped and looked at her intently. "I want you to be happy, Amice."

She just stared at him. Happy? With Lugh? Not unhappy surely, but happy? She could not envision it.

"Come, break your fast."

Amice let him guide her to the dais and took her usual seat between Cain and Lugh. She reached for a cup of ale and trickled some down her dry throat.

Lugh thumped her knee. "Are you recovered from your ordeal, Amice?"

"Aye." She sipped more ale. "Though I shall be happy to stay out of the water for a while."

Lugh's face darkened and he snarled out a curse. "We shall see to that whoreson. Worry not, his crime shall not go unpunished."

"Thank you for your aid, Lugh."

Gifford leaned forward with a mischievous grin. "The MacKeir has been telling us the story." He shot an approving glance toward Cain. "Quite a magnificent rescue."

"Yes." Amice turned toward Cain. His warm, blue eyes held her fast and she slowly smiled. "Magnificent, indeed, my lord."

"My name is Cain." His gaze slid into her like a crack of heat lightning.

Amice's smile faded. He was right, it was ridiculous to cling to her intention to not call him by name now. Too much had happened to keep the distance. "Thank you for my life. Cain."

He nodded. "My pleasure, Amice. I am only sorry I could not take down Woodford at the same time."

"As am I," Amice said, recalling the night spent with the man. "He is mad."

"Aye."

Rand passed her a piece of bread with a chunk of white cheese. "Have you accomplished your task here, Amice? Mother is . . . most anxious for your return."

Amice sighed and took the food. "Not yet, but soon I hope."

Piers jumped up and refilled her cup of ale. "What is your plan, my lady?"

"Laila and I are going to search further. We need to find out more about Muriel."

"Would you like help?" Gifford asked with a twinkle in his eye.

Amice grinned at him. "Nay, my lord, 'tis not necessary. I am sure you have work to do."

He blinked and sprang up. "Aye, indeed. Excuse me, my lady." Gifford waved a hand. "And the rest of you." He trotted off toward his workroom.

Cain stared after him. "I hope nothing explodes."

Amice giggled. "Perhaps today is the day he finds Merlin."

"Aye, right after the pigs take flight." Cain shook his

head and stood. "Search anywhere you like. If you need me, I shall be with Nyle."

Amice watched him walk away, sensing Lugh's and Rand's eyes on her. She forced a casual smile to her lips.

"Rand?" Lugh asked.

"Aye."

"I am in need of a bit of swordplay. There is no one here worth my talent. What say you?"

"My pleasure." Rand chuckled as Piers drew himself up in mock affront.

The two big men rose and headed toward the training field. When they reached the door to the hall, Lugh looked back.

He looked at Agatha, who stared after him with a bemused expression. In a few minutes, she left as well.

In the direction of the training field.

Amice turned toward Piers and raised a brow.

He merely shrugged and wandered out, whistling.

🐚 🐚 🐚

As Agatha exited the hall and followed in the wake of Lugh MacKeir, she recited all the reasons she should turn right around.

He was a barbarous Highlander.

He was dark, not fair-haired.

He was too big and fearsomely skilled with weapons.

He said and did outrageous things.

He was arrogant.

He attacked every meal as if it were his last and fought like a demon.

He did not live life, he glutted himself on it.

She stared at the wide set of his shoulders and hastened her pace.

❧ ❧ ❧

By late afternoon, Amice was ready to concede defeat. She and Laila had explored one chamber after another, particularly in the east tower, and found nothing. She plopped down on a trunk in the ground level chamber and sighed. "Mayhap I am mistaken."

Laila absently pushed at stones in the wall. "Do not give up yet."

Amice stood and stretched her back. She stared at the opposite wall, nearly covered by a wall hanging. It was of a mailed knight kneeling beside a pool. Looking back at him from within the water was a beautiful woman with one slender hand outstretched.

A woman with red hair.

Her heart picked up in pace and Amice moved closer to the hanging. "Laila?"

"Aye."

She pointed at the woman. The hanging was old and faded, but it was still clear that the woman had long, red hair. "Does this resemble Muriel?"

Laila came beside her and peered at the hanging. "It does."

They shared a look, then gently lifted the hanging from the wall. Amice groaned in frustration. The wall appeared solid.

"Nay, wait," Laila murmured. "This stone is different."

She slowly pushed against the stone and a door appeared, opening with the slightest touch.

Amice stepped forward and her mouth dropped open. "A hidden room."

Laila handed her a candle. "Come."

They stepped down into the small chamber carved from the outer wall. The aura hit Amice at once. A warm, happy kind of feeling swelled in her chest as she took in the room.

She stopped before a mattress piled with cushions and soft furs, noting the jeweled goblets and ewer on the adjacent table. A low brazier stood against the wall close to the makeshift bed. "This is where they met."

"Muriel and Gerard?"

"Aye." Amice twirled around, sighting the rush mats on the floor and the basin for water. "Met and loved. 'Twas their secret, special place."

Laila ran a finger across the surface of the table. "There is not even any dust."

Gulping, Amice knelt before a trunk. She slowly lifted the lid, reached in and took out one of the rolls of parchment. The paper crinkled as she unrolled it. Age had darkened the color and softened the markings.

"What is it?"

Amice sat back on her heels. "Drawings."

Laila knelt beside her. "Oh, my."

Amice felt a flush of heat rise in her cheeks. The drawings were beautiful. And very detailed.

"That looks like—"

"Cain," Amice finished. "He looks just like Cain." As she gazed at the drawings, her body clenched inside itself.

"And this is unmistakably Muriel."

"Aye."

"Which one drew them, do you think?"

"Gerard. Look at the way Muriel is portrayed. Only a man in love would draw a woman in passion like that." Amice shivered and looked down at the other drawings. They were all similar, portrayals of the lovers in various positions, losing themselves in their desires.

Laila pointed down at the parchment. "Is that possible?"

Amice giggled and turned the paper one way and then the other. "I am not sure." She laughed again. " 'Twould take a great deal of agility."

"Aye." Laila chuckled and looked down into the trunk. She lifted out a flat wooden box.

With more reluctance than she would admit, Amice set the drawings aside. She watched as Laila opened the lid and blinked in wonder. " 'Tis just like Beornwynne's Kiss, only with rubies instead of amethysts."

Laila ran her fingers over the heavy gold necklace, set with large, blood red rubies. Suddenly, she stilled and stared hard at the piece.

"What is it, Laila?"

"It should be returned," Laila said in a distant voice.

"Returned? To whom? Cain?"

"Nay." Laila met Amice's gaze. "To Muriel."

"It was hers?"

"Aye." Laila unrolled the parchment and ran her finger down the drawings. "There, see. She wears it."

Amice studied the drawing. It was the most sensuous of them all. Muriel was astride Gerard, her back arched, her eyes closed, and he gazed up at her with an expression of awe. The necklace was the only thing she wore.

"How did it end up here, do you think?"

Laila put her palm over the necklace and closed her eyes. She shook her head. "I am not sure, but Muriel did not willingly give it up."

"How can we return a tangible object to a ghost? Bury it in her grave?"

" 'Tis the only way I know."

Amice stared down at the piece. " 'Tis worth a great deal of coin."

"A King's ransom."

"We must show it to Cain." Amice rose to her feet, cradling the box in one hand, the parchment in the other.

Laila stood also. "And then we need to talk to Muriel."

❦ ❦ ❦

Agatha walked into the bathhouse, humming as she considered which of her new bliauts to wear for supper. She set down a stack of linen and unplaited her hair, running her fingers through the tight plaits. With a happy sigh, she stripped off her bliaut and undertunic and laid them carefully on a bench.

It was then she heard breathing. Harsh breathing.

Her throat tight, Agatha slowly turned to look at the bath. "Oh," she gasped.

Lugh MacKeir rose to his feet and gave her a look even she could not mistake.

Agatha's breath left her body. His emerald eyes smouldered. Actually smouldered. She had heard of such a thing, but never imagined a man would direct such a look toward her.

"Agatha," he rumbled.

With her name, Agatha felt her legs start to shake.

Lugh parted the water in sure strides until he stood only inches away, the water sluicing down his chest.

His very big, thickly muscled chest, covered with springy black hair that trailed down to... *Oh, my God*.

Agatha blinked and licked her lips.

Lugh growled deep in his throat.

She took a step back.

His nostrils flared as if he scented her, knew her to be as aroused as he obviously was. He was all raw sensuality, unabashed hunger, and his eyes drew her in as if she were caught in a powerful wave.

"You . . . you are betrothed," Agatha finally squeaked.

"Aye, to a woman who clearly loves another."

Agatha's lips parted. "I should leave," she whispered.

His face tightened and he took a step forward. "Stay."

Agatha inched around the bath toward the door, and Lugh followed her. She felt as if she were being stalked by some great beast of prey. What the beast might intend turned her insides to melted butter. She put her hand on the door, but another, much larger one covered hers.

He was right behind her. She could feel the heat of him through her chemise. He pressed his body against hers and Agatha trembled.

"Stay," he rasped in her ear. "You know I want you. And I have seen the way you look at me. You want me too."

"Nay," Agatha said weakly. Lugh MacKeir could not be more different than the suitor she had envisioned. He was rough, dark as night, and she very much doubted the man even knew what poetry was. Dear God, but it did not matter.

"Aye." He brushed her hair away from her neck with his other hand and smoothed his lips across her skin.

She shivered.

Then he nudged his heavy thigh between her legs and Agatha knew she was lost. Sheer lust ripped through her as she felt him prod her most hidden folds with his sex. Her body clenched and quivered, overriding all reason. She moaned and arched her back, pressing against his heat.

Lugh let out a hiss and put his hand on her thigh, bunching the fabric of her chemise in his fist. With agonizing slowness, he gathered the folds of the linen, exposing her calves, her thighs, and finally her buttocks to the warm air.

Would he take her like this? Standing? Leaning against the door? At the very idea, Agatha felt a bolt of desire rip through her and knew she would let him, would love every part of it. This big man could do anything to her.

"*Breagha*," he whispered. "Your skin is like the softest velvet." He smoothed his fingers down her buttocks. "The color of rich cream."

His fingers moved lower and Agatha closed her eyes.

"Your hair is a fine, bright silk," he said softly.

And then he slid his calloused fingers across her dampness, and Agatha fought to stay on her feet. It was impossible.

Her legs would not support her, and she slipped down to the floor.

Lugh let her slide but never moved his hand, teasing her with slow strokes, exploring her in a way she had never felt.

Agatha pushed against his hand, filled with an odd anxiousness.

"Easy, love." He wrapped a thick arm around her waist and found a place on Agatha's body that took the last scrap of her sanity and threw it to the heavens.

"Ahh," she moaned. What was he doing? With flicks of his finger, he brought forth a pressure in her center, rising with each touch. She gasped for breath and could not find it.

He pushed a finger into her body and stroked her swollen nub in circles.

"Lugh," she gasped. "I—"

"Let go, my love. This is for you," he said with a groan. He intensified his movements and Agatha surrendered.

She bucked against his hand, keening her pleasure as a tidal wave rose within her, burning, tightening until she exploded, convulsing around his finger and crying out her release.

Within an instant, he flipped her around and kissed her. Kissed her as if she were the most beautiful, precious woman in all the world.

He drew back and smiled. "You bring me to my knees."

Agatha crooked a smile. "I think that was my position."

Lugh threw his head back and laughed, then picked her

up as if she weighed no more than a butterfly and carried her into the bath.

Then he taught her just how much pleasure could be had in mating, and Agatha knew her life had taken an irrevocable change.

Chapter 12

It took Amice over an hour of searching and when she finally found Cain, she halted in disbelief. He was outside, flat on his back with a child balanced atop his raised legs, her small hands outstretched in his. The girl was shrieking with laughter, yelling "Again, again," and Cain was rocking her back and forth.

The expression on Cain's face was one Amice had not seen in five years. Carefree, unrestrained happiness. He laughed with the child, voicing protests but continuing to play.

She must have made some sound, because he looked back and spotted her. His smile eased, and he set the child back on the ground.

When the girl stood, Amice saw that one of her legs was shorter than the other. Her brown curls bobbed when she moved in a kind of hop.

Cain got up and the girl took his hand.

For a moment, Amice could only stare at them, caught in a vision of what might have been. The girl looked to be about five years of age. The same age Cain and her daughter would have been.

"Amice?" Cain asked, a frown crossing his face. "Are you all right?"

She gulped. "Nay. I have something to show you though."

He raised a brow.

" 'Tis not for the eyes of a child."

Cain leaned down and whispered something to the girl. She grinned and scampered off toward the kitchen, hitching along with her odd gait.

Amice's heart tightened in her chest. "Who is she?"

"Her name is Olive. She is from Hazelstone."

"Her parents?"

" 'Twas only the mother. Her father abandoned them when Olive's condition became apparent." His mouth flattened. "Woodford butchered her mother."

"What is to become of her now?"

"She shall stay here." He gave her a soft smile. "She seems to have adopted me."

Amice's eyes burned and she looked down.

Cain coughed. "What is it you have to show me?"

"Is there a place we can sit?"

Cain looked around and pointed toward the garden. "The garden. 'Twould be best."

Amice walked beside him in silence. She tried hard to avoid speculating on what her child might have been like, what life could have been if Cain had married her and she had borne their daughter. It was too painful, too heart wrenching to think about. But to see him playing with Olive brought it all to mind.

She hardened her heart. She would have a child of her own to hold if naught for Cain's betrayal.

They settled on a stone bench, and Amice handed him the box.

Cain looked at her with curiosity.

"Laila and I found a hidden chamber at the ground level of the east tower."

"A hidden room?"

"Aye."

Cain shook his head. "What was in it? What was it used for?"

Amice bit her lip. "We think it was a place where Muriel and Gerard met in secret."

"Why?"

She handed him the roll of parchment and looked away.

"My God," he whispered as he took in the drawings. "Damn, but my ancestor was a fine artist. And *quite* a handsome man."

At the laughter in his voice, Amice turned back.

Cain was doing much the same thing she had done, tilting his head from side to side as if trying to determine how such a position might be accomplished. He laughed aloud and put the drawing in front of Amice's face.

Her cheeks heated and she could not meet his gaze.

"What think you of this one?"

Amice rolled her eyes. "I think a person would need to train for that one, my lord."

"Pleasurable training, indeed."

She did meet his gaze then and was caught by the hunger glittering in his eyes. "Indeed," she choked out.

Cain cleared his throat and put the drawings down. "So, Gerard and Muriel were lovers."

"Obviously." Amice gestured toward the box. "Open it."

When he flipped open the lid, the rubies caught the sunlight and gleamed bright red against the burnished gold. It was as if the stones absorbed the sun and reflected it back threefold. Cain stared, openmouthed, then looked at Amice in clear puzzlement.

Cain held the necklace up in the light. "All this time. A fortune lay within my own walls," he said softly.

"It belonged to Muriel."

"How do you know?"

Reluctantly, Amice unrolled the parchment and held up the drawing of Muriel wearing the jewelry.

Cain slowly lowered the necklace and stared at the picture. "He *did* love her."

Amice cautioned a glance at the drawing and came to a heartrending realization. She knew that look. On that face. Or rather, on Cain's face when he looked at her during their lovemaking. She swallowed. "Perhaps. Or mayhap he was simply caught up in the moment."

With a snort, Cain shook his head. "He loved her. That look is not mere lust."

Embarrassed, Amice looked down at her hands. "Laila believes the necklace must be returned to Muriel."

"Returned? To a ghost?"

"Aye."

"And how might we accomplish that?"

Amice lifted her brows. "Bury it with her, I suppose."

Cain gazed at her incredulously. "Bury a fortune just to appease that troublesome wraith? You jest."

"You *do* want to get rid of her."

"And you think this will do it?"

"I do not know," Amice admitted with a sigh. "I intend to try to find out more from Muriel."

Cain frowned and turned the necklace over in his hands. "I will need a very good reason to give up something so valuable."

"I understand." And well she did. Cain's quest for wealth and security governed his life.

"You shall try to summon her this eve?"

"Aye."

"I want to be there."

Amice opened her mouth to protest, then stopped. Perhaps having the man there who happened to look just like Gerard Veuxfort would prompt Muriel to reveal more about their relationship. "Very well." She stood and looked toward the bathhouse.

And gasped in astonishment.

Before she could help it, Amice let out a little cry, then pressed her hand against her mouth.

Cain leapt up beside her. "What the hell?"

Lugh and Agatha did not even see them. They gazed at each other with reverence between exchanging long, deep kisses. From the dampness of their hair, it was apparent they had been together in the bathhouse.

"MacKeir!" Cain shouted. "What are you doing to my sister?"

Lugh stopped short and dropped his arms. Wide-eyed, he looked first at Cain, then at Amice, then back at Agatha. Agatha looked as if she had just swallowed something too big to chew.

Amice started laughing. "I should think it obvious," she managed to spit out.

Cain gave her a black look. "Well?" he said to Lugh.

"I . . . ah, well hell," Lugh finished. He held up his palms and looked at Amice. "I am sorry. I was overcome."

Amice beamed a smile toward Agatha, who inched closer to Lugh. "I am happy for you, Lugh."

"You shall marry her," Cain ordered in a tight voice.

Lugh's eyes lit up, then he gave Cain a measuring look. " 'Twould be my *privilege*. I would not disgrace your sister." He pulled Agatha away, murmuring soft words of reassurance amidst Agatha's squeaks of embarrassment.

Cain rubbed the back of his neck and muttered, "What next?"

"At least Agatha will be married," Amice said in a low tone. *At least Lugh has the honor to do right by her*, she wanted to say. *At least he does not use her, then walk away as if naught of significance transpired.*

He turned his probing gaze on her. "But what of you?"

"I am free." Amice suddenly realized what this meant. She was not bound for the cold, remoteness of Tunvegan, but could journey to Villa Delphino when this was all over. Away from Cain, she thought with a painful thud.

"You are not dismayed?"

Amice shook her head. "Nay. I am not the right

woman for Lugh. Though I would not have predicted the one would be Agatha."

"I should have seen it coming. The first time he saw her, I half thought he would leap upon her right in the hall."

"Agatha is strong enough to handle Lugh."

"From the look on his face, 'twill not take much." He sighed and gathered up the parchment and the box. "Lugh MacKeir for a brother-in-law."

"He is a good man."

Cain paused and gazed closely at her. "It was never my intention to dishonor you, Amice."

Her throat closed and she looked away. "Leave it be, Cain."

She sensed the heat of his stare, and then he walked out of the garden. Amice fisted her hands and forced back the burning tears.

Chapter 13

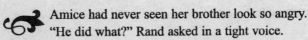 Amice had never seen her brother look so angry.
"He did what?" Rand asked in a tight voice.

"You heard me. 'Twas obvious he and Agatha had been together in the bathhouse."

Rand's face reddened. "I shall beat him into the dirt for this insult."

Amice laid a hand on his arm. "Nay, Rand, leave it be. I did not wish to marry Lugh, you know that."

"But he was betrothed to *you*."

"He knew I did not love him," Amice said softly.

"What does that have to with anything? People do not marry for love."

"Some do."

"Peasants. We do not have that luxury."

Amice stared at him. "I am happy for them, Rand.

And I am happy to be free of the betrothal."

Rand took her hands. "Are you sure? I can force him to marry you."

"Nay. That is not the life I want."

"What kind of life *do* you want, Amice?"

"Once Mother is gone," she said slowly, "I shall journey to this Villa Delphino."

"Why must you leave England? You can stay at Wareham, you know that. You shall always have a place there."

Amice turned to stare out the window. "There is nothing in England for me but heartbreak, Rand."

"So you wish to run away."

Amice bit her lip and nodded. "I suppose I do."

"Is it Cain Veuxfort?"

"Aye."

Rand was silent so long Amice finally turned back to look at him. He gazed at her thoughtfully. "Do you wish to wed him?"

Amice's breath caught in her throat. "Nay," she said flatly.

"Why not?"

"He . . . will never see me for who I really am. In his eyes, I am incapable of loving one man and just short of being a witch."

"Idiot."

"Aye, but there it is."

"We need to get back to Wareham."

"You go. I shall not return until I possess the villa. It is my salvation," she finished in a whisper.

Rand dropped a kiss on her forehead. "I shall leave on

the morrow." He frowned. "But not before I have a talk with Lugh MacKeir."

"Rand."

"A talk. I feel partly responsible for this muddle. Lugh was insistent on wedding you. And I thought it would make you happy once you accepted it." He shook his head. "But he should have spoken to me before taking another woman."

Amice's lips twitched. "I got the impression it was not something he planned."

"Even so. A man should have more control than that."

Amice thought of Cain. It was obvious how much he hated losing control. How he could love her with such savage gentleness, then turn a cool gaze on her was unfathomable. It was as if there were two Cains.

She managed a shrug. "Do not be too hard on Lugh, Rand. I truly am happy for both of them and happy to be free of the betrothal."

"Very well." He pressed another kiss to her forehead. "I shall see you at supper."

"Aye. I am going to rest a bit."

"You do look tired. Are you ill?"

"Nay."

He peered closely at her, and Amice felt as if he could see Cain's brand on her face. "Are you sure? You look a bit flushed."

"I am just tired." She smiled and pushed him toward the door. "Now, go so I can rest."

With a last glance of concern, Rand mercifully left. Amice sat on the windowseat gazing out at the sea. As she watched the waves pound ceaselessly against the shore, she felt an odd calm descend over her.

It was time she moved forward with her life. Relegate Cain to a buried, painful part of the past and build some kind of future. She realized she had always been waiting for him to come back to her. Against all odds, without even knowing of his wife's death. Holding herself suspended, her heart carefully preserved for him.

But he did not want her heart.

It was time she faced the truth.

Amice lay on the bed, curled into a ball, and buried her face in the pillow.

It was time to give up and pursue a new dream.

❧ ❧ ❧

Piers found Gifford and Laila huddled close together in Gifford's workroom, Laila gazing at Gifford's palm. Their conversation broke off abruptly when he walked in.

"Piers, my boy, what brings you here?"

He looked suspiciously at Gifford, then Laila. "What are you two doing?"

Gifford took a gulp of ale. "Laila is telling my fortune."

Piers blinked. "Can you do that?"

Laila sent him a serene smile. "Sometimes."

He moved to take a stool next to Gifford and tipped ale down his throat. "Well, what lies in Gifford's future?"

Gifford cracked out a laugh. "A long life, many grand-nieces and -nephews and maybe, just maybe a chance to meet the great Merlin himself."

"Good tidings, indeed."

"You do not believe me," Laila commented.

Piers shrugged. "I doubt anyone can see into the future."

"Give me your hand," she said.

When Piers hesitated, Gifford gave him a nudge. "Go on, do not be afraid."

"I am not afraid."

"Then give her your hand."

Piers gulped down more ale and put his hand into Laila's smaller ones. She traced the lines in his palm and touched her fingertips against the pulse in his wrist. Her gaze narrowed in concentration and she closed her eyes.

"Well?" Gifford asked.

Fighting the urge to snatch back his hand, Piers forced himself to patience. It was a silly trick, but he liked Laila enough to humor her.

"You run from one experience to another without really appreciating any of them," Laila began.

"Women," Gifford quipped. "She has you there, boy."

Piers rolled his eyes. " 'Tis no secret I enjoy women."

"Shh," Laila whispered. She furrowed her brow and slowly smiled. "You shall soon face a great challenge that will test your ability to slow down and focus. And you will discover a great love. But," she looked up at him, "she will not be at all what you expected and to win her you must uncover what lies deepest in your heart."

Piers stared at her. *Become more like Cain? Settle with one woman?* He shook his head. "Interesting."

Laila smiled knowingly at him. "Remember my words when your destiny finds you."

Gifford slapped him on the back. "Mayhap some of my great-nieces and -nephews will be *yours*."

"I doubt that, Uncle." Piers reached for the jug of ale. He hoped neither Laila nor Gifford noticed his hand shook. "Cain is the one who needs to beget children."

"Hmm." Gifford stroked his chin. "Any ideas on that, Laila?"

"He and Amice belong to each other. They have been heartmates in many lives."

Her voice held such certainty Piers felt a chill across the back of his neck. "Not sure it is going to happen in this one."

Gifford tossed back a drink and slapped his hands on the table. "We need to do something! I am tired of watching Cain go through life without living it."

"He is stubborn," Piers said. "Consumed by duty. And too serious and judgmental."

"Not exactly a list of favorable qualities," Laila commented.

"But also passionate, deeply emotional, and terribly lonely," Piers finished. "My brother hides himself well."

Laila sighed. "He does not think Amice is good enough for him."

Piers gave her a keen look. "Nay, it is the opposite. He fears he is not worthy of *her*."

"Foolish boy," Gifford muttered. "Should lock them both in a chamber until they talk about their past and resolve things."

"Not a bad idea, Uncle. What think you, Laila?"

"I can guess one thing that would happen in those circumstances."

Gifford took a drink and chuckled. "Mayhap that is the way to bring them together."

"Perhaps the past is too much of an obstacle to overcome," Laila mused.

"Do you know what happened?"

"Some."

Piers lifted a brow.

"I swore to Amice that I would not speak of it. But I will tell you this. When Cain left her to marry Luce, it nearly destroyed her. And she is not the kind of woman who forgives easily."

"Damn."

"I must go. Amice and I are going to confront Muriel this eve, if we can."

Gifford's gaze brightened. "When?

"At dusk."

"In the east tower again?" Gifford's enthusiasm was apparent.

Laila laughed. "Aye, but in another chamber at the base. 'Tis hidden."

"A hidden chamber?"

"Where Muriel and Gerard met." Laila giggled. "Have Cain show you Gerard's drawings. Quite impressive."

Gifford just blinked. "I pray this time you succeed in getting rid of that damned wraith."

"We shall see." Laila turned to go.

Gifford picked up a chunk of pink crystal and smashed it into bits.

❧ ❧ ❧

Amice woke to a banging on the door. She rubbed her

eyes and walked over to open it.

Cain stood in the doorway.

She wrapped cool reserve around herself. "What is it?"

"Will you show me the chamber you found? I have looked but I cannot locate it."

It was a reasonable request. "Aye." Amice drew on her shoes and followed Cain down the steps and across the bailey toward the east tower. Amice blinked when they entered the tower. "How odd."

"What?"

"When we left, the door was open." She pointed to the wall hanging. "Now, 'tis back the way it was."

Cain glanced around. "Meddlesome ghosts." He took the wall hanging down, and Amice moved to press on the stone.

The door slowly swung open, and Amice followed Cain down into the chamber. As she stepped into the room, it hit her again, the utter joy and peace emitted by the place, as if the stones themselves had absorbed the emotions of the people within.

"I cannot believe no one ever found this chamber," Cain murmured as he walked around.

"No one probably looked."

Idly, Cain picked up an embroidered pillow and lifted it to his nose. He stiffened and said, "Lavender."

Amice felt a chill roll down her spine. The same scent she wore.

Cain's eyes locked with hers, and all at once the chamber became too small and far too hot. He dropped the pillow back onto the fur-covered pallet.

To Amice, it all seemed to happen slowly, as if she

watched from within a heavy, languorous fog. From the corner of her eye, she glimpsed a flash of movement. She stepped forward, intent on escaping the chamber.

The door was closed.

She pushed on it and nothing happened. Amice laid her forehead against the stone. "We are trapped."

Cain moved beside her. "Let me try." He pushed and shoved against the door to no avail. "Damned ghost," he swore.

"I do not understand why Muriel would do this."

With a frown, Cain shook his head. "Nor I. The last thing she appears to want is for you and I to be together." He turned to stare at Amice.

And just like that, hunger slammed through her blood like thunder.

Amice's mouth went dry.

"I suppose you are no longer betrothed."

Amice gulped. "Nay, I suppose not."

Cain's eyes glittered like sapphires in a blazing fire. "There is no way out of here until Muriel tires of her game."

"Nay," Amice whispered.

"I want you," Cain said, his face tense. He fisted his hands. "I do not want to, but there it is."

"Cain—"

"I want to be inside you. I *need* to be inside you." He moved forward and wrapped his hands around her waist. His whole body felt like a coil of energy ready to explode.

Amice could not move. "I—"

"Let me come inside you." His voice was low and his eyes gleamed with dark knowledge.

"Nay," she choked out.

His fingers tightened on her waist and his expression turned to torment. "Your being here is burning me alive. I cannot sleep for dreams of you," he haltingly admitted.

"We should not."

"True enough, but I am past caring." He pulled her full against him. "Feel me. Feel how much I want you."

Amice closed her eyes. She did feel him, a hard lance of heat against her belly. Her body convulsed deep inside, wet with wanting.

"Let me in, Amice."

She licked her lips and opened her eyes to gaze into his. His ocean eyes had always undone her. She put her hands on his shoulders and pulled his head down for a kiss.

God, how she loved kissing him, loved the feel of his firm lips, the taste of him like the richest wine. She could kiss him forever just like this.

But it was not enough. Never enough.

In what seemed like too long a time, they finally shed their clothes and lay atop the furs. Cain leaned up on one elbow and looked down at her. "God, you are beautiful."

"As are you." Amice reached up and trailed her fingertips down his cheek.

Cain took her hand and kissed each finger, then her palm.

Amice's heart hitched in her chest.

He kissed his way down her arm, across her shoulder and grazed her neck.

Then he moved lower and all Amice could do was to curl her hands into fists and hold on as he kissed, licked and sucked his way over her body. He moved leisurely, in an almost worshipful, slow exploration of her skin, as if he were committing her to memory. With every kiss, her body rippled in response. She thought she might go mad with the waiting.

And then he finally stroked her where her body burned, rubbing his thumb in slow, fluid circles against her. Amice arched into his hand as her body flooded with sharp pleasure. Again and again he coaxed her with gentle strokes, spreading molten fire into her veins. Amice writhed against his warm fingers, silently pleading with him to end her torment.

When he slid a finger into her, she came up off the furs and cried out. Desire rolled in waves through her blood.

"Cain," she cried.

So quickly she could barely react, Cain raised her hips and plunged deep into her body.

What blessed relief. Amice met his thrusts, arching up off the bed and clinging to his shoulders. How she loved him inside her, his thick length filling her, completing her.

"Oh, God, yes," she moaned.

She gazed into his eyes, deep blue with passion, and tightened around him.

He let out a groan.

"I am only alive when you are inside me," Amice whispered.

With that, Cain froze for a moment, then slowed his thrusts. He drew back and slid his hands beneath her buttocks, lifting her up onto his sinewy thighs. Amice glanced down to where their bodies joined and stared, transfixed.

Slowly, Cain pushed deep, then withdrew, again and again and again.

The sight of it sent a jagged bolt of craving straight to her center, and Amice felt herself begin to come apart. Helplessly, she gazed up at him but there was no mercy in his piercing eyes.

"Cain, please," she gasped, teetering on the edge, her body desperate for release.

He only gazed at her intently and said, "Nay," through gritted teeth.

Amice whimpered. Her legs trembled and turned to melted butter, shaking uncontrollably and falling open in silent supplication

Cain let out a low hiss of satisfaction. A drop of sweat ran down his face. "Amice."

She reached for him.

He swore a curse and slid into her inch by agonizing inch until he was in deep, then stopped.

"I never want this to end," he rasped.

Tears burned the backs of Amice's eyes. She drew his head down and kissed him, telling him with her body what she could not say in words.

With that, Cain took her hands and changed the pace, finally giving Amice what she so desperately needed, driving into her faster and faster until it seemed he was always there, sending her into a spiraling wave of desire.

The intensity of her release shocked her. Amice screamed as it ripped through her body and clenched around Cain's sex, convulsing in harsh, rapid beats.

He roared her name and filled her with wet warmth.

When they finally found the energy to try the door, it was open.

❧ ❧ ❧

After his appalling loss of control with Amice, Cain hid himself in his solar and pretended to go over Nyle's records. What had possessed him to take her like that? It was as if she had cast a spell on him. When Amice was near, his will turned to water. Boiling water.

He tapped the quill against the table and frowned at the listing of supplies and costs. Maybe he should just accept Muriel's presence and ship Amice back to Wareham with ownership of Villa Delphino. At least he would not continue to make a fool of himself.

The door swung open and Piers ambled in. He took one look at Cain and stopped short. His eyes grew wide and his mouth dropped open.

"What?" Cain snapped.

"You were right."

"About what?"

"This place *is* going mad. 'Tis most aggrieving." Piers took a stool.

Cain rubbed the back of his neck. "What in Hades are you talking about?"

His brother gave him a discerning stare. "Sex."

Oh, Lord. Cain looked down at himself and briefly closed his eyes in dismay. His tunic was on backwards.

"Aye, 'tis madness, indeed."

"Am I to assume you spoke to Agatha and that huge Scot she has apparently taken a liking to?"

Piers laughed and slapped his knee. "By God, I never thought I would see the day when our dour sister found a mate. And Lugh MacKeir. Hah!"

"You should have seen them coming out of the bath-house," Cain said with a grin. "I have never seen such a look on Agatha's face."

"Amazing. And then, I venture to the stable to check on Pagan's leg splints and find our fair cousin and one of the grooms making so much noise even the horses were riled up."

"Morganna was in the stable?"

"Aye. She was so busy screaming, 'Faster, faster,' she did not even know I was there." Piers shook his head. "Damned fine set of tits, though."

Cain frowned. "She put some kind of drug in my wine the other night and tried to get me to bed her."

Piers blinked. "What kind of drug?"

"I do not know. Morganna claimed not to know either."

"Where did she get it?"

Cain shook his head. "I did not wait to ask. I needed to get her out of my chamber fast."

"Oh."

"Aye. Whatever it was, I was hard as iron and damned near desperate enough to take even Morganna."

"I shall have to ask her about that." Piers raised his eyebrows. "Might be a useful substance to have around."

Cain rolled his eyes. "Best make sure you have an energetic companion."

"Which brings me to you."

"Piers."

His brother waved a hand. " 'Tis not my affair, I know, but Cain," he fixed him with a serious look, "what in the hell are you doing with Amice?"

For a moment, Cain just stared at Piers. "A fair question. The problem is I have no idea."

"What do you mean?"

"I feel . . . great desire for her, I cannot deny that."

"Desire?"

"Lust. Powerful, undeniable, uncontrollable lust." Cain shifted uncomfortably on his chair.

"A woman who can make *you* lose control is admirable, indeed."

Cain scowled.

"Is that all?"

Cain's scowl deepened. "I do not know."

"He who lies to himself shall never know his true soul."

Instead of responding to Pier's ridiculous statement, Cain pushed the box across the table toward him. "Amice and Laila found this in a secret chamber in the east tower."

Piers took the box and opened it. He stared for a moment, then raised gleaming eyes to Cain. " 'Tis a treasure."

"Aye. But Amice is of the opinion I should bury it with Muriel, who owned it."

"Bury this? Nay."

"I agree."

Piers took out the necklace and laid it on the table. "What kind of secret chamber?"

Cain tossed the roll of parchment at his brother. "This may even give you an idea or two."

The expression on his brother's face was so comical Cain had to laugh.

"Damn." Piers looked at the drawings one by one, tilting

his head this way and that. "Done that. That one too. Definitely that one." Then he stopped and looked at Cain with a grin. "Inventive man, our ancestor."

"Aye. And very handsome, do you not agree?"

"Not bad." Piers shook his head. "I suppose now we know why Muriel hates you so much. You look just like the man who rejected her." He peered at Cain over the drawings. "This eve, Amice is going to try to reach Muriel."

"Piers, this is not entertainment, for God's sake."

His brother just grinned at him. "Cain, will you at least *try* not to be so damn sober. After all, *I* am the one who has not lain with a woman for a fortnight."

"Why not? Are you ill?"

Piers chuckled and shook his head. "Have not had a taste for it. Strange." He stood and stopped at the door. "You know, that gives me an idea."

"What now?"

"Well, you claim that the Lady Amice could not be true to you, aye?"

Cain stiffened, his mind suddenly flooded with images. Images of what had just occurred between Amice and him. Then, images of her body entwined with another, faceless man. He gritted his teeth. "Nay."

"Why not put it to the test?" Piers's tone was light but he watched Cain carefully.

"What are you blathering about?"

Piers shrugged. "I have enjoyed a certain amount of success with women."

Cain stood and walked toward his brother. Sudden anger bubbled up inside him. As he neared Piers, his brother gave him a smug smile.

"Mayhap I should try my hand at seducing the fair Lady Amice. 'Twill not be hard duty. I can tell that beneath her bliaut she possesses a lush body, full breasts, long legs. And her mouth—"

Cain punched him so hard Piers went flying into the wall. Stunned at his action, Cain stared down at him.

Piers was laughing. "Simply lust?"

Cain glowered at him. "You shall not aim your sights on Amice."

"I like her," Piers said, his laughter fading in an instant. He stood back up and crossed his arms. "I think you delude yourself about her failings."

"Stay. Away. From. Amice." Cain fisted his hands.

"Why, Cain? Why?"

She is mine, he wanted to bellow, but he swallowed the words.

"Why, Cain?" Piers asked again softly. He smoothed down his tunic. "As you so oft point out, I have few responsibilities. *I* could accompany her to Villa Delphino, see to her welfare. Her comfort."

Cain bared his teeth. "You are taunting me. You have no intentions toward Amice."

"Mayhap not. Or," Piers shot Cain a challenging look, "mayhap I see the treasure my brother refuses to." He winked and sprang out of the chamber before Cain could reply.

Piers is just trying to provoke me, Cain told himself.

The saints save me, he thought. *'Tis working.*

❧ ❧ ❧

Cain was drawing on a new tunic to wear for supper when he felt cold air brush his face. He snapped a look toward the window but the shutters were closed.

Then he turned back and faced an older version of himself.

"Gerard Veuxfort, I presume," he managed to say calmly.

"Aye."

"Tell me there are no more of you lurking about."

Gerard grinned. "Nay, just the two of us."

Cain glanced around him. "Where is she?"

"In her usual place."

"The east tower?"

Gerard nodded. "Never go there, myself." He floated across the chamber and appeared to sit on a trunk and cross his legs.

"Why not?"

The spirit blinked. "Woman hates me. And for good reason."

Cain rubbed the back of his neck. "Have you tried to explain why you did whatever you did? Ask her forgiveness?"

Gerard just looked at him and smiled. "Is it that easy?"

Damn these ghosts and their perceptiveness. "She is wreaking havoc with my life simply because I happen to resemble you."

"And I am sorry for that."

"*Have* you at least attempted to talk to her?"

"Oh, yes. For the first ten or so years, I was too embarrassed, too filled with guilt to even think about it. Later, I tried, but every time I approached her, she cursed me and I ended up in some strange, dark place for a long while."

Cain swallowed. "What kind of place?"

"The kind I do not wish to return to. Ever."

"So you gave up."

"Aye." He straightened and came close to Cain. "Now, I hide from her. But you know all about that yourself."

"I have responsibilities," Cain bit out. "When Father died, Falcon's Craig was on the edge of ruin. The King's amercement would have taken everything from us if I had not married well and brought the estate back into profit."

"Duty makes a cold companion."

Cain rolled his eyes. "You sound like Piers."

"Your brother is wiser than he knows."

"Why are you here?"

Suddenly, Gerard's head lifted and his eyes opened wide. "She is near." He started to fade.

Cain reached out and passed through a light blue tunic. "Wait! Why did you come?"

"To warn you not to make the same mistake I did."

Chapter 14

Amice knew Laila was right to contact Muriel here, but the last place she ever wanted to see again was the room where she had revealed too much of herself to Cain. Though he lounged in one corner watching her, she refused to look at him.

He had not spoken one word to her since that afternoon.

She bent down and tossed more sage on the fire burning in the brazier.

"Courage, *te'sorthene*," Laila whispered.

"Tonight she will come. I can feel her in the air."

Out of the corner of her eye, Amice saw Cain unbend and walk toward her. She stiffened and finally looked at him, blanking her eyes of any expression.

He looked grave. "Gerard Veuxfort paid me a visit."

"What? When?"

"Before supper."

Amice frowned. "Why did you not mention it at supper?"

He did not answer.

Amice crossed her arms. "What did he say?"

"He has tried to apologize, explain to Muriel, but she will not listen." Cain gave her a wry look. "Gerard claims when he attempted to talk to her, Muriel cursed him to some awful place for a time."

"Did he tell you what he did to her, what happened?"

"Nay. He sensed Muriel and . . . dissolved before I could question him."

Amice and Laila shared a look. "Why did he appear to you?"

Cain shrugged and shifted his gaze away.

He was lying. Hiding something. Which probably meant it had something to do with *them*. With her. "What else did he say?"

"That is all."

Amice stared at him until he looked into her eyes. "Are you sure?"

Cain's jaw tensed. "Aye."

Amice turned away to find Muriel with an expression of utter outrage on her face. Her hands were fisted at her sides, and her form was so solid Amice had to remind herself she was a spirit.

"How dare you?" she hissed.

For a moment, Amice floundered, wondering whether Muriel referred to her being in the chamber or what had transpired earlier with Cain. She bit her lip.

Laila stepped forward and raised her palms. "We only seek to help you."

"By invading my privacy, exposing my secrets? This is how you help?"

A cold breeze snapped through the room.

"Tell me why you linger," Amice said.

Muriel glared at her, but Amice saw something else in her eyes. She drew in a breath.

"You want in death what you could not have in life."

"Nay." Muriel turned vaporous. "You are wrong."

"I am right. You stay for him, for Gerard." Amice walked toward her. "And he is here for the same reason."

Abruptly, Muriel became solid, fury radiating from her.

"He wants to apologize."

"Apologize," Muriel snarled. " 'Tis far too late for that."

Amice took a deep breath. "But it is clear he loved you."

"Oh, yes." Muriel's lips twisted into a bitter smile. "Loved me so much he broke our betrothal. Loved me so much he believed Elena's lies." She advanced on Amice. "Loved me so much he would not even listen to me! Loved me so much he stripped my precious necklace from my dead body and gave it to his *wife*!"

"But, Muriel, perhaps there is an explanation."

"There is no explanation. He used my body and threw me away when a more advantageous match came along."

"The . . . his drawings do not look that way," Amice said softly. "They look like love." She sensed Cain move behind her, felt the force of his stare at her back, but she could not look at him.

"You want to know what really happened?"

Amice nodded.

Muriel's gaze turned so bleak Amice's heart ached for her. "I loved him. Loved him with all my heart and soul. When we were together, 'twas so perfect to be almost like a dream. I gave him everything.

"And then he turned away. Believed that I had betrayed him." Her eyes narrowed. "Refused to believe the babe I carried was his."

Amice gasped. Dear Lord, not this too.

Muriel nodded. "Aye, I had a child growing inside me. Gerard's child."

How could she kill herself with an innocent babe inside? Amice's horror must have shown in her face, because Muriel shook her head.

"Nay, I did not kill the babe." Muriel came so close that the edge of her gown fluttered over Amice's bare feet. "When Gerard broke the betrothal, my sire was most displeased. Of course, he did not believe me either. He beat me so badly I lost the babe," she spit out.

"Oh, my God."

"I wished I had died too. Somehow I survived." Her voice dropped to a whisper. "But I did not want to live anymore."

Amice reached up and felt tears on her cheeks. "I understand."

"Aye, you do."

"Then what *do* you want, if not to be reunited with Gerard?" Cain suddenly asked. "Do you stay solely to plague me?"

Muriel glowered at him, then started laughing. "Aye, my lord. And I shall until the end of your miserable days." With that, she was gone.

Cain smashed a hand against the wall. "Damn her."

As Gifford and Piers crept into the chamber, Amice slowly turned toward Cain. "I do not entirely believe her, Cain."

"Neither do I," added Laila.

He turned anguished eyes on them. "What do you mean?"

Amice shook her head and tried very hard to separate Muriel and Gerard's saga from her own. "I still think the reason she stays is to be with Gerard."

"She hates him."

"I am not so sure about that."

"He certainly thinks so." Cain's voice sounded strained and Amice had to look away from his gaze.

"Aye, but it makes the most sense."

Cain raised his palms. "What can we do?"

"Got to bring them together," Piers offered. "Make them confront the past."

Amice was glad the light in the chamber was dim as she was sure her face reddened.

Gifford rubbed his hands together. "Aye, that is the thing to do."

"How?" Cain asked. "How can we force them to do what they have spent so many years avoiding? Amice?"

"I . . . I must think on this," Amice managed to stutter. She felt as if she were breaking apart from the inside. "There must be a way to help Muriel achieve the peace she needs."

Laila took her arm. "Come, Amice. You need to rest."

"Aye." She ventured a last glance at Cain. Frustration was stamped on his features, and she fought back a longing to soothe the strain from his face.

"Mayhap Muriel must learn to forgive Gerard," Piers mused.

Amice turned to look at him. "But why should she?"

Piers's eyes widened with suspicion.

Suddenly, it was all too much. From a place deep in her soul, sobs erupted like a great tidal wave. Tremendous, wrenching sobs, her tears flowing like an erupting storm. As Piers looked at her in confusion, Amice bent over, gasping for air.

Laila pulled at her arm but Amice could not move.

All she could think was how she had lost her child. How her grief at Cain's betrayal was so great her body could no longer function as it should. How she lay bleeding to death in the grass before Laila had found her. How tiny her daughter's body was.

She blinked through tears and saw Cain standing in front of her.

"What is wrong, Amice?" His gaze held a mixture of concern and bafflement.

Fury ripped through her like thunder. Amice looked over at Piers and Gifford. "Please leave," she managed to whisper.

They filed out, followed by a clearly reluctant Laila.

Cain's expression of confusion deepened, and he crossed his arms.

She shook her head in disgust. Disgust at him and at herself. "Give me the villa. Let me leave here."

He set his jaw. "I cannot until that . . . apparition is gone."

"Find another way."

"How?"

Tears pooled in her eyes.

"Why has this upset you so? I do not understand."

"Nay. You do not." Her voice was raw. " 'Tis the shame of it."

"Were you carrying a man's babe once?" he asked in a whisper.

She could not believe it. After everything, he still did not believe in her. "You bastard," she spat. "I was carrying *your* babe."

"What?" Cain took a step closer and his arms dropped.

"Aye. And when you calmly informed me you were leaving to marry, I lost her."

"Oh, my God, Amice. Why did you not tell me you had conceived?"

"I never had the chance."

"Amice, I am sorry. I did not know."

"Nay, how could you? You were gone."

She could see Cain's throat working and the look he sent her was bleak. "I am so sorry," he whispered.

"Sorry." Amice laughed. "Such a mild word. I nearly bled to death by the time I lost my child. I shall probably never be able to bear another child because of it."

Cain's face turned bone-white, and he took another step toward her.

"Get out," she rasped. "Leave me be."

He bowed his head and left.

❦ ❦ ❦

The next morning, Lugh MacKeir sought out Cain on the training field. At the man's approach, Cain held up a hand to his training partner and lowered his sword. "What do you want?"

The MacKeir barreled to a stop and put his hands on his hips. "My Agatha wishes me to take her to Tunvegen. Soon."

"You have no shame in you at all, do you?"

"No. And even if I did succumb to such a weak emotion, I would not feel it over this."

Cain stepped up and scowled at him. "You dishonored my sister *and* Amice."

The MacKeir did not even flinch. "I did not shame Agatha as I fully intend to wed her as soon as possible. And *I* did not lay with Amice."

"She was your betrothed."

"Aye, but 'tis clear she cares for another," he paused, "for some reason I cannot fathom. I cannot accept a wife who longs for a different man in her bed." He looked pointedly at Cain.

Cain rubbed the back of his neck and scowled at The MacKeir. Would that his words were true, but he knew Amice better than that. She cared for him once, true, and obviously their physical desire for each other had not abated, but he had only to recall her words to Piers to know they had no future.

Amice would never forgive him. Why should she? His chest tightened as he remembered her revelation. Dear God, a child. She had lost a child because of him. *Their* child.

"She intends to leave England, you know," The MacKeir said conversationally. "Forever."

"What?" Cain barked.

He looked smug. "Aye. As soon as her mother passes."

Cain felt as if The MacKeir had driven a blade into his heart. "Why would she do such a thing? Leave her family and all that she knows? Why would her brother allow it?"

"Looks to me like she is running away from something. Or someone. And Rand loves her enough to grant her wish."

Was she so determined to avoid him she would put countries between them? Aye, she would. Amice possessed the most independent will of any woman he had ever known. The sharp edge of loss cut through his belly.

The MacKeir put his hands out, palms up. "I am a simple man. If I want something, I go after it. If I think or feel something, I say it. But you, Hawksdown, you are an onion."

Cain raised his brows. "An onion?"

"Aye, with too many hidden layers." He leaned toward Cain and fixed him with an intent stare. "Take some advice. If you want her, seize her! Do not let her leave."

"You do not understand."

The MacKeir sighed and shook his head. "Aye, I do. But about Agatha——"

"You shall wed my sister before taking her anywhere."

"Agreed. Now, there is one more thing."

"More comparisons to vegetables?"

"Woodford." MacKeir's expression turned grim. "I would like to help you finish that whoreson before I return to Tunvegen."

"I can fight my own battles, MacKeir."

"I feel obligated to Amice to assist you."

"Very well." Cain sheathed his sword. "Now, here is my plan."

❦ ❦ ❦

Amice entered the bailey and saw Cain and Lugh over on the training field deep in discussion. Good. She walked quickly across the open ground and into the tower containing Cain's solar.

The document transferring Villa Delphino to her had to be either here or in Cain's chamber, and she would prefer to avoid that place.

Anger and shame swirled in her belly. She could not bear to stay at Falcon's Craig any longer. Once she found the document, she would try one more time with Muriel, then leave. Surely, she had earned Villa Delphino by now.

Slowly, she pushed open the door and peeked in to make sure the room was empty. With a sigh of relief, she went in and shut the door behind her.

For a moment, she simply absorbed the room, sensing Cain's essence, smelling the lingering scent of cedar.

A table stood in the center of the room, stacked with rolls of parchment. Against one wall was a cupboard stuffed with more papers. Where could it be?

Amice walked around the table and saw a small trunk. It was a beautifully carved piece, made of mahogany and gilded with gold paint.

She bent down and jiggled the lid. Locked.

Knowing Cain, he probably kept the key with him. Amice stood and shuffled through the piles on the desk, looking for something to use. A dagger lay next to a stack of quills.

She snatched it up and went to work on the lock. This

had to be it. She twisted one way and then the other, all the while feeling as if the door would open at any instant and she would be discovered. Determinedly, she attacked the lock. If Cain walked in, so be it. She would simply demand her due.

With a soft click, the lock parted.

Holding her breath, Amice slowly lifted the lid and lowered her head to peer inside.

Her heart dropped and she gasped. With unsteady fingers, she reached down into the velvet-lined interior. Two objects lay inside, carefully nestled in the rich, blue velvet.

The purple ribbon she had worn in her hair the last time she and Cain had been together.

And the ring she gave him when they secretly promised to each other. She turned it over in her palm, her vision blurring with tears.

Why had he kept the tokens? And why in such a special place?

Suddenly, the door crashed open and Amice whirled around, her hand to her mouth.

Cain's face could have been chiseled from granite. "What are you doing?" He stalked toward her, his cheeks tight, his eyes glittering.

Amice swallowed her embarrassment and stood, still clutching the ring in her hand. She held it out in her palm. "Why did you keep this?"

He clenched his hands. "It has some value. There was no reason to toss it away. I had forgotten about it, truth be told." Cain moved closer, crowding her. "Why are you skulking around in here?"

His body trapped her behind the table. Amice dropped the ring back into the trunk and lifted her chin. "I want Villa Delphino."

"Muriel is not gone."

"You have had enough of me," Amice snapped.

Cain's eyes flashed and he curved his mouth. "Oh, no, my sweet. Never enough."

His words shot through Amice's brain like a bolt of lightning.

Just before he kissed her.

Cain tangled his fingers in her hair, imprisoning her head, plunging his tongue in deep, ravishing her mouth in long, smooth strokes. She wound her arms around him and held on, meeting his hunger with her own, their mouths and tongues mating feverishly. God, she wanted this, needed this. It was as if without his mouth, his taste, she was forever doomed to hunger.

He slid one hand down to her buttocks and thrust her against him, rubbing against her center as he plundered her mouth.

Amice whimpered.

At the sound, Cain growled a curse and shoved her away from him.

Amice stood staring wide eyed, her arms hanging limply at her sides.

"What do you do to me?" Cain bit out.

"I—"

"What in the hell am I going to do with you?"

Love me! Amice wanted to scream, but she bit her lip instead. "Give me Villa Delphino," she whispered. "Let me go."

Cain stared back at her, his face set into grim lines, his eyes like fire-lit sapphires. "Nay," he said in a low voice, then whipped around and stalked out of the room.

Amice looked down at the ribbon and ring and felt something inside her set adrift. Surely, he lied about the tokens. He kept them too close.

It was as if he deliberately distanced himself. As if he imposed an iron will upon his wants, his emotions, buried them in a huge pile of responsibility.

But why?

Amice slammed the lid back on the trunk and turned toward the door. It was time she discovered the truth about Cain and Luce.

Chapter 15

Cain left Falcon's Craig the next day. He had to. Amice's arrival had awakened something dormant within him. He had spent years burying himself in the business of being the Earl of Hawksdown.

He had only to look at Amice and the most elemental part of him thought, *That is mine. Mine to possess, mine to sink my body into until my skin is permanently stamped upon hers.*

Mine to love.

It was madness.

"Think you he will come?" The MacKeir asked from the horse beside him.

"Aye." He glanced at the other man. "The guards watched Jack, the traitor, slip out the postern gate last night. He is undoubtedly on his way to Hexham now."

"Good. How long have you known Woodford had a spy in the castle?"

"Not long. After Woodford attacked Hazelstone, I realized someone must have told him of Amice." Cain fingered the pommel of his sword.

The MacKeir grunted a Gaelic curse.

Eight men rode behind them, made up equally of members of the garrison and the Highlanders. To a man, each wanted a piece of Henry Woodford.

But Woodford was his. "We wait a few days at Styrling, then go to the cottage. He will be there. He will not take the chance that I will burn down the place where he spent so much time with Luce."

"Have you been there before?"

Cain shook his head.

"Bad bit of business, that," MacKeir muttered.

"Aye." Cain did not say any more on the subject but urged his mount to a faster pace. Initially, his announced intention to destroy the cottage was solely to draw Woodford out, but Cain had decided to make it a fact. *After* he killed the skulking bastard.

No man touched Amice and lived to tell of it.

❧ ❧ ❧

Amice walked into the stable. "Piers?" she called out.

"Over here," a muffled voice replied.

Sidestepping a groom at work brushing another horse, Amice followed the sound of Piers's voice to the last stall on the right.

Piers looked up with a quick grin. "Give me a minute to finish, my lady."

Amice squatted down in the straw. "What is wrong with him?"

"Leg splints. I am applying a warm poultice to ease the swelling." He wrapped a linen bandage around the horse's foreleg. "Easy, boy," he crooned.

Amice sniffed. "Camphor?"

"Aye, and pennyroyal." He stood and brushed straw off his tunic. "What may I do for you?"

"I want to talk to you about Cain," Amice blurted out.

Piers raised a brow. "Oh?"

"Halden, are you in here?" a feminine voice purred.

Piers rolled his eyes. "Morganna." He stepped out of the stall and crossed his arms. "Halden," he called.

As Amice stood, a big man with bushy black hair emerged from another stall. He gave Morganna a sly smile before turning to Piers. "My lord?"

"Saddle Gabriel and Pleasance." He took Amice's arm. "The *lady* and I are going for a ride."

Morganna glared at them, and Piers shot her a grin.

Amice hid her smile behind her hand. Morganna clearly had come in search of Halden for one thing and was *very* irked at being, at the least, delayed.

"Like a bitch in heat," Piers whispered, with a wink.

While they waited, Morganna spoke to Halden in soft tones, touching him on the arm, the shoulder, the back as he tightened saddles on the horses.

"Halden, hurry up," Piers called. "For God's sake, keep your hands off him for a minute, Morganna."

Amice had to turn around. She could not help but

laugh at the look of outrage on Morganna's face.

"Do you wish to fetch a mantle, my lady?" Piers said over his shoulder.

Finally, Amice reined in her mirth and turned back. "Nay, the day is fair."

Halden led Pleasance over, and assisted Amice into the saddle.

"Enjoy your ride, Lady Amice," Morganna said in a sugary voice.

As Amice rode past her, she leaned down and said, "Enjoy *yours*, Morganna."

Piers's raucous laughter followed them out of the stable. "Well put, my lady." He shook his head and started laughing again. "Just wait until she finds out what Cain plans for her."

Hopefully, something far away, Amice thought. "What is that?"

They rode toward the gatehouse and Piers gestured to a heavyset man standing by the portcullis. "See him?"

"Yes." Amice studied the man. He reminded her of a boar, big and meaty with a crudely sensual curve to his mouth.

"Sir Edrick. Reportedly enough of a man to handle even Morganna. She will soon find herself wed to him and shipped off to Casswell Manor."

"Good." At least Morganna would not have Cain.

"Aye. We all tire of the wench's antics." Piers fell silent as they passed under the gatehouse and rode across the drawbridge.

Amice drew in a deep breath and looked around the countryside. The ground spread out before them in low, rolling expanses of green, and the roar of the ocean flowed over the earth. A light mist danced across the grass. "Falcon's Craig is a lovely place."

Piers tilted his head back and looked at the sky. "I cannot imagine living anywhere but by the sea."

"It is very exhilarating."

"What is Wareham like?"

"Much different. Smaller. It is made of grey stone and has a main tower, a great hall, and four corner towers. Wareham is more refined, romantic, while Falcon's Craig is more imposing, wild."

Piers sidled his mount close to hers. "What did you want to talk about?"

Amice bit her lip. "Why is Cain so . . . controlled? So . . ."

"Stubborn? Mule-headed? Determined to do what he perceives to be his duty at all costs?"

"Aye." Amice smiled at him. "All of those things."

Piers sighed. "Somewhere along the road of learning to do and be all the things necessary for the Earl of Hawksdown, Cain lost the ability to look at himself honestly. He has sacrificed much to hold Falcon's Craig for the family."

"What was Luce like?"

"Strange."

Amice remembered the dingy little chamber at Woodford's castle and shivered. "How so?"

"She looked like an angel but she was devious, sneaky. Half the time, no one knew where she was."

"Was Cain . . . happy with her?"

Piers halted his horse and stared intently at her. "No."

Amice swallowed. "How did she die?"

"She killed herself."

"What?" Amice froze in disbelief.

"Accidentally. All she wanted to do was get rid of Woodford's babe growing in her belly. She bled to death."

"Oh, my God."

" 'Twas a dark time." For a moment, Piers's face looked savage.

"Cain must have been devastated." Now, it all made sense. He withheld himself because of the pain he endured from his wife's betrayal. She knew Cain. Such a betrayal would wound him deeply.

"Aye." Piers took a deep breath and pointed at a copse of trees in the distance. "I am in the mood for a race, my lady. Shake off such grim talk. What say you?"

"A race it is."

"Wager?" Piers wore a mischievous grin.

Amice's horse pranced beneath her. "If I win, you convince Cain to give me Villa Delphino. Now."

"Done." Piers leaned close. "And if *I* win, you will tell Cain how you really feel about him."

Before Amice could stutter a reply, Piers kicked his horse and they dashed forward.

Amice bent down low over the saddle, urging her palfrey on. "Come on, girl. Come on."

They thundered across the grass, nearly nose to nose. As they neared the trees, Amice pulled ahead. "Yes!" she cried, giddy with the thought of victory. "Almost there, girl."

And then her saddle slipped. Amice clutched at Pleasance's mane, but it was too hard to hold on. For an agonizing moment, she felt her body slipping over the horse's side, then she went hurtling to the ground and everything went black.

❧ ❧ ❧

Cain looked around the cottage in disgust. He had never bothered to come here after Luce's confession and death. In the end, the true Luce had come out. Informing him in scathing tones that she could never love anyone but Woodford, could never be satisfied by *him*.

The irony was that he really did not care.

A big bed took up most of the space, piled with silk bedcovers and pillows. Lengths of silk were tied to each of the four posts and a box on the floor held a truly amazing collection of sex devices, not the least of which was a big, leather covered item shaped like a man's staff.

He thought of taking the box back to Piers, but decided against it. He wanted no reminder of how base and deceptive Luce had been.

With a last glance, Cain walked out of the cottage.

Woodford and a band of fifteen men sat on horses in a circle around the cottage. The one guard who had accompanied Cain was securely bound.

Cain suppressed a smile. How predictable Woodford was. He knew his own men and The MacKeir's were well hidden in the trees.

"Leave this place alone," Woodford ordered.

Cain leaned against the doorframe and crossed his arms. "I see Jack gave you my message."

Woodford's eyes glowed like burning obsidian. "You shall not burn the cottage."

"Oh? Luce is *dead*, Woodford. What difference does it make? You shall never meet her here again."

"Her memory is alive." Woodford's mount shifted back and forth, its bridle jangling.

Cain laughed. "You think this place some kind of shrine? A shrine to what? Depravity? Betrayal?"

"To love," Woodford shouted. "Something you know nothing about."

"You sick bastard," Cain swore. He picked up a torch.

Woodford inched forward. "Put that down."

The MacKeir and the other men emerged from the trees, encircling Woodford and his men. Each held their swords at the ready, their expressions fierce. Each remembered Hazelstone.

"I offer you a bargain, Woodford."

The other man's gaze narrowed. "What?"

"Fight me. Now. Just you and me."

Woodford leapt down from his horse. "To the death?"

"Aye." Cain glared at him. "To the death. With no interference from your men."

"Done."

Cain dropped the torch, stepped forward, and raised his sword and shield.

Woodford rushed him with a roar and the battle began. He swung his sword down toward Cain's neck, but Cain easily danced away.

As they exchanged blows, the sounds of the forest

faded away. Cain grunted as he smashed into Woodford's shield. The man was smaller than Cain, but what he lacked in strength he made up for in sheer, mad rage.

"You never deserved my Luce," Woodford hissed.

Cain swung his sword toward Woodford's knees. "I never wanted her."

Woodford jumped over the blade and whirled back. "You are a liar."

"I only bed her once to consummate the marriage."

"She denied you."

Cain dodged a blow aimed at his head. "You did not know her as well as you thought you did. She begged me to take her."

"Liar!" Woodford thundered as he spun to the left, his sword flashing in the sunlight.

"Pleaded with me to swive her over and over." Cain laughed. "I told her I did not want another man's leavings."

"Bastard," Woodford rasped.

Cain turned and brought his sword up with every bit of his strength. The blades crashed, and Cain forced his arm to remain steady, grimacing with the effort. Woodford's sword arched into the air.

"No, Woodford, you are the bastard," Cain growled, just before he turned his wrist and sliced his blade through Woodford's neck.

Woodford's head landed by his horse's hooves, his body crumpling to the ground at Cain's feet.

Complete silence blanketed the clearing.

Cain raised his head and stared at Woodford's men, one by one. " 'Tis your choice. Leave here with your lives, or die today with your lord."

They filed away without a word.

The MacKeir rode up and dismounted. He clasped Cain's hand with his. "Well done, my lord. Well done."

Cain gave him a grim smile. "Now, let us burn this damn place to cinders." He went back into the cottage and lit the torch. The old wood sparked quickly, and as Cain and the other men moved back, the cottage went up in flames, the roof caving in with a great whoosh.

The men cheered.

❧ ❧ ❧

Gradually, Amice became aware that someone was yelling her name. She blinked open her eyes and winced at the sunlight. She was lying flat on her back in the grass.

What had happened?

Piers's face slowly came into focus, his gaze wide with obvious worry. "Amice?"

"Piers."

"Are you all right? Can you move?"

She wiggled her toes, then shifted her legs. "I think so." Amice pushed herself into a sitting position. "My head hurts."

Piers ran his hands over the back of her head and frowned. "You have a good sized lump."

Her stomach gave a lurch. "I feel like I am going to be sick," she said softly. Her head pounded and her stomach rolled.

"Just stay still." Piers stood. "There is a pool not far from here. I will fetch you some water."

"Thank you." She swallowed and watched Piers gallop off. Pleasance nudged her shoulder, and Amice reached up to stroke the horse's muzzle. The saddle lay in a heap next to her. Amice stared at it for a moment before she realized what she was seeing. "Oh, my God," she whispered and put her hand to her mouth.

Pleasance nudged her shoulder again as if to soothe her.

Amice reached out a trembling hand to touch the leather. The girth had been sliced nearly through, the stress of riding causing it to break completely.

Out of the corner of her eye she saw Piers return. He knelt down and handed her a skin of water. "Drink."

Before she did, she pointed at the girth. " 'Twas deliberate."

Piers cursed low and lifted the girth to inspect it. "Morganna."

"Think you she would do such a thing?"

"Who else could it be? Halden has no reason to harm you."

"I cannot believe Morganna hates me that much."

Piers shrugged. "She is avaricious."

Amice took a long drink of water. "Can you help me up?"

"Aye." To Amice's surprise, he simply picked her up and put her on his horse. He gathered up the broken girth and saddle and secured it to his own. Then, he leapt up behind her and wrapped a surprisingly strong arm around her waist. "Pleasance will follow us," he murmured, and set off.

Amice fell asleep halfway to the castle.

❧ ❧ ❧

Cain faced Morganna and fought to control his anger long enough to hear her tale. His fingers itched to draw his sword and chop off her scheming head. He had just gone to see Amice and found her sleeping, pale as bone.

"I did nothing," Morganna insisted, with a mulish cast to her mouth.

"The girth was cut," Piers reminded her.

She turned on him with a glare. "Anyone could have cut it."

"But you were there," Cain said, fingering the pommel of his sword.

Morganna took a step back. "So was Halden. It was he who saddled the mounts, not me."

"I have spoken to Halden. I do not believe he would endanger his life by tampering with Amice's saddle. Why would he?"

"Mayhap he mistakenly thought it would please me to see her injured."

Cain barked a mirthless laugh. "Do not flatter yourself. You are naught to Halden but a willing body to ease his lust upon."

Morganna looked mad enough to spit. "I did not cut the girth," she gritted out.

"Then who did?"

"I do not know! Maybe your ghost did it. She has tried to harm Amice before."

"Has she?" Cain stalked forward. "Or has Muriel received aid? Aid from a living being."

Morganna's face leached of color. "I did nothing."

Piers walked to her other side. "Where did you get the drug you gave Cain?"

"I . . . from some old woman I met at the market in Neubiginge."

"What was it?"

"I told Cain, I do not know. It was just supposed to . . . speed things up a bit."

Cain snarled. "You are a liar and a whore. And you shall be gone from Falcon's Craig this very day."

"What? But where can I go? This is my home," she shrieked.

"No longer." Cain went to the door of his solar and opened it. "Come in, Edrick."

At the sight of Sir Edrick, Morganna's mouth dropped open and she shot Cain a beseeching look.

He ignored her. "You know Edrick, I believe," he said smoothly.

Morganna just shook her head.

"I have decided he will make a fine husband for you. You will be married in the chapel immediately and leave for Casswell Manor this day."

"Nay," she whispered, giving Edrick a fearful look. "You cannot give me to *him*. He is a brute."

Edrick moved to stand in front of Morganna. "I am not a cruel man."

"Nay," Morganna choked.

"But I will not allow my wife to swive another," Edrick continued. "You will be most satisfied with me in that regard, I wager." He slowly smiled.

Cain thought Morganna might swoon at that, but she

lifted her chin and met Edrick's leer with a haughty look. "Cain, do not do this to me," she pleaded.

"Either way, you are gone. Take Edrick and you will have a place to live, a man to take care of you." Cain shrugged. "Refuse and you will be cast out with nothing."

Tears sparkled in Morganna's eyes, but Cain felt no remorse. She tried to kill Amice. He would just as soon see her put to death. "Make your decision, Morganna. Now."

She gazed at Edrick in horror, tears welling in her eyes.

Edrick looked like a man about to enjoy a fine sweet-meat.

"Well?" Cain asked.

"I . . . I will marry him."

Edrick's smile widened and he took hold of Morganna's arm. "Do not worry. Obey me and all will be fine."

Morganna let herself be led away.

Piers clapped Cain on the back. " 'Bout time we rid ourselves of the wench. She was upsetting my horses, for God's sake."

Cain raised a brow. "I am more concerned about her attempts to harm Amice."

"Yes, I imagine you are."

"Do you think Morganna cut the girth?"

Piers nodded. "Had to be her. Nobody else around."

"Perhaps I am being too lenient with her."

"Oh, I don't know. Life with Edrick is punishment enough, I am thinking." Piers chuckled. "He will not hurt her but he will use her well."

"She will probably enjoy that," Cain said with a grin.

"Aye."

Cain's face darkened. "I am going to check on Amice."

Piers gazed at him knowingly. "When times are darkest, the heart seeks the light."

"Piers, please. No sage words today."

His brother just winked.

Chapter 16

The next time Amice opened her eyes she looked into Cain's. Confused, she sat up in bed and blinked at the pain in her head.

Cain sat on the edge of the bed. "How are you feeling?"

Their gazes caught, and for a moment Amice said nothing, simply returned his stare. A fire sparked in the fireplace but the chamber was quiet, the kind of quiet that carried an air of expectancy. A sense of intimacy wrapped around her, and Amice was content simply to look into his beautiful eyes.

"Amice?"

"I . . . I am fine."

His jaw tightened. "Morganna will be gone this day."

"Do you really think she is responsible?"

Cain rubbed the back of his neck. "It makes the most

sense. And it is past time I see her settled."

"Sir Edrick?"

"Aye. He will manage her well enough."

Amice looked down. "I must admit I shall not be sorry to see her go."

For a moment, Cain did not say anything and Amice finally lifted her gaze. "Nor I," he said. He reached out and smoothed Amice's hair back from her face.

Amice swallowed.

"Woodford is dead."

"You killed him?"

Cain nodded. " 'Twas a fair fight." He took her hand in his and stroked her fingers.

Amice held her breath. Surely he did not realize what he was doing.

"And then I burned the cottage to the ground."

"What cottage?"

His fingers ceased their motion and he flashed her a surprised look. "I forgot. You did not know."

"About what? What are you talking about."

Abruptly, Cain rose to his feet and paced across the room. "A cottage where my late wife met her lover."

It was the first time he had spoken of Luce. So many questions Amice wanted to ask tumbled through her brain she could not sort them out. "I am sorry, Cain. You must have been terribly hurt by her disloyalty."

He did not look at her. "A breach of faith is always hurtful."

The pain in his voice wound through Amice's veins and settled into an ache low in her stomach. "You must have loved her very much."

Slowly, he turned and gazed at her. "Actually, I never loved Luce at all. She was merely another duty." He turned and walked out of her chamber.

Amice just stared at the open door, her mind whirling with the import of his words. She had assumed he fell in love with another woman. Assumed the *real* reason for his abandonment was that he found a woman he wanted more than her.

She got out of bed and dressed. For the first time she wondered if she bore some responsibility for what had happened between them. She had told Cain she loved him, true, but talking of her feelings had always been difficult for her. Did he not understand how much he meant to her? Was that her fault?

Her mind spun with questions.

One swirled through her brain like a mounting storm.

Was it possible there might be another chance for them?

❧ ❧ ❧

"I cannot believe this is happening," Morganna hissed.

The apparition in front of her laughed.

"You were supposed to help me win Cain." She threw an armful of bliauts into a trunk.

"You truly are a pathetic creature," Muriel remarked.

"*I* am pathetic?" Morganna slammed the lid of the trunk. "*I* am not the one who killed myself over my poor broken heart."

"No, but you are the one who thinks the answer to any problem is to spread your legs."

"For a woman, it often is."

"You should have been more subtle."

"I did not have time." She glared at Muriel. "He grows more besotted with Amice every day," she spat. " 'Tis unbelievable."

Muriel frowned. "Aye. There may truly be a chance the earl will find happiness."

"This is all *your* fault."

"*My* fault? You are the one who failed to get rid of Amice despite ample opportunities. And even with the aid of my potion, you still could not manage to entice the earl." Her lips twisted into a bitter smile. "You deserve Edrick."

Morganna sank to the floor and buried her face in her hands. "Oh, God, what am I to do? The man is an animal."

"I imagine you shall suit each other very well," Muriel said dryly.

When Morganna looked up to dispute her words, the ghost was gone.

ᵍᴼ ᵍᴼ ᵍᴼ

Early that evening, Cain stood in the chapel and watched his sister exchange vows with The MacKeir. He still could scarcely believe Agatha, for whom he had given up finding a husband, would be taking as her mate a massive Highlander who looked at her as if he were contemplating which part to savor first.

Agatha beamed up at The MacKeir as if he were the answer to her every prayer.

The MacKeir placed a ring on Agatha's right thumb, saying, "In the name of the Father," then on her index finger with the words, "and of the Son," and then finally on her middle finger, adding, "and of the Holy Spirit. Amen."

Cain cast a glance toward Amice. She watched the couple with what looked like pride.

As he patted Agatha's hand, The MacKeir said,

"With this ring I thee wed."

"This gold and silver I thee give."

"With my body, I thee worship." The MacKeir paused and winked at Agatha, who flushed deep red.

"And with this dowry, I thee endow."

Tears glimmered in Agatha's eyes. Cain snuck another glance at Amice and noticed her eyes gleaming.

Father Colbert stepped forward.

"Do you, Lugh MacKeir, give your body to Agatha Veuxfort, in holy matrimony?"

"I do," The MacKeir affirmed in a loud rumble.

Agatha swayed toward him. "And I receive it."

"And do you, Agatha Veuxfort, give your body to Lugh MacKeir, in holy matrimony?"

This time when Cain looked over at Amice, he found her gazing at him. Their eyes locked, and he felt as if he fell into a deep, dark well. Warm, inviting, bringing him the only peace he would ever know.

He vaguely heard Agatha say, "I do."

Cain's breath caught in his chest when Amice bit her lower lip. He took a step toward her before he could think.

"And *I* receive it," MacKeir roared.

The Highlanders in the rear of the chapel broke out into cheers, nearly drowning out Father Colbert's blessing.

Amice blinked.

It was as if Cain woke from a dream. His skin felt warm and prickly and something in the region of his heart ached with a dull throb. He forced himself to break away and look at Agatha, who was being thoroughly kissed by The MacKeir, to the cheering of his men.

"Good to see the lass properly wed," Gifford commented. "And The MacKeir was not the man for our Amice."

Cain raised a brow. "*Our* Amice?"

"Aye."

When his uncle did not say any more, Cain turned and looked at him. Gifford's stare was clear challenge. He opened his mouth to refute his uncle's implication but the words would not come. *My Amice,* he said in his mind. *Mine.* It sounded so right. He glowered at Gifford. "Leave be."

Gifford sniffed and looked away, muttering, "Foolish boy," half under his breath.

The MacKeir finally stopped kissing Agatha and turned to yell, "Now, we feast! A man needs his strength to handle a wife like my woman."

Agatha looked somewhat dazed but she was smiling when The MacKeir dragged her out the door of the chapel.

Piers stood shaking his head and laughing. "Madness." He strode over to Amice and offered her his arm. "May I escort you, fair lady?"

Cain frowned.

Amice put her hand on Piers's arm and looked up at him from beneath her lashes." 'Twould be my pleasure, kind sir."

Gifford cackled.

Cain's eyes narrowed to slits and he glowered at his brother. Piers blithely ignored him, other than to send Cain an exaggerated wink as he sailed by with Amice.

❧ ❧ ❧

As Cain sat at the wedding feast, trying his damnedest to accept the fact that Lugh MacKeir was now his brother-in-law, and to suppress the growing feeling that this should be *his* wedding feast to celebrate his marriage to Amice, a page slipped him a note. He unfolded the parchment and frowned. It was a plea from Morganna to speak to him before she departed.

Piers craned his neck to read the note. "Toss it on the floor, Cain. The wench has caused enough trouble already."

But duty made Cain rise. He would listen to Morganna and then see the last of her. Forcing himself not to look at Amice, he left the hall and sought his solar.

Morganna stood within, an odd expression on her face. Sir Edrick was not present. "Cain," she said.

He stopped at the doorway. "Where is your husband?"

"Seeing to my belongings." She frowned. "Meager as they might be."

"What do you want, Morganna?"

She rushed across the solar and took the sleeve of his tunic in her hand. "Cain, please do not do this to me! The man is a pig."

He yanked his arm free. "On the contrary, I think you and Sir Edrick shall suit each other quite well."

Her face colored. "He is . . . huge. He has already

taken me twice. I am so sore I am not sure I can ride."

Cain fought the urge to laugh, and lost.

Morganna's face drew into harsh lines. "Ismena always hated you, you know," she hissed. "If she were yet alive, she would never allow you to condemn me to the likes of Sir Edrick."

"Morganna, cease with your stories. Your future has been decided. Be thankful I did not do worse."

" 'Tis no story," she spat. "Ismena told me herself. How she hated you. Just as she hated the weakling who sired you."

His mother was hardly a loving woman, but hate? He knew he never measured up to her expectations, had received her contempt often enough, but hate was too much to believe. Scenes of his mother shifted through his mind, bringing with them a hint of doubt. "What are you talking about?"

"She hated you both. Hated that she had to marry him and birth you. She wanted the Earl of Holstoke, had loved him forever."

Cain blinked. "Luce's father?"

"Aye." Morganna looked smug. "And she did have him, in her way."

Unease swirled through Cain's belly, and he grabbed her shoulders. "What are you saying?"

She curved her lips in a hateful smile. "Piers is not your brother, not your full brother. He is the Earl of Holstoke's."

Cain shook her hard. "You lie."

"Nay, 'tis the truth. He is a bastard, unacknowledged by his father. Your mother barely tolerated him, told me often Piers wasn't anything like his sire."

"You lying bitch."

Her expression turned sly. "Save me from Sir Edrick and I shall not tell a soul."

"Why did you not mention this before?"

"I only found out today while packing."

Cain sneered. "You belong to Edrick now."

"Get rid of him. Send him on to Casswell Manor without me."

"And you will remain here?"

"Aye."

"You have no proof of this farfetched claim."

"Do I not?" She withdrew a piece of vellum from a pouch around her waist. " 'Tis in Ismena's own hand."

He snatched the sheet from her and read. "Damn the old spider to hell," he said. It was all there, her disdain for her husband and first born, her obsession with the Earl of Holstoke, her betrayal of her husband that resulted in a second son. "Where did you get this?"

Her smile was mocking. "Your mother *liked* me. Keep me here, Cain," she whispered. "I could be good for you. You shall not regret it."

Cain stared at the woman he had taken in, tolerated, made excuses for, and who now threatened the tattered fabric of his life. "You. Shall. Go. With. Your. Husband. *Now.*"

"You will not risk exposing your brother's disgrace. Your family's disgrace."

He reached out and wrapped his hands around her throat. "You are an evil, grasping witch, and your time here is done."

She tried to swallow but could not.

Cain squeezed harder. "Listen well to me, bitch. Tell your tale to another soul and," he bent his head until they were eye to eye, "I will find you and I will kill you." He eased up on the pressure.

Her eyes were twin moons of blue. "You would not."

This time, he laughed. "Oh, Morganna, you are so wrong. I can and I will. With pleasure."

She paled and turned to leave.

He kept hold of her throat. "Remember, Morganna. I shall hear of it if you speak your fable. Sir Edrick is my loyal and now," he smirked, "grateful man."

When he let her go, she bolted through the doorway.

He took a deep breath and tried to make his hands unclench. By the saints, Piers a bastard?

Piers would never know. He would never know and nothing would change.

Cain tossed his mother's venom into the fire and watched it burn.

❦ ❦ ❦

At midnight, Cain abruptly awoke. For a few minutes, he lay in bed listening for what might have awakened him. Nothing.

He sat up and swung his legs out of bed. Was this another annoying antic by Muriel?

But when he reached for his braies, he froze. A strange hum began in his veins. His breath quickened and he hurriedly threw on braies and a loose tunic. He felt as if something called to him with an odd sense of urgency, and he quickly left his chamber and strode down the steps.

It was the thirtieth day of April. Beltane.

Once in the bailey, the feeling grew stronger. Cain looked around and froze when he spotted a small fire, half hidden within the grove of apple trees. He slowly approached the spot.

When he arrived, his mouth went dry.

Amice danced around the burning fire, her face flushed and glowing. She wore only her white bliaut and her feet were bare. Flowers wound through her unbound hair, which swirled around her as she twirled and jumped to some silent music.

She had never looked more beguiling, all mystery and woman blended into perfection.

His Amice.

His pagan.

He was Christian. He renounced pagan practices.

But Beltane . . . A celebration of life, of fertility.

Even as he reminded himself of his deeply held religious beliefs, he walked toward the fire and held out his hands to Amice.

She stopped so suddenly she would have fallen into the flames if he had not caught her around the waist. "What are you doing here?" she panted.

Her skin was warm beneath his hands and he suddenly felt recklessly alive. "You summoned me."

"What?" Her eyes widened.

"Aye. You beckoned me from a deep sleep."

Amice stilled and put her hands on his arms. "I possess no such power."

"It seems you do." Cain felt as if another man had

taken him over, a wild, dangerous man who took what he wanted. And ever since he had seen Gerard's drawings, he had dreamed of taking Amice in so many new ways, ways he would not have thought of five years ago. He slid his hands up Amice's back and tangled them in her hair, holding her head fast. "I felt you," he whispered. "I know you."

She parted her lips.

"This Beltane we shall celebrate together."

"Are you going to dance?" she whispered.

He drew in a deep breath. "A kind of a dance. The kind when I am deep inside you." He rocked against her. "The kind you want. As I want."

Cain could see Amice's pulse at her throat. He bent down to nuzzle her skin, pressing a kiss to the tender flesh. "Tonight, we celebrate life," he murmured.

When he let go of her waist to free himself of his braies, she turned and took a quick step away.

He pulled her against him and put his face against her neck. "You will not run from me now."

Amice stiffened at the growl in his voice. He was hard and hot against her body, his heart a steady thud, his breathing harsh against her ear. This was not the controlled Cain she knew. She should be strong, she told herself. Resist him. But a part of her was wildly curious about what this Cain would do.

With his other hand he began unlacing her bliaut, pressing open-mouthed kisses across the back of her neck.

"Cain."

"Do not deny me. Not tonight."

Tonight. Beltane. Amice stared at the shooting flames and felt her will unravel.

Her bliaut fell to the ground.

"Mayhap you *are* a witch," Cain said, as he smoothed his long hands up her belly to caress her breasts. Amice fell back against him.

Cain laughed in her ear.

For a moment, his touch withdrew, then he was all there against her. Hot and naked, his arousal prodding her.

She tried to turn but his hands held her. Her woman's place ached, clenched, and her stomach churned. When Cain pulled her to the ground, she went easily, her limbs boneless.

He lay on top of her, covering her with his heavy, sleek body. "Tell me you want me inside you. Tell me you need me." He eased off his weight and slid a hand under her, pulling her up onto her knees.

Amice closed her eyes as he slowly drew his fingers through her body's opening. She panted for breath, anticipation melding with just a touch of fear.

"Tell me," he demanded in a rough voice.

"Please."

"Say the words." He stroked and spread her open, torturing her center with soft, slow circles.

God, yes, she needed. She wanted with everything she was. "Please, Cain." She pushed against his hand and fisted the grass, needing to hold onto something, some anchor.

His hand stopped and Amice cried out. Then he slid his staff between her legs, rubbing himself against her and she forgot to breathe.

"Say it, dammit," he said roughly.

"I want you," she cried. "Please, I need you, Cain. Now!"

He growled low in his throat and buried himself in her.

Amice collapsed onto her arms and gave herself up to the night.

He took her with such raw hunger Amice was unable to do anything but lay her head in the grass and accept him. Harsh, untamed, there was nothing measured in the way Cain invaded her body, claimed her soul even as he brought her to such a release she saw stars behind her eyes.

And when it was over, he gathered her in his arms and held her close, taking her mouth, her tongue, with the same sweet abandon.

She fell asleep with the sight of a tear on his cheek.

❧ ❧ ❧

Amice awoke in her own chamber. Without Cain. She opened her eyes and found a man casually perched on the end of the bed. A partially transparent man who happened to look exactly like Cain, only older. Amice groaned and shut her eyes.

He laughed.

With a sigh, Amice sat up and studied the ghost. "I assume you are Gerard Veuxfort?"

With a glimmer of blue and white, the spirit gave a small bow with his head. "That I am, Lady Amice."

Had last night been a dream? She took a quick look around her chamber but there was no sign Cain had been there. The bed had clearly been slept in by one person, not two.

"No, it was not a dream," Gerard said with a smile.

Amice gave him a sharp look.

The ghost drifted closer, settled next to her, and crossed his legs. "I have wanted to meet you but," his shoulders moved, "Muriel is usually lurking about."

"She is?" Amice peered into the corners of the room. "Is she here now?"

"Oh, no. I would not be if she was."

"How can I help her?"

Gerard uncrossed his legs and stood. "The only way for her to find peace is in forgiveness."

"Forgiveness of you."

"Aye."

"Why should she? You misused her and tossed her away."

"I had reasons."

"What reasons? How can you justify what you did?"

"I am not trying to justify it. I know I made mistakes, acted foolishly. But I did not hurt Muriel on a whim."

"Why, then?"

He started to fade, blending into a swirl of blue and white. "Find my journal."

Amice shot out of bed, clutching the bedcover to her chest. "What? Where is it?"

"Cain knows. 'Tis with the rest of our family records." Gerard disappeared.

"What?" Amice called, but there was no answer. She shook her head, gazing at the space the ghost had just inhabited. Piers was right. Madness *was* descending upon them.

She clutched the bedcovers around her and sank back onto the bed, briefly closing her eyes. What had possessed her to . . . celebrate Beltane with Cain, of all people. When she remembered how he had taken her, she cringed in embarrassment while heat rose to her cheeks. God, but it had been intoxicating. She clenched her fingers in the covers at the memory.

Cain had never been like that, so bare and unrestrained. But then he had left. Dumped her in her chamber and run.

Nothing had changed. She was a fool to think it ever would.

❧ ❧ ❧

Cain stood in the bailey flanked by Gifford and Piers, watching Agatha coo and giggle at her new husband, who gazed at her with prideful possession. At least a few things were going well. Morganna was gone and Agatha truly appeared happy.

Agatha came over and smiled at them. She looked around and asked, "Where is Amice? I wanted to say farewell."

Probably plotting how soon she can escape Falcon's Craig, Cain thought. *Escape the man who took her like some kind of animal last eve.* "I—"

"Here, Agatha," another voice interrupted. A voice that sent a surge of heat straight to his rod.

Cain took a deep breath and cautioned a look at her. Damn, but she stole his reason. She wore a deep purple silk bliaut with a lighter shade of purple undertunic, midnight hair framing her striking face. When Agatha took her hands, she smiled and Cain's stomach turned over.

"Amice, well, I hardly know what to say."

The MacKeir moved up behind Agatha and put a heavy

hand on her shoulder. He shot Cain a hard look.

"Be happy, Agatha. And you as well, Lugh."

"You are not angry with me?"

Amice chuckled and shook her head. "Nay. I am pleased for you both."

"Amice is a wise woman, Agatha," The MacKeir said. "She knows the heart will not be denied. Is that not right, Hawksdown?"

Cain resisted the urge to roll his eyes. When would the man leave? "Should you not be on your way?"

The MacKeir rumbled a laugh. "Aye." He stepped around Agatha and embraced Amice in a tight hug, whispering something to her that Cain could not hear. Amice's face paled.

Agatha hugged Piers and Gifford, then turned to Cain. "Do not let happiness elude you, Brother."

"Be well, Agatha. Send us news when you arrive at Tunvegen."

Concern clouded her eyes for a moment, then she nodded. "Farewell."

With a final jaunty wave, The MacKeir led Agatha and his troop of Highlanders out of the bailey.

"I am going to miss that man," Gifford commented. "Livened things up around here."

Cain rubbed the back of his neck. "We have enough to occupy our attention without the complication of Lugh MacKeir."

Gifford sniffed.

He *had* to do something. Something active. Every instinct in him screamed to throw Amice over his shoulder, take her to his chamber, and do all the things he dreamed of. Dreams that left him feeling increasingly restless and empty. "Piers?"

His brother stood looking at him with a mocking smile.

Did everyone have to guess his pathetic lack of control when it came to Amice? "I want to practice a new tactic The MacKeir told me about. Will you join me?"

Piers grinned. "Are you sure there is not something else you would rather be doing?"

Cain gritted his teeth. "Nay." He turned toward the training field and began walking. "Come," he called over his shoulder.

Piers chuckled as he followed Cain. "Desire swells when fulfillment is delayed."

"Shut up," Cain snapped.

Chapter 17

With every swipe of his sword, Cain felt Amice's eyes upon him. He struggled to ignore her, reminding himself that it was his duty to train, to keep his battle skills honed. Did the woman not have something better to do? Like get rid of that blasted ghost?

And it did not help that Piers wore some silly grin on his face that widened each time Cain snuck a glance over at her.

Finally, after an hour of exchanging blows and coming perilously close to losing a body part from his inability to concentrate, Cain lowered his sword. "Well? What do you want?" he barked.

Amice flinched.

Cain felt like a churl. It wasn't her fault he felt such torment every time he looked at her. Or did not look at her.

Or smelled her. Or heard her voice. Or thought about her. *Damn it*. "What is it, Amice," he tried in a calmer tone.

"I need to speak with you."

Piers immediately turned to engage one of the garrison, leaving Cain and Amice alone.

Cain studied her face but could find no hint of her intention. He sheathed his sword and walked over to her. "Very well."

Her gaze could have frozen water in fire. "Where is Gerard's journal?"

He blinked in shock. "What?" Casting his voice low, he took her arm and led her away from the men.

"His journal."

"How did you hear of a journal?"

"From Gerard."

"What did he say about it?"

"He said I should find his journal and that you know where it is." She glared at him. "Why did you not tell me of this?"

Cain rubbed the back of his neck. Was he to have no secrets? Damn these meddlesome ghosts.

"Where would it be? Gerard said the journal was with the other family records." Amice lifted her chin and Cain's stomach sank. He knew that look. She would not be put off by vague explanations.

" 'Tis a secret, known only to the earls of Hawksdown. Not even Piers knows."

Amice's eyes gleamed with curiosity. "Why is it secret?"

"Amice, I—"

"We need to find the journal." Her mouth was set. "I

shall not reveal your secret to anyone; I give you my oath."

Could he trust her? Could he afford not to? Gerard would probably show her himself if Cain did not. "Come with me."

❧ ❧ ❧

Amice walked with Cain in silence, her curiosity mounting with each step. She glanced at him and bit back a question. His face was taut, his eyes glowing, as if he kept some wildness leashed within him.

A part of her wanted to see if she could make him loosen the leash, but she sternly reminded herself to focus on her task.

They left the training field and crossed the bailey. The day was grey, the clouds low overhead, and a cool, salty breeze lifted from the sea to wash over them as they walked. Amice lifted her skirts and concentrated on keeping up with Cain's long-legged stride.

Cain said nothing but led the way into the garden and past the grove of apple trees. A huge arbor of grape vines spread across the back of the garden.

Amice blinked in astonishment when Cain took out a key, reached through the arbor and unlocked a door covered with vines.

Cain reached back and took her hand without looking at her. He pulled her through and shut the doorway.

"What is this?" Amice wrinkled her nose at the musty smell in the tiny chamber.

"Just as Gerard said. Where our family's records are kept." Cain lit a pair of candles and set them on a table.

Amice peered around her, noting the chests stacked against the walls. "Why is it secret?"

He turned then and looked at her. "For a very good reason. And it must remain so."

"I told you I would honor your wish in that regard."

Cain's jaw tightened. "Be sure that you do."

Amice looked away. "The journal must be in one of the trunks." She dropped to her knees and reached out to open the lid of the closest one.

"Not that one."

She looked up.

"They are arranged by date." He gestured to another trunk. "That would be the one from Gerard's time."

"Do you want to look?" Amice was dying to know what lay in the other trunks, but the expression on Cain's face stopped her from moving. What was he hiding?

"Aye." He opened the trunk and began pulling our bundled sheets of vellum.

Amice inched closer.

"This looks to be Gerard's," Cain said, and handed her a bundle.

Amice began reading. She was immediately entranced. "He writes of Muriel. This must be it!"

Cain shoved the rest of the books back into the trunk and clicked it shut. "What does he say?"

"How beautiful she is, how much he loves her." Amice squinted to make out the words. "How much he looks forward to being with her always." As Amice read, she felt Cain's intense gaze and sat back on her heels to continue reading.

"He . . . he writes, 'She is so beautiful, she steals the

breath from my body, so passionate, I could lie with her a thousand times and still starve for her.' " Amice stopped and swallowed, her throat suddenly dry.

" 'Tis clear from the drawings they desired each other greatly." Cain's voice was close. Too close.

Amice snapped up a look to find him nearly on top of her. She opened her mouth, but no words came out.

His eyes glittered and Cain stared at her mouth. "What else does he write?"

Amice dragged her gaze back to the journal. She sucked in a breath as a rush of heat sped to her face. "He, he says, 'My desire for her is like a fever burning in my blood. I spend each day dreaming of sinking into the sweet oblivion of her body, our hearts merging as one.' "

"Does he write anything about what happened?" Cain's voice was hoarse.

Afraid to look at him, Amice forced herself to remain focused on Gerard's writing. She feared if she saw the same hunger in Cain's eyes as she heard in his voice, she would be lost.

"Amice?"

She scanned the page and flipped to the next, skipping Gerard's lengthy reflections on the joy of mating with Muriel.

Amice stopped on the thirteenth page. "Here it is."

Cain peered over her shoulder. "He believed Elena."

"Aye. He did think Muriel disloyal. It broke his heart," she said softly. She would *not* look at Cain. "But look at this." Amice pointed to the center of the page.

" 'Even though my Muriel betrayed me, I still could not imagine life without her. But then Magda visited me and everything changed. All know of the old woman's strange powers. She sees things. And today she told me my future if I should take Muriel to wife,' " Cain read aloud.

Amice gasped.

Cain read on. " 'If I marry Muriel, I shall lose everything. That, I could accept if not for the worst part. Magda tells me that I will lose Muriel too. To death. I cannot allow that to happen, even if it means denying my own happiness. I shall send her away today.' "

"So that is the real reason he broke the betrothal," Amice breathed. She snuck a look at Cain.

He scowled at the journal. "Elena probably paid the old woman to come up with Gerard's 'future.' "

"Or Magda saw that Elena would have Muriel killed if she married Gerard."

"Mayhap."

Amice turned the page.

Out of the corner of her eye, she saw Cain stiffen. He yanked the journal from her hands, but not before Amice read the words.

When she looked at Cain, his face was bone white.

"What . . . what does he mean?"

"What are you talking about?"

She pointed to the journal. "I saw it, Cain. He says he is not really a Veuxfort, that the name and title were gained by deceit and treachery."

Cain turned a shade paler. "Amice, let it go."

"Nay." She stood and crossed her arms. "I want to read the rest of the journal."

Cain jumped to his feet, holding the journal tight against his chest. "You found what you sought."

"I do not know that. There may be more."

"You know why Gerard felt he had to give her up. That should be enough for Muriel to forgive him," Cain insisted.

Amice dropped her arms and walked forward until she was so close to Cain she could feel the heat radiate from him. "Who are you?" she asked.

For a moment, he just stared down at her, his throat working, his nostrils flared. "I am the Earl of Hawksdown."

"Cain *Veuxfort*?"

"You know my name."

"How did you come by it?"

He gave her a mocking smile. "From my sire."

"Who got it from?"

"His sire."

"Who got it from?"

"Amice. Cease."

"No, I shall *not* cease." Unreasoning fury surged in her. She had given everything to a man who concealed his very identity.

"Amice, this is not something I am free to speak of."

"I want to know who the hell you are!" she shouted. "I want to know who I gave my heart to!"

Cain froze. "Your heart?"

Amice blinked. She could not believe she had blurted that out. "Answer my question," she hissed.

He dropped the journal to the floor.

"My life is a lie," he whispered. "The real Veuxfort was foolish enough to trust a man who happened to look identical to him. A nobody, who was hard, ruthless and able with a sword. A man who decided it would be easy to become

Veuxfort and take his young bride at the same time."

Amice stared at him. "He . . . killed the real Veuxfort?"

Cain nodded. "And took his place. Anyone who raised a question disappeared."

"My God."

"Now, you understand the need for secrecy."

Amice gestured around the room. "But why keep the records at all? Why not burn them?"

"There is much in the journals besides the shame of our lineage. And no one knows of this chamber."

"Did all of the Earls of Hawksdown keep journals?"

"Aye, every one. Some are quite detailed in their description of life, our family history."

"Do *you* write in a journal?"

Cain stilled. "Yes," he admitted haltingly.

"Is it here?" God, what she would give to read Cain's journal. To know his true thoughts, his innermost feelings would be like solving a tantalizing mystery.

Cain shook his head, but his eyes shot to another trunk and Amice knew he lied.

She lunged for the trunk and threw open the lid, seizing the top journal.

Cain stood over her, bristling. "Put that back. 'Tis private."

"Are you afraid I will find out who you really are?" Amice opened the journal.

"You know who I am."

Amice stared at him. "Do I?" she asked softly. "Do I, Cain?" She dropped her gaze to the journal.

"As much as anyone." He snatched the journal from her hands and closed it.

"I wonder."

Cain tossed the journal back into the trunk. He leaned down and retrieved Gerard's journal before placing it into her hands. "Now that you know our secret, there is no reason for you not to read it." His voice was cool and impersonal.

Damn him for his controlled indifference. Amice fingered the edges of the vellum. Pain and sorrow flooded her as she looked up at Cain's set face. "Why did you leave me?"

He flinched as if she had thrust a dagger home. "I had to."

"Why?"

His gaze blanked of emotion. "The King levied a huge amercement upon us due to my father's stupidity," he bit out. "In one of his innumerable drunken binges, Father suggested to Richard that the reason he was so consumed by warring was because he preferred men to women."

Amice opened her eyes wide. "He *said* that to the King?"

"Aye. And Richard responded by fining him the sum of two hundred thousand shillings to help fund his crusade."

It was a huge sum of money. More than Wareham could spare, she was sure.

"And Mother presented me with Luce. Along with sufficient coin to pay the King and Styrling Castle, which Mother had long coveted."

"I see."

"I did my duty, Amice. 'Twas the right thing to do."

Awareness seeped into her heart, along with a profound sense of irretrievable loss. "As you do still."

"Aye." He opened the door and waited for Amice to

exit before securely locking it and smoothing the vines back into place. "As I always will."

Amice returned to her chamber in silence.

There was nothing more to say.

❦ ❦ ❦

When Amice entered her chamber, she found Hawis tidying up. "Hello, my lady."

Amice poked her head into the adjacent chamber.

"Your friend is not here."

"Do you know where Laila is?"

Hawis moved closer and dropped her voice to a whisper. "Aye, I saw her when she left." She paused and gave Amice a secretive smile. "She said her people were camped nearby, and she was going to pay them a visit."

"Oh." Amice's spirits sank further. She wished Laila had waited for her.

"Can I get you anything, my lady?"

Amice looked around, noting the ewer of wine, covered basket, and fresh bowl of water. "Nay, thank you, Hawis."

The other woman bowed and left the chamber.

Amice poured a cup of wine, settled onto the windowseat, and opened Gerard's journal.

But the words blurred until she could not see anything but the first page of Cain's journal. No wonder he had so quickly grabbed it away from her.

Tonight Amice's father came to see me. He knows everything, even my family's secret. I have

*no idea how he found out. The earl told me I must
stay away from Amice or he would expose us. He
claims to have proof. He told me I would never be
good enough for a de Monceaux, not even his use-
less daughter. The earl is a callous brute but I
know he is right. I shall never be worthy of Amice's
love. She knows it too. 'Tis why she would never
be faithful.*

A tear trickled down her cheek and she blinked. How
she hated her father. Amice knew he had not demanded
Cain leave because of his ancestry, but solely to take something away from *her*. Despair surged through her stomach
with a burning ache.

She took a sip of wine and started laughing. It was all
so tragically pathetic.

There was no way for her to prove to Cain he was
wrong. All the love in the world could not make him see
how fine a man he fundamentally was, whether noble or
peasant. No words could convince him her heart knew
him as her soulmate, and she could never give her heart to
anyone else.

Amice gazed out at the endless expanse of blue-grey
sea. She felt as if her face was frozen into a perpetual
expression of confusion. How could God allow this to
happen? How could He let her know such perfect love,
then tear it away?

She buried her face in her hands, and her laughter
turned to sobs. It was hopeless.

Amice drew a shuddering breath, lifted her head, and
put her shoulders back. She swiped the tears from her eyes

and started reading Gerard's journal.

Bring Muriel peace and get away, she told herself. It is the only thing to think about. Maybe if she were far away from Cain and exploring a new world she could find a measure of contentment, if not happiness. Maybe in time she could stop seeing his ocean eyes, banish the memory of his skin against hers, and forget the way she felt when he did no more than hold her hand.

And maybe Cain's pigs *would* fly.

❦ ❦ ❦

Cain decided to ride out to Hazelstone to check on the status of repairs and went to find Olive to accompany him. He looked in the kitchen first, where he knew she spent much time, but Malina shook her head at his question. An hour later, he had checked the garden, her chamber, his solar, and even the fishpond, but Olive was nowhere to be found.

Annoyance turned to worry, and he cautioned a visit to Gifford's chamber to see if his uncle had seen her. When he opened the door, his jaw dropped.

Olive sat cross-legged atop Gifford's table, intently wielding a mallet against some kind of pink rock. Whack! Whack! Pieces flew across the table, and Gifford scurried to gather them into a pot.

"Good job, Olive," his uncle praised.

She shot him a gamine grin, before bringing the mallet down again, her teeth worrying her lower lip.

So as not to startle her, Cain slowly walked to the table.

Olive looked up and gave him such an open smile, his heart warmed. "What are you doing, little one?"

"Helping Uncle Gifford," she announced.

"I see."

She jumped down from the table and threw her skinny arms around his waist. "Where have you been, Lancelot?"

Cain rubbed her back and looked over at Gifford who was sweeping pink fragments from the table. His uncle lifted his brows. "Lancelot?"

"Aye," Olive answered, as she hopped around the table to help Gifford. "My mother always told me stories about a brave knight called Lancelot who was a true and valiant hero."

"Hmm," Gifford answered. "And do you see my nephew as a hero?"

"Oh, yes." Olive's face drew into a fierce look. "He killed that bad man who murdered my mother, you know. Chopped his head right off," she added, wide-eyed.

Cain frowned. "Where did you hear that?"

Olive shrugged. "Everyone knows how fearless and strong you were." She turned her big, round brown eyes on him and Cain felt as if he really could be a hero. "I tried to explain that to the lady, but she would not listen."

Cain prayed "the lady" was not who he feared, but he had a strong feeling she was. "What lady?"

Olive tilted her head. "The one with the pretty red hair. She is not very nice, though."

For a moment Cain was not sure what to say.

Gifford put a hand on Olive's shoulder. "That lady is not real."

Olive nodded gravely. "Aye, I know. She told me she was a spirit named Muriel." Olive said it as if encountering a ghost was not particularly strange.

"What did Muriel say to you?" Cain asked.

She wrinkled her nose. "She said you wanted to drive her out but she would not leave." Olive plucked at the fabric of her little bliaut. "I told her she should be in heaven like my mother, but she said she could not go yet."

"Did she say why?"

"Nay." Olive walked over and put her thin hand in his. "She kind of faded away then. I have not seen her since."

Thank God for that, Cain thought. He would see Olive spared Muriel's bitter truths. He squeezed her hand. "I was going to ride over to Hazelstone. Do you wish to come with me?"

Olive jumped up and down, yelling, "Yea!"

Cain chuckled. "I assume that is a yes."

"Yes! I can see Nona. I miss her."

Cain crouched down so his face was at Olive's level. "Are you happy here, or would you rather I find a place for you in the village?"

She threw her arms around his neck and planted a big kiss on his cheek. "I want to stay with you."

To his surprise, Cain felt tears burn the backs of his eyes. In a short time, his little Olive had become an important part of his life. "Good." He stood and took her hand.

Gifford gazed at him with a thoughtful expression.

"What?" Cain asked.

His uncle hung the pot over a fire. "The child is good for you. You should have some of your own."

Cain sensed Olive wilt a bit, and he pulled her close. "Olive *is* my own, now."

She brightened.

Gifford crossed his arms. "You know what I mean."

"As always, Uncle, I appreciate your counsel."

"Where is the Lady Amice?"

"I know," Olive said. "She is in her chamber reading. Hawis told me." Her mouth turned down and she gazed up at Cain. "Do you think Lady Amice would teach *me* to read?"

"She will not be here long, sweeting."

Gifford loudly cleared his throat.

"But I shall be happy to teach you," Cain added, ignoring his uncle.

"You will?"

"Aye."

"Thank you, Lancelot."

Cain grinned at her. "Shall we be off, my lady fair?"

Olive giggled. "Aye. Maybe we shall come across the Rom's camp. I should love to see their wagons."

"The Rom's camp?"

"Aye. Hawis told me they were near. Lancelot, can I have my fortune told?"

She looked so hopeful Cain hated to deny her. "Sweeting, you know no one can really predict your future."

Gifford cleared his throat again.

Cain gave him a stern look.

"But it would be fun," Olive insisted.

"We shall see," Cain said. "But for now, let us check on Hazelstone. You can play with Nona while I see how the rebuilding progresses."

Olive pulled him out of the workroom, skipping in her excitement.

Chapter 18

Amice closed Gerard's journal as Laila entered the chamber. Her friend's gaze was bright, her mouth curved into a slight smile. "Did you see Milosh?" Amice teased.

"Aye. He is as much a rogue as always and sends his love." Laila sat down beside her and pointed to the journal. "What is that?"

"Gerard's journal. I have been reading it."

"And?"

" 'Tis a sad tale." Amice set the journal aside and poured a cup of wine, swirling the liquid around in her mouth.

"We guessed as much."

"He *did* love her, that is apparent." Amice looked out the window. "But he hurt her anyway."

Laila reached out and squeezed Amice's shoulder. "Does he say why?"

Amice nodded. "He claims a woman told him his fortune. She told Gerard if he married Muriel he would lose everything, and Muriel would lose her life."

"Who told him that? What was her name?"

"Magda. Have you heard of her?"

Laila jumped up and retrieved her string of polished, blue stones, which she fingered as if to soothe herself. "Aye. There are stories about a woman called Magda. Tales of a great seer."

"So it *was* true."

"Perhaps. But a person's future is never fully predestined."

"Cain thinks 'tis more likely that Elena paid this Magda to convince Gerard."

"Aye, he would think that. He would not believe in something like the ability to see through time."

Amice looked down at the journal. "There is more."

"Something to help us?"

"One thing. Gerard claims Elena is the one who stole Muriel's necklace. When he discovered it, he hid it in their secret chamber."

"Hmm. From what we have learned of this Elena, that makes sense." Laila shook her head and crossed herself. "A wicked woman."

Amice took a deep breath. She would not tell Laila of Cain's ancestor's evil deed. But there was something more she found in the journal. Another link between her and the Veuxforts. "After Muriel's death, Gerard ensured he had a son, then left Falcon's Craig."

"Left? But Muriel said nothing of that."

"He was gone two years, traveling first toward the Holy Land and eventually seeking out what remained of his ancestral family."

Amice ran a finger down the journal. "He stopped in Italy, Laila. He loved it so much he stayed for months." She lifted her gaze. "You should read his descriptions. It truly sounds like paradise."

"Why did he leave?"

"He grew curious about what had happened to the family of . . . Harding Veuxfort. And when he finally found what was left of them, they were barely surviving."

"What did he do?"

"He brought them back here and settled them in Hazelstone."

"I imagine Elena did not approve of that."

Amice shook her head. "According to Gerard, she was furious that he would associate in any way with such 'filthy peasants.'"

"What happened then?"

"The journal ends."

Laila frowned. " 'Tis odd he would stop so suddenly."

"Aye. Perhaps there is another book somewhere." She bit her lip, wishing she could share with Laila the amazing secret chamber she had seen.

"Laila, I think with all we have learned, we can free Muriel from this place."

Her friend sat and gave Amice an intent stare. "What shall you do when we have succeeded, *te' sorthene*?"

A sliver of pain broke free of its bonds to swirl through her belly. She resolutely pushed it down. "Return to

Wareham for a time. When Mother . . . passes on, I shall go to Villa Delphino. Live where the sun shines nearly all the time, the air is warm, and the sea is turquoise blue."

"Are you sure 'tis the right course? I thought perhaps now that Morganna is gone—"

"Nay," Amice said softly. " 'Twould be better if there was a great distance between me and Cain Veuxfort. I have finally accepted that."

Laila nodded, but her eyes held doubt. "As you wish."

"Will you go with me?"

"I shall stay with you until you find your destiny."

"My destiny is in Italy."

Laila stood. "Perhaps." She turned toward the door. "I need to deliver some mugwort I promised to Gifford."

Amice watched her friend leave and forced herself to make a list of what she would need when she finally left England. They would need passage on a ship. Horses, food, clothing, furniture. So many things to consider.

Could she really do it? Leave all she knew? Was she brave enough? Desperate enough?

Aye, she was.

❧ ❧ ❧

In the late afternoon, Cain rode back into the bailey of Falcon's Craig to find Laila waiting for him. He slowed his mount as he approached her and dismounted with a sleeping Olive cuddled against his chest. "What is it?"

She flattened her palms against her skirts. "My lord, I am concerned about Amice."

"Where is she?"

"I do not know. She went out for a ride earlier today and has not returned." Laila looked up at the dull, grey sky. "She should be back by now."

"Do you know where she intended to ride?"

"She said along the coast."

Cain frowned. "Who went with her?"

"She went alone, my lord."

"What?" Cain's voice roused Olive, and she rubbed her eyes. In a calmer tone, he asked, "What was she thinking?"

Laila gave him a hard look. "Amice said she needed the fresh air to clear her thoughts. She insisted on going alone."

"What is wrong?" Olive asked in a sleepy voice.

"There is a storm headed in," Cain said to Laila.

"I know."

Cain handed Olive to Laila and started toward the stable. "I need a fresh horse."

"You will go after her?"

"Aye." He led his mount into the stable and found Piers emerging from one of the stalls holding a bucket full of oats. "Which of your horses is the fastest?"

Piers stopped and leaned against the door to a stall. A horse pushed its head over the top and nudged his shoulder. "Pagan, now that his leg splints are healed. Why?"

"Amice is out there somewhere," Cain bit out. "Alone. And Laila says she has been gone too long."

"Do you want me to go with you?"

"Nay, just help me saddle Pagan."

Within a few moments, the stallion was saddled and prancing, picking up on Cain's sense of urgency. Cain leapt on his back and grabbed the reins. "If the storm is as bad as it looks to be, we may have to seek shelter until morning."

Piers lifted a brow.

Cain slapped Pagan's rump, and they thundered out of the stable. Once across the drawbridge, Cain turned north and rode close to the cliff over the shoreline, scanning the countryside for any sign of Amice. A long, vast emptiness stretched out before him as he and Pagan galloped atop the sparse grass.

Low clouds moved in, masking the sky in a grey fog. The scent of the sea was strong, the waves cresting in white before smashing against the sand and rocks below.

Where was she?

How could she be so foolish as to ride out alone? And why not return when it became clear a storm was moving in?

He leaned down against Pagan, urging the horse to speed.

How far would she have gone?

Far enough to escape you, his inner voice mocked. You know why she felt compelled to leave Falcon's Craig without a guard. You know why she remains outside despite the approaching rain. 'Tis because you drove her out.

A few drops of rain struck his face, and Cain reined in to look at the sky. Over the ocean, dark grey clouds roiled and the wind blew in gusts, scuttling the clouds across the sky and lifting his hair. Cain watched as the rain moved onto shore, then turned back to drive Pagan forward once more.

Rain pelted him as he rode, the few drops turning to heavy sheets. Mist rose from the grass and the sky darkened to slate. He peered through the veil of water for Amice.

"Amice!" he yelled. "Where are you?"

There was no answer but the moan of the wind.

"Damn it," Cain swore. He turned inland and rode toward the hills. Where was she?

The ground dipped and rolled, the grass turning slick beneath Pagan's hooves. Cain slowed the horse and looked around. It was strangely still. Wreaths of mist and fog carpeted the grass and obscured the trees.

"Amice!" he hollered.

Then he heard it. A voice, somewhere ahead. He kicked Pagan and galloped forward, his heart clenching in relief when he finally saw her.

She was on foot. Her bliaut was soaked to her skin, her hair slicked back from her face.

He jumped off Pagan and ran to her. "Are you all right?"

Amice nodded tiredly, but as she took a step forward, her face tightened and she stumbled.

Cain caught her shoulders and steadied her. "What happened?"

"My horse took a fright when she saw a wolf and threw me, before running off. I did something to my ankle."

Cain bent down and ran his hands up her ankle. It was swollen. "You should not have been out by yourself."

Amice did not say anything.

"You will ride back with me," he said. But just as he took Amice's arm, lightning cracked across the sky in a blinding, jagged arc, and Pagan reared up with a scream. Cain ran forward, but another bolt of lightning crackled and Pagan took off at a gallop before Cain could catch the reins.

He stood watching the horse flee and let out a long curse. They were leagues from Falcon's Craig, and Amice should not be walking on her ankle.

As he considered their options, Amice limped past him. He caught her arm. "What are you doing?"

She looked at him as if he were addlepated. "Walking back to Falcon's Craig."

"You cannot walk all the way to the castle on that ankle."

"Yes, I can." She took a couple of steps forward, her mouth drawn into a thin line, her gaze focused.

"Pagan will return to Falcon's Craig. Someone will come to find us."

"I am not waiting out here in the rain." She shoved a wet tangle of hair from her face and kept walking.

Cain caught up with her. "At least lean on me to take weight off your ankle."

"I am fine."

The rain came down so heavily, it seemed as if they were caught in some kind of isolated waterworld. Mud sucked at Cain's boots, and he could not see far in front of him.

Amice sailed on as if she were taking a stroll in a sun-lit garden.

"Let me help you," he repeated.

"I do not need your help."

"Damn it, Amice, you do not have to do everything on your own."

She glared at him. "Aye, I do. I always do."

"Sometimes, you need to depend on someone else."

Amice laughed in his face. "Like you? Surely, you jest."

Her jibe struck him in the gut and Cain sucked in a breath. "You cannot bring yourself to depend on any man, can you?"

"No. Why should I?"

"Give me your arm," he ordered.

"Nay."

"Why do you have to be so stubborn?"

"Why do you have to be so controlled?"

Cain rubbed the back of his neck. " 'Tis safer," he admitted.

"Easier," she sneered.

"Aye."

Amice stepped forward and gave a cry before she went down to the ground. She knelt on the grass and closed her eyes.

Cain squatted beside her and waited for her to look at him.

"I do not like to be dependent on anyone," she finally said. "I cannot. You are right."

"But sometimes you do *need* someone. I understand why I am the last person you would wish to rely on. But I am the only person here and you need help." He reached out.

Slowly, Amice took his hand and let him pull her to her feet. He took her arm, wrapping his own around her waist. Amice stared straight ahead.

They moved forward, making slow progress as Amice

half walked, half hopped along. Night was falling and a cool breeze floated in from the sea.

Amice shivered. "I shall be happy where the days are warm and sunny," she said softly.

Cain stiffened. "Amice, you cannot be serious about leaving England to live in Italy."

"Why not?"

" 'Tis madness. A woman has no business going on such a journey alone. You should be content to stay at home."

He knew he had made a mistake when she narrowed her eyes and glared at him, before attempting to pull away. "It is not your affair, Cain."

"You barely know anything about this place, other than some story your brother told you."

"As well as *your* ancestor's journal."

Cain drew his brows together. "What are you talking about?"

"Gerard's journal. After Muriel died and he sired a son, he left Falcon's Craig and ended up for a time on the Italian coast."

"How long was he gone?"

"Two years in total."

"I wonder why he came back."

"He traced his true origins and brought his blood relations back to settle at Hazelstone. But then, the journal ends."

Cain stared at her in astonishment. "Do you mean I am related to some of the villagers?"

"Aye."

"Olive," he said.

" 'Twould explain the strong bond between you."

Cain shook his head to clear it. "All of that is interesting, but still, you cannot think to live at the villa. What will you do there?"

She stiffened her lips. "Whatever I wish. Leave be, Cain."

"Am I so abhorrent to you that you must run so far?"

When she looked at him, there were tears in her eyes. "You can never let it go, can you? You have to push and prod and peel away the layers."

" 'Tis my way. And I am not ashamed that I seek the truth."

"Do you, Cain? What about the truth from yourself?"

"What?"

Amice prodded him in the chest. "The truth about what you really want in life. When you take away duty, the important image of the Earl of Hawksdown, what is left?"

"I do not know what you mean."

At his words, her expression turned to bleak sadness. "Nay, you do not, and that is the shame of it."

"Amice, I—"

Out of the grey rain and fog emerged a group of horses led by Piers. "Cain!" he shouted. Behind him rode a troop of men from the garrison, one leading Pagan by the reins.

He heard Amice's sigh of relief before she stepped away from him. She stumbled a bit, but when he reached for her, she managed to elude his hand.

"Stubborn," he muttered.

Piers jumped down and wrapped a mantle around Amice. "Are you all right?"

"My ankle is twisted."

Cain vaulted onto Pagan and nudged the horse to where Amice stood in the rain. "Lift her up. She rides with me."

Before Amice could protest, Piers lifted her onto Pagan.

Cain wrapped his arm around her and drew her close.

She pulled the hood of the mantle down over her face.

✿ ✿ ✿

While Amice rested in her chamber, Cain met with Nyle and tried to pay attention to his seneschal's report. "How many of the barley fields are planted?"

"All." Nyle looked down at a diagram. "And we are nearly finished with the wheat, oats, peas, and beans."

"Good." Cain opened his mouth, then snapped it shut as Gifford barreled through the door, Piers following close behind him. His uncle, naturally, carried a jug of wine with him and careened to a stop before Cain's worktable without acknowledging Nyle's presence.

"Want to talk to you." Gifford took a gulp of wine and wiped his mouth.

"Uncle Gifford, can it wait? Nyle and I are going over the progress of the planting." *At least Nyle is going over it, and I am trying without success to listen,* Cain thought.

"Nay." Gifford took a stool and gazed at Cain expectantly. " 'Tis *important.*"

"It always is." His uncle's visit reminded him of when Gifford and Piers came to ask about Amice.

"Would you like to finish later, my lord?" Nyle asked.

"I can take the time to check on the harrowing."

"Very well. We shall meet on the morrow at sext."

Nyle gathered up his records and nodded before walking out.

Piers took his seat and reached for Gifford's jug. "Amice's horse made it back to the stable."

Cain frowned. "Was there anything wrong with the horse?"

"Nay."

"Amice said a wolf scared her."

Gifford grabbed back the jug. "I do not want to talk about poor Amice's accident."

"What is it, Gifford? More supplies for your experiments?"

His uncle wagged a finger at him. "I know better than to ask *you* to get me what I need. No, this is about something even more pressing than finding the great Merlin."

Cain raised a brow. "It must be very critical, indeed."

Piers crossed his arms and grinned at Cain.

"Marriage," Gifford announced.

Oh, no. "Gifford, we have had this discussion before."

"Different now. Amice is no longer betrothed."

Piers leaned forward. "And 'tis obvious you want her."

Want her. Want was too mild a word for the way he felt toward Amice. Maybe craved, or ached for with an intensity that would not be controlled. Cain rubbed the back of his neck. "I do not deny my desire for Amice."

Gifford tossed back a drink and fixed Cain with a disapproving stare. "You belittle the girl. 'Tis not 'desire' you feel, and you know it."

"Oh, but it certainly is."

"Not only that."

"Uncle Gifford, let it be."

"Are you going to let her leave? Travel to some far-away land? Where you will never see her again?"

Pain sliced through his chest at the thought. "I—"

"Can do the right thing by her now," Piers commented. "There is no amercement to pay, Mother is long dead, and you are free to *choose* a wife."

Cain blinked at him. The right thing.

"Think of it as doing your *duty*," Gifford said, unable to completely hide his smile.

"Aye," Piers added. "After all, you did dally with her, then marry another. Not right, that. And if not for you demanding she come here, her betrothed would never have met Agatha. Amice would be married to The MacKeir."

Gifford set down the jug and clapped his hands. "Right. When you look at it that way, 'tis the only thing to do. Offer for her. Give her a home to take charge of."

Piers took the jug. "Olive would love a babe to help take care of."

Cain looked back and forth between Gifford and Piers and a wall within him gave way.

The hell of it was they were both right. He had the chance to make something up to Amice.

Perhaps he could marry her then spend more of his time traveling to his other manors rather than sending Nyle or his assistants.

Or maybe he could stay right here and spend every night learning new ways to pleasure Amice. A bead of sweat coursed down his back.

"Well?" Gifford barked. "What are you going to do?"

Cain stared at him and a strangely wonderful feeling unfurled in his chest. "Offer for her."

❧ ❧ ❧

The morning after her accident, Amice looked at Cain in complete bewilderment. "What did you say?"

"Marry me." He stood absolutely still, his gaze unreadable.

"Why?"

Cain gave a dry laugh. "Are you wanting some great proclamation of love?"

Yes, Amice wanted to scream. *Of course, that is what I want.* She crossed her arms. "I do not understand. Why ask me to marry you now?"

"As Gifford and Piers continually remind me, 'tis my duty to take a wife."

Amice's heart sank. "Is there naught for you but duty?"

He took a step closer. "We desire each other," he said softly. "That part of our marriage will be good."

"And the rest?"

Cain shrugged. "Amice, I do feel badly about how things ended between us before. And if I had not asked you to come to Falcon's Craig to oust Muriel, The MacKeir would not have come here either. You would be securely married by now."

"I see." Amice felt as if her chest was slowly cracking open like an eggshell, her heart oozing out onto the floor. "You feel responsible for my unmarried state."

"Aye." He rubbed the back of his neck.

"I made my own choices, Cain."

"But—"

"The answer is no. I shall not marry you."

Cain looked at her as if she had lost her wits. "What?"

"I will not marry you."

"Why not? 'Tis a good offer." He gestured to her chamber. "Falcon's Craig is a fine castle now. I have ample coin to indulge you." He glanced at her. "But I will insist on your loyalty."

Rage ripped through Amice's blood with such force, she half expected it to erupt in thunderbolts from her fingertips. He spoke as if he made her some kind of business proposition. A partnership of sorts, with an untrustworthy spouse. "I told you. I am going to Italy."

"To live alone?" he asked incredulously.

"Perhaps. Or maybe I shall find one of the Italian men to my liking."

Cain's face blanched. "You cannot be serious."

"Why not? The Italians are rumored to be a handsome people."

"Amice, do not do this."

She walked over until their faces nearly touched and glared at him. "How dare you ask me to marry you like this? As if it were no more than the fulfillment of another duty."

"I did not mean to make it sound like that," he said stiffly.

"Aye, you did. And do you know why?"

"Why?"

"Because you are still hiding," she spat. "You want the truth from everyone else but not from yourself. You run from yourself and hide behind duty and responsibility. What do *you* want?"

His jaw wrenched. "You, damn it. I want you."

"You want to have me in your bed," she said softly. "I know that."

"Or out of the bed. Anywhere I can," he answered just as softly.

"Even though you do not trust me."

Cain just looked at her.

"Even though you cannot bring yourself to say you love me."

He said nothing.

"Even though you will not admit your life is empty without me."

Cain gazed down at her, his eyes unfathomable pools of blue. "I said I want you. That should be enough."

Amice gave a bitter laugh. "It is not enough for me." She walked back across the chamber and gazed out the window. "My answer is no."

"I am not the only one who runs, Amice." Cain left without another word.

❦ ❦ ❦

Amice held herself rigid until she heard the door shut behind Cain. Her whole body shook, and she could only breathe in short, shallow gasps.

How could he do this? How could he be so damned indifferent? She could not understand it. She never would.

Marry me, he had said. God, once she would have

given everything in the world to hear those two words. Had thought she *would* hear them, had created the joyful picture in her mind over and over.

But not phrased as duty. Or as simple lust. And how could she be with him when Cain still did not trust her?

Amice bowed her head and clenched the material of her bliaut in her fists. Damn him. She tried to tell herself to be strong, to accept what could never be, but her heart would not allow it. Cain had finally broken through her defensive walls, and it was as if flaming oil seared deep, wounding and scarring as it went.

"It is all quite ironic, you must admit," a voice said.

"Aye," Amice whispered in a broken voice, before turning to face Muriel.

The spirit floated closer. "Veuxfort men are incredibly stupid. They destroy any chance they have at true happiness."

"So it seems."

"Unfortunate for the women who love them."

Amice stared at Muriel, feeling more depleted than she ever had in her life. She sat on the windowseat. "Why do you stay, then?"

Muriel glided over and sat beside her. "For the same reason you came here. Beyond hope, beyond prayers, beyond any realistic chance, I hope one day Gerard will know himself, will know his heart and that it belongs to me." She gave Amice a sad smile. " 'Tis pathetic, I know."

"But Muriel, I am not so sure of that. You should talk to him."

"I cannot. He destroyed me in life. I cannot give him

the opportunity to do the same in death."

" 'Tis the only way to free yourself from this," Amice gestured around the chamber, "empty existence."

"Free myself? You are a fine one to give advice on the matter."

"I—"

"Just refused marriage to the man you love because of *pride*." Muriel lifted her hands and gold shimmers spilled from her fingertips. "How can you possibly think to free me when you cannot free *yourself*?"

Amice watched as Muriel faded away. So, it had come to this. She was receiving advice first from Lugh MacKeir, and now from a ghost. She was going mad.

For they were both right.

Chapter 19

Cain stormed into Gifford's workroom and slammed the door. Gifford's and Piers's heads snapped up with identical expressions of surprise.

"Oh, no," Piers said.

"Damned right," Cain snarled. He spotted the pink crystal in Gifford's hand and pointed to it. "And forget your elixirs, old man. I have had enough!"

"What did you do?" Gifford asked before calmly smashing the rock.

Cain rubbed the back of his neck and paced across the chamber. "Offered to marry Amice."

Piers beamed a smile at him.

"She refused," he snapped. God, he still could not believe it. Thanks to these two and their scheming, he had made a fool of himself once again.

Gifford got out another jar holding some dried green substance. "Why?"

"She says she is going to Italy." He smashed a fist down onto the table. "Damn it!"

"How did you ask her?"

Cain glowered at his uncle. "I said, 'marry me.' 'Twas plain enough."

"Did you tell her you love her?" Piers asked.

"Nay."

Gifford rolled his eyes. "Well, then, of course she said no. A woman needs to hear she is loved."

"When did *you* become an expert on women?"

"I told my Marna every day until she died that I loved her. You have to say the words in your heart, boy."

Piers sat on the edge of the table and crossed his arms. "A man may desire a woman, but a woman desires the desire of a man."

"What the hell does that mean?"

"It means she needs to know what she means to you, simpkin."

"Next, you will have me writing poetry."

Piers cocked his head. "Not a bad idea, but I doubt your ability."

"It is done. I let you two talk me into this, and she said no. That is it. I do not want to hear any more talk from either of you about Amice. Understood?"

"Went about it all wrong," Gifford muttered.

Piers gazed at him and shook his head, his mouth turning down. "You probably told her you felt it was your duty."

Cain gritted his teeth. "I do."

"Oh, for God's sake," Gifford swore.

"Life is more than duty, Cain."

" 'Tis easy for you, Piers. *You* are not the earl. *You* do not have charge of Falcon's Craig and the safety of our people. You play with your horses and women. *I* have responsibilities."

His brother's face looked as if Cain had struck him. "You *are* a fool," Piers finally said. "You do not deserve a woman like Amice." He popped off the table and went out.

Cain felt like the worst of churls. "I should not have said that," he murmured.

Gifford dumped the pink pieces into a pot already holding ground herbs. "Aye, you should not have. Piers is a good boy. He wants the best for you." His uncle gave him a sad look. "As I do." He shook his head. "But you keep mucking it up."

"He is right, you know. I do not deserve Amice." Cain turned and left.

❧ ❧ ❧

That afternoon, Amice packed her trunks. Tomorrow she was leaving this place, Villa Delphino or no. She would just find another way to find her paradise. As she tossed in a pale yellow bliaut, Laila walked in.

"Are we leaving?"

Amice put in a chemise and pressed the stack flat. "Aye. On the morrow. We shall try one more time with Muriel."

Laila put her arms around Amice and hugged her.

" 'Twill be all right, *te' sorthene*."

"I need to return to Mother."

"Aye." Laila rubbed her back. "Lady Eleanora's journey to the other side comes soon."

"I fear you are right."

Laila smiled brightly. "And then you shall go on your adventure to this Villa Delphino."

Amice blinked back a tear. "Yes. Where the sun and warmth shall soothe my heart."

"I stopped in to see Gifford on my way here."

"He told you about Cain?"

"Aye. I am sorry."

Amice just shook her head, tears welling up in her eyes and spilling down her cheeks in a torrent. She could not seem to stop, and Laila clucked in concern. " 'Twas terrible, Laila," she finally managed to choke out. "He looked at me, and there was nothing in his eyes at all. Nothing."

"I do not understand these *gadje*."

"Apparently, neither do I." Amice drew in a shuddering breath and wiped her eyes. "I am going to bathe. Can you find Hawis and ask her to send food and drink later?"

"Of course."

"I cannot bear to sit next to Cain at supper this eve."

"I understand. I shall stay here with you. And after we dine, we shall contact Muriel and send her on her way."

Laila sounded so determined, Amice had to smile. "I pray you are right."

When Laila looked at her, there was an odd glint in her eyes. "I am."

As Amice prepared for that eve's attempt to summon Muriel, she made herself list all the things she needed to do before leaving Falcon's Craig. See her three trunks loaded. Make sure Hawis packed sufficient food to last them four days. Inform Thomas of their imminent departure so he could ensure the horses and men were ready. It would be difficult to manage, but they would.

On the morrow, she would leave. Amice knew Cain was right. She was running. From him, but also from herself. From her own weakness. Cain sapped all will from her with just a look.

He did not understand. To him, it was a simple matter. He would remain the Earl of Hawksdown no matter how many times he joined his body with hers. But for her, the risk was too high. Perhaps it would be a gradual thing, but over time she would be consumed by him, a slave to her emotions, her abiding need for him. His simple presence engulfed her free will.

She had to get away from Cain before she crumbled like a dry fall leaf.

❦ ❦ ❦

Amice knelt in the center of a ring of candles arranged in the pattern of a five-point star. Between Laila and her was a tall, fat candle scented with myrrh.

Like spectators at a tournament, Cain, Gifford, and Piers stood along one wall. Amice glanced over at them. Gifford fairly quivered with excitement. Piers gave her a supportive look.

Cain, of course, bore an impassive expression, his legs braced apart, his arms crossed.

The candlelight wavered and moonbeams shifted

across the tower floor with the night wind.

Amice held out her hands, palms up. *"Togaidh mise chlach, Mar a thog Moire da Mac—"*

In a bright flash of gold and green, Muriel appeared. " 'Tis not necessary to go to all this trouble," she said with impatience. "If it pleases me, I shall appear to you, and if it does not, no amount of incantations shall bring me to you."

Amice sat back on her heels. "You *must* talk to Gerard," she said softly.

Muriel's shape gleamed and she narrowed her green gaze. "Why?"

"I found his journal."

"What interest is that to me?" Muriel floated closer to the candle star.

"He writes of you. There is much you do not know. Reasons for his actions."

"What difference does it make? He wronged me, no matter his reasons. Shamed me. Cleaved my heart into so many pieces it could never be made whole. And all the while looking at me with blank eyes, as if it meant naught to him."

Amice tried to find the right words to convince Muriel, but in truth she was right. Amice felt the same. Why *should* Muriel listen to Gerard?

Then the answer struck her. Because Muriel *needed* to. Because she *wanted* to forgive Gerard.

And, after all, Muriel *was* dead.

"Cease this foolishness, Lady Amice," Muriel mocked. "Run away to your pretty villa and forget about the Veuxforts and the tragedy they wreak."

Amice stood. "Nay."

Muriel turned her gaze on Cain. "Why not give the girl the villa? Set her free."

Cain's jaw clenched. "You know why."

"Aye, I do." Muriel's expression was smug. "What think you, Cain? Should I let Gerard tell me his story? Explain why he destroyed me?"

Cain looked only at Amice. "Aye. What is the cost of that?"

"Greater than you can imagine," Muriel whispered.

"He still loves you," Laila said.

Amice's face burned and she looked away from Cain. For a moment, she thought Muriel would disappear, but her image fluttered and remained.

"Then let him be brave enough to face me," Muriel snapped.

"Mayhap if you promise not to curse him this time?" Cain suggested.

"I make no promises. Either he is courageous enough, or not. This is the only chance I shall give him."

Amice's breath lodged in her throat as a glimmer of blue slowly transformed into the spirit of Gerard Veuxfort. He stared at Muriel with a sort of wonderment.

"I have missed you," he said.

Muriel blinked. She pointed at Amice. "The girl claims you have something you wish to say to me."

"Aye, love, I do. Will you listen?"

"I have said I will."

Amice looked from Muriel to Gerard then back again. Even though she had brought two spirits together before, it had never been like this. It was as if the very air held itself still as the two old spirits faced each other across the expanse of a chamber. As if time paused.

Gerard drifted a bit closer to Muriel. "I am so sorry for everything, Muriel. I was a stupid fool."

"Aye, you were stupid."

"I did not see Elena's black heart. She tricked me."

"Because you would not believe in me. Believe in the strength of our love."

"You are right." Gerard hung his head, then lifted his gaze to Muriel's. "I was wrong. I made a terrible mistake."

"I lost our child," Muriel responded, her voice anguished. "Our daughter."

Gerard closed his eyes. When he opened them, there were tears on his face.

Amice sucked in a breath. She had never known a spirit to shed tears. Laila stood and took Amice's hand.

"God, Muriel, I never knew." Gerard shook his head. "The pathetic part of it all is that I broke the betrothal to *save* you."

Muriel moved a few feet toward Gerard. "What do you mean? Save me from what?"

"Death." Gerard took a step forward. "The old witch, Magda, she told me if I married you, you would die."

"What?"

Gerard nodded. "That is the real reason I did not marry you." He held out his hands. "It killed a part of me, my love. The best part. Aye, I married Elena, but I never loved her. I could never love a woman other than you. And when you jumped to your death…" He broke off and scrunched up his face. " There was nothing left for me."

Muriel inched closer, and Amice held her breath.

"I did my duty for the Veuxfort line and left Falcon's Craig. I became a wanderer for a time."

"I know you left."

"Aye. I only came back to see to my family. My *real* family." He waved a hand. "But that is another story."

"Did you order my gravestone?"

"Nay."

Muriel dimmed a touch.

"I *made* it myself. I found the stone. I carved the words with my own hands. And I carried it to the place I chose to bury you."

Muriel put a hand to her mouth.

"I love you." Gerard reached out a hand. "Be with me forever, my love."

"But . . . what of my necklace? Why did you take it from me? Give it to *her*?"

Gerard's expression grew fierce. "I did *not* take it from you. That bitch, Elena, stripped it from your body without my knowing. She actually dared to wear it in front of me." His lips twisted. "I yanked it from her neck and put it in our chamber." He shook his head. "I am sorry."

Amice squeezed Laila's hand as Muriel slowly lifted her hand. She placed it in Gerard's and they glowed bright, blending together like two fires becoming one.

Muriel turned to Amice with a smile on her face. "Thank you."

"You are most welcome. May God keep you."

"And you, my lady."

In a whoosh, both spirits disappeared.

"They are gone," Laila said.

Amice fastened her gaze on Cain. "Give me Villa Delphino."

He reached inside his tunic and drew out a rolled piece of vellum.

Amice stepped over the candles and held out her hand.

Without a word, Cain gave her the document.

Amice turned and left.

❧ ❧ ❧

The next day, Cain watched Amice and her companions ride out of the bailey and felt as if his lifeblood slowly seeped out of his veins into the dirt.

She had really left. Gone with no more than a cursory farewell.

Gifford shuffled up beside him. "Damned disappointed in you, boy. Thought you were smarter than this."

Cain could not find it in himself to rebuff his uncle. "Where is Piers?"

"*Playing* with his horses, no doubt." Gifford let out a loud huff. "Should have told her how you feel."

"How is that, Uncle?" Cain lashed out. "You seem to know me better than I know myself."

"That I do," Gifford replied with a frown. "And if you would be honest with yourself, you would see I am right. Forget about what you *should* do for a moment, who you *should* be. Look inside yourself for once! Think about who you *are*, what you truly *want*."

"Peace. Prosperity. And I finally have that."

Gifford just shook his head. "Head like a rock," he murmured and walked away.

Cain climbed to the battlements and watched Amice depart. He set his jaw and reminded himself of all he needed to do. On the morrow was court day. Now that Agatha had departed for Tunvegen, a visit to Styrling Castle was overdue.

Amice looked over her shoulder toward the castle, and Cain's heart pounded. Would she turn back? He half opened his mouth to speak, then realized there was no way she could hear him. Cain slowly lifted a hand.

She turned back around and urged her mount to a gallop. Within a few minutes, she was gone from view.

And Cain finally saw the clear truth. Gifford was absolutely right. He *was* a stupid fool. He had made terrible, irrevocable mistakes, much like his ancestor. Had thrown aside the woman of his heart.

But there, the similarity between their situations parted. For it was obvious Muriel had loved Gerard with everything she had. Still loved him even after he betrayed her. Remained a spirit trapped at Falcon's Craig by her love for him.

Amice could not run away from *him* fast enough. If she had loved him once, it was gone now. And he had only himself to blame.

He had killed any feelings Amice might have held for him by his own blind stupidity, his devotion to duty.

It was as he told Gifford. He did not deserve Amice. He never had. He was lucky that for a time she did not realize it.

She surely did now.

❧ ❧ ❧

Four days later, Amice wearily dragged herself into the hall at Wareham. God, she was happy to be home. The journey from Falcon's Craig had seemed to take forever, every step haunted by the sight of Cain standing alone on the battlements watching her leave.

Pain snapped through her chest, and Amice made a fist. She would *not* cry. She would not give in to the bleak hopelessness that invaded her soul.

Rand burst into the hall and rushed over to her. He took her hands, his face drawn into lines of sorrow. "Amice, thank God you are here."

She looked dully at him.

"It is Mother. She is barely hanging on, keeps asking for you."

Sharp pain turned to an overwhelming ache. Rand took her arm. "Come."

Amice let him tug her out of the hall and across the bailey to the south tower. She felt as if a turbulent wave of emotion carried her, helpless to do aught but keep her head above water. As she followed Rand up the narrow stone steps, she struggled to gather her strength, her composure. Something deep within her had begun unraveling upon her departure from Falcon's Craig, and she could not seem to weave the threads back together.

They reached the door to her mother's chamber, and Rand paused. "She is not well," he said softly. "Her mind, well, you will see. She is nearly gone."

Though she knew her mother faded with each day, Amice had held out the hope that somehow her mother would find renewed strength. She nodded. "I understand, Rand."

But when they entered the chamber and Amice saw her mother, she realized she did not understand at all. She walked to her parent's bedside. "Mother?"

Her mother's eyes fluttered open. She stared at Amice as if she did not know who she was.

Fighting back tears, Amice sat on the bed.

Her mother gripped Beornwynne's Kiss in her thin fingers, gazing at it in wonder. " 'Tis so beautiful," she said in a watery voice.

Amice's throat was so tight she could not speak.

Her mother turned her gaze to Amice and smiled. "What of the Earl of Hawksdown?"

Amice's heart clenched in her chest. "What of him, Mother?"

"I thought perhaps…" her mother paused, her eyes clouding. She smiled. "My mother and sisters wait for me."

"Nay," Amice said, taking her mother's other hand. "Not yet."

"Yes."

"I do not want to lose you, Mother," Amice said, her voice breaking. "I need you."

"No, Amice, you do not need me. You are the strong one now. You always have been. Do not be afraid to fight for what you want. Be happy."

"I shall try."

Her mother's gaze suddenly bored into hers. "Do more than that. Do not let your father's legacy deprive you of happiness."

Amice swallowed hard.

"Rand, you shall take care of her."

"Of course, Mother," Rand said, and he kissed her forehead.

"I shall miss you both. It has been my honor to call you both mine."

"We shall miss you too, Mother," Amice whispered.

Her mother smiled softly and closed her eyes.

For a moment, Amice just stared, then yelled, "Nay." She gripped her mother's hand tight, keening sobs of grief ripping from her mouth.

Her mother's maid dropped to her knees and silently prayed.

Rand gently removed their mother's hand from hers and pulled Amice into his arms, rubbing her back as one might soothe a child. Only the shaking of his own body revealed his grief.

They stood like that for a long time. Amice closed her eyes and gradually managed to control her sobs. She was vaguely aware of other people entering and leaving the chamber, but she had not the strength to care who or what they were doing.

Her mother was dead.

Until this moment, she had not realized how much she had depended on the bond, on having her mother's presence in her life. Even though her mind was not capable of listening to Amice's troubles, she still was an anchor of warmth, of caring.

But for Rand, Amice was now adrift. The only man she would ever love lost to her forever; her mother gone. She drew in a rough breath and gazed up at her brother.

His eyes were damp with tears, and he gave her a shaky smile. "She is at peace now."

"Aye." Amice took a deep breath and wiped her eyes. "And I am free to go to Italy."

"That is still your wish?"

"Very much. I need to build a new life."

Rand sighed. "I shall send Guy with you."

Amice smiled at him, silently thanking God for giving her a brother like Rand. "I had a feeling you might let me have your second-in-command. Are you sure you do not wish to come yourself?"

"I cannot be gone that long." He caught her chin with his hand. "Are you *sure* you want to go, Amice?"

She stared back at him, the memory of Cain waving farewell winding through her mind. "Yes. As soon as possible."

Chapter 20

Piers walked into Cain's workroom, his features set into unusually somber lines. He tossed a roll of parchment on the table in front of Cain.

"What is this?" Cain picked up the parchment.

"Laila left it with me to give to you." Piers's voice was clipped.

"When?"

"Gave it to me last eve, but told me to wait until they were away to give it to you." Piers turned and took a step toward the door.

"Piers. Wait."

His brother paused but did not turn around. Cain fingered the leather cord around the parchment. "I was wrong the other day. I offended you and I apologize."

At that, Piers turned, but his expression remained cool. "My stock is well reputed. The destriers I breed bring much coin to Falcon's Craig."

"I know that."

" 'Tis not by accident."

"I know you work hard with the horses. I spoke from my own frustration, naught more." Cain rubbed the back of his neck.

"But you still meant it. You see yourself as the only responsible one, the one upon whom all the burdens rest. If not for *you*, Falcon's Craig would wither and be lost."

"It is my responsibility."

"How selfimportant you have become."

Cain stiffened.

"You have accomplished much, there is no denying that. You sacrificed yourself in marriage to pay the King's amercement and acquire Styrling Castle for Mother. You brought the castle back from poverty to abundance. You fought alongside Richard, and men still talk of your bravery and skill. The great Earl of Hawksdown."

"I will not apologize for trying to distinguish myself. There is naught wrong with that."

Piers leaned close. "But at what cost, Cain? Can you ever be good *enough*?"

"No one is perfect."

"Ah." Piers laughed. "Well, that is a relief to hear. I feared I was the only one with flaws."

"I have plenty of flaws, Piers. I never claimed otherwise."

Piers's face grew serious, and he poked Cain in the chest. "What is in *there*, Cain? Have you ever stopped to think of that?"

"I do not have time to sit around contemplating my *feelings*."

"God forbid."

Cain scowled. "You sound like Amice." When he said

her name, a wave of sheer agony wrapped around his heart.

"Wise woman. But she too guards herself. You are a pair."

"What do you mean?"

Piers shrugged. " 'Tis obvious. She shields her emotions just as you do. 'Twould be quite interesting if you both let down your guard."

"Amice is gone. Probably halfway to Italy by now."

"I see. Sounds like a nice place. Mayhap one day I shall pay her a visit."

Cain's scowl deepened.

"A man who follows his heart follows a sage, but a man who follows his head follows a fool." Piers gave him a discerning look and left.

As Cain unrolled the parchment, he could not help but wonder over Piers's words. Had he become a man who believed himself better than others? His life a quest to prove his value? Was there nothing else?

He shoved the questions aside and concentrated on making out Laila's spidery handwriting.

To the Earl of Hawksdown,

It is not my place to write this letter to you but I feel I must. No, I feel it is part of fate that I do so. Amice is the child of my heart. Above all things, I wish for her happiness. I had hoped she would find it without my aid, but I see that is not to be so.

Her destiny does not lie in Italy. It lies with you as yours lies with her. You are true heartmates and have been together through many lifetimes.

Come for her now. Do not let your fears and ambitions blind you. She loves you as you love her. Move beyond the past and forge a new future.

Come for her.

Laila.

Cain stared at the letter until the words blurred. He saw the rest of his life stretched out before him. Empty. Lonely. Devoid of warmth, of joy. Without Amice.

Could he take the risk?

Could he bare his heart to her?

Could he afford not to?

A glimmer of movement slowly took shape before him, and separated into two distinct forms, though they stood so close together with hands entwined that they almost seemed one. Cain buried his face in his hands. "I thought I was rid of you two."

Muriel laughed softly.

"You are," Gerard said. "Muriel, behave yourself."

The two ghosts stared at him.

"What do you want?" Cain asked.

"Now that I . . . understand, I have changed my mind about you," Muriel said, her image becoming brighter.

"Oh?"

"Do not waste your life, Cain. Go to her! Tell her what lies in your heart. Beg and plead, if need be. But do not let her go!"

"I—" Cain's protest died in his throat.

"Go after her, lad," Gerard urged. "Do not let the time slip away until you are an old, lonely man full of regrets."

Muriel stroked his shoulder.

Well, hell. They were right. As was everyone.

He would have to go after Amice.

He nodded and the spirits disappeared.

And for the first time in five years, his heart felt light and free.

❧ ❧ ❧

"I am leaving," Cain said.

"What?" Piers asked, his usually blithe expression frozen.

Cain grinned. "I am doing what Gifford and you have been badgering me to do for days. I am going after her."

"But, how can you? I mean, who will manage Falcon's Craig? When will you return?"

"I do not know." Cain leveled him a look.

"What?" Piers looked so panicked Cain had to thrust down the urge to laugh.

" 'Tis yours."

"Nay."

"Aye. I am giving it up." Cain felt the absurd urge to throw up his hands and dance.

"Cain." Piers's voice was so sober Cain's euphoria vanished.

"You can handle it."

"It is not my place."

"Do not be ridiculous. You happened to be born a younger son, but you are fully capable. You shall be fine."

"Cain." Something in Piers's voice stopped him, and Cain looked at his brother, really looked at him. "I know," Piers said.

"No, you do not know. You have always . . . well, you have suffered from having me as the eldest. You can handle things as well, if not better than I."

"No, Cain, I mean I *know*."

Cain saw the truth in his brother's yes. His brother. None of Ismena's failings would change that. He put his arms around Piers and clasped him close. "You. Are. My. Brother. Nothing and no one shall ever change that. Not our

. . . mother, not Morganna, not anyone. You are my brother."
Cain's voice broke. "And no one shall ever say otherwise."

"Dear God, Cain," Piers whispered. "You have found
your heart."

When Cain released Piers, he found both their eyes
were damp. "Do this for me, Piers. Please. I need to go."

"Go then," Piers said, his voice cracking. "I would be
proud to take over." He winked. "After all, I have Gifford
to aid me."

"Oh, no," Cain groaned, and then grinned. "Enjoy
yourselves."

"We shall."

❧ ❧ ❧

Amice adjusted Belle's saddle and checked the girth.
Ever since her fall, she checked her mount herself. Rand
helped her up into the saddle. They were in the bailey surrounded by people, horses, pack animals, and carts.

" 'Tis very exciting," Laila commented from the horse
next to hers.

"Aye." Amice looked around at the chaos and smiled.
"I can scarcely believe we are going. Just think of all the
wonderful things we will see!" They were to journey by
land to the port at Dover, cross the English Channel by
boat, then through France to board a ship at the port of
Marseilles for their voyage to Italy.

"Are you ready, Lady Amice?" Guy called over. His
eyes were bright, his mail gleaming in the sunlight. A group
of twenty men accompanied them, with double that number
of donkeys, packhorses, and carts to carry their belongings.

Amice took a last look at Wareham. She would probably

never see it again. A ribbon of sadness wound through her, but she pushed it back. Today, she began a new life. "Aye."

They rode out of the gatehouse to the cheers of the castle people. Rand stood by the gatehouse and waved a solemn goodbye.

But as Amice rode outside the castle walls, she saw horses in the distance. She halted Belle and pointed. "Guy, do you see that?"

He moved his mount closer to hers and drew his sword. "Aye."

"Who is it?"

"I cannot make out the banner." Guy squinted his eyes and peered at the approaching riders.

" 'Tis the Earl of Hawksdown," Laila said.

Amice's stomach dropped. "What?"

"She is right," Guy added. "I can see the banner now. Azure with an argent lion courant and a single star."

"But . . . why is he here?" Amice asked, half to herself. The riders drew closer, and she could see Cain at the forefront. Her heart clenched and she tightened her hold on the reins. Belle sidestepped, bumping into Laila's horse.

Laila lifted a brow. "I doubt it is to pay *your brother* a visit."

Amice shook her head in bewilderment. "I do not understand."

Laila just smiled.

Cain pounded to a halt before them, his destrier's coat slick with sweat. "Amice."

A tiny flicker of hope awakened in her chest. "Why are you here? We are leaving to journey to Italy, as you can see."

He moved his mount closer. His eyes were a deeper blue than Amice had ever seen, and his features were drawn into harsh planes and angles. "I need to talk with you. In private."

"I—"

"Grant me that, Amice. Please."

How could she refuse? It would be the last time. "Very well. Guy?"

"As you wish, my lady." He called an order to his men and they returned inside the castle walls.

As Cain's guards dismounted and streamed into the hall, Cain jumped down from his own mount and held out his hand to her. For a moment, Amice stared down at him. So many questions pounded against fear and hope that she was not sure what to do.

"Take my hand, Amice."

She slowly reached out and he took her hand, then lifted her by the waist from her horse, bracing her against his body. Amice's breath hitched and her stomach flipped over.

"Where may we talk?" he asked.

"The garden, I suppose." She turned and walked across the bailey. Cain strode beside her in silence. When they finally entered the walled garden, Amice paused and buried her hands in the folds of her mantle. She gazed up at Cain and waited.

His throat worked and he said, "Do not leave for Italy today."

"Why not?"

His gaze glittered with fire. "Because I want you to stay with me."

Amice ached with such pain she could barely find the breath to speak. "We have already discussed this, Cain. You do not owe me anything. I release you from any sense of responsibility you have created for me in your mind."

Cain closed his eyes briefly, as if he were in pain. "It is not that." He rubbed the back of his neck. "I have been wrong, Amice. In so many things. I hardly know where to start." He fixed her with a steady gaze. "But know that what I feel for you has naught to do with duty."

Amice bit her lip. God, she was afraid. What was he saying?

"Marry me." Cain took her hands. "I shall take you to Italy myself as a wedding gift."

He said nothing of love. Amice's heart twisted and gut-wrenching pain pooled in her belly. "Why do you torture me like this?" she cried. "Does it satisfy you in some perverse way to expose how desperately I want you?"

"No."

"Then why?"

"Because I love you, dammit! I have *always* loved you. So much that it scares me. Now, do you see?"

Amice opened her eyes wide. Feelings swelled within her so strong she was surprised the very air did not whirl with them. "What did you say?"

Cain's gaze was stark. "I said I love you. Too much."

"Why does it scare you?" She knew, but she wanted to hear it from him. She knew because the strength of her love for him terrified her.

"Because it makes me vulnerable. Utterly, pathetically defenseless." He put out his hands, palms up. "I can wield a sword with no small skill. I can manage Falcon's Craig and protect my people." He gazed at her in naked desperation.

"Cain."

"But I cannot survive you not wanting me."

She squeezed his hands. "I will always want you."

"Most of all because I am afraid I will fail," he whispered.

"That I will not be enough of a man to hold you."

"You shall always hold me. Do you not understand, still?" Tears trickled out of her eyes, and Amice let them fall. Her last shield crumbled, and she gazed up at Cain without hiding her feelings.

Cain stared at her, his gaze raw.

Amice gulped and took a deep breath. "I have loved you more in a heartbeat than anyone could in a lifetime. I could never love another man the way I love you."

Tears appeared in Cain's eyes. "Truly?"

"You are my heartmate. I knew from the first. And you have owned my heart ever since. You have the power to grant me the greatest joy, or deliver me into the deepest misery. And yes, that scares me too."

His mouth twisted. "Be with me always, love. I am empty if I cannot be with you."

She smiled as joy flooded her heart. "Yes."

Cain bent and kissed her, capturing her lips in a soft, then hungry kiss. He braced her head with one hand, and she clung to his shoulders. Amice felt her tears fall, but she did not care. The only thing she cared about was this man who had enslaved her from the beginning.

"I shall never let you go," he rasped into her ear. "Never. And I shall love you until the end of time."

"As I shall love you."

Epilogue

The Italian Coast

Cain sat on the sunny beach and grinned at his wife. His wife. It still seemed like a dream. One he had dreamt so many times, but never truly thought to live. Down the beach a bit, Olive frolicked in the calm, turquoise water.

"Be careful, husband. You look relaxed. Even happy." Amice slid her hand into his.

"I am happy." He stroked a fingertip down Amice's cheek, and her toes curled into the sand. "Deliriously happy." He waved a hand at the lush hills surrounding the beach, the clear blue water. "I am in paradise with the woman I love."

"Mmm. Do you not worry about Falcon's Craig?"

"Nay. I received a letter from Piers." Cain quirked a grin. "Though he complains, it is clear he is managing."

"I still cannot believe you turned Falcon's Craig over to Piers."

"It no longer seemed important."

Tears clouded her vision, and Cain wrapped his fingers around hers. "I never thought I would be this happy again," Amice whispered.

"You shall always be this happy, if there is aught I can do to make it so."

"Just be with me."

"Always," he promised, squeezing her hand.

"Always," Amice said, and placed her other atop his.

And somewhere, in a far away eternity, Gerard and Muriel smiled.

Dance of Desire
Catherine Kean

Desperate to save her brother Rudd from being condemned as a traitor, Lady Rexana Villeaux must dance in disguise at a feast for the High Sheriff of Warringham. Her goal is to distract him so her servant can steal a damning missive from the sheriff's solar. Dressed in the gauzy costume of a desert courtesan, dancing with all the passion and sensuality in her soul, she succeeds in her mission. And, at the same time, condemns herself.

Fane Linford, the banished son of an English earl, joined King Richard's crusade only to find himself a captive in a hellish eastern prison. He survived the years of torment, it's rumored, because of the love of a Saracen courtesan. The rumors are true. And when he sees Rexana dance . . .

Richard has promised Fane an English bride, yet he desires only one woman – the exotic dancer who tempted him. Then he discovers the dancer's identity. And learns her brother is in his dungeon, accused of plotting against the throne. It is more temptation than Fane can resist.

The last thing Rexana wants is marriage to the dark and brooding Sheriff of Warringham. But her brother is his prisoner, and there may be only one way to save him. Taking the greatest chance of her life, Rexana becomes the sheriff's bride. And learns that the Dance of Desire was only a beginning . . .

ISBN# 1-932815-35-X • Sapphire Imprint • $6.99 US
Historical Romance • March 2005

Knight's Legacy
Trenae Sumter

On location in Scotland for a film shoot, stuntwoman Cat Terril is waiting to film an action scene when she takes a stroll through the ancient castle that is their set.

Then she meets an old man in black robes who gives her a set of keys and directs her to . . .

"Follow your heart . . ."

Thinking it is a harmless prank designed by fellow stuntmen, Cat follows the old man's direction to a locked door around which swirls a strange, lavender mist.

Using the set of keys, she opens the door, steps into the mist and falls, literally, into a frigid lake in thirteenth century Scotland.

There was no 'harmless prank' involved. Cat is in desperate peril, finding herself suddenly the hostage of vicious, brutal clan leader, Calum Mackay. To obtain clemency from the Scottish king, the renegade Mackay must give his daughter, Brianna, to Englishman Roderic de Montwain in marriage. Brianna, however, in love with another, has run away. And Cat bears a striking resemblance to Mackay's absent daughter.

It is unbelievable enough to find herself in medieval Scotland. It is beyond comprehension to find herself abruptly married to a stranger. A stranger, moreover, who unlocks a passion and sensuality within her Cat never suspected she harbored. And Roderic, who has vowed to never lose his heart, finds himself falling for the mysterious, flame-haired bride he has taken to his bed. A bride some say is mad . . . and others claim is an imposter . . .

ISBN# 1-932815-00-7 • Amethyst Imprint • $6.99 US
Paranormal Romance • November 2005